THE BO

THE BOY WHO LOVED RAIN

"The reader is drawn ever deeper into a labyrinth of lies, truths and half-truths, of guilt, shams, of shallow-buried regrets, walled-up secrets and harsh recriminations. Before the stumbling in the gloom can lead out into the daylight where hope becomes a possibility, the dark places must be explored where psychosis, religiosity, and faith jostle in disequilibrium. It is not only Colom who has to discover his identity; his parents and others at the centre of the tale have to face their own mirrors of truth.

"This is a compelling debut novel, written in a style that combines elegance and passion. Like all good fiction, it turns the reader's gaze inwards."

Derek Wilson, historian and novelist

A pastor, poet, and missionary, **Gerard Kelly** lives in Normandy, France. He is author of fourteen books and the founder of the popular twitter prayer stream @twitturgies. He blogs at godseesdiamonds.tumblr.com.

THE
BOY WHO
LOVED
RAIN

*They say that what you
don't know can't hurt you.
They're wrong.*

GERARD KELLY

LION FICTION

Published by Lion Fiction
an imprint of
Lion Hudson plc
Wilkinson House, Jordan Hill Road
Oxford OX2 8DR, England
www.lionhudson.com/fiction

ISBN 978 1 78264 129 2
e-ISBN 978 1 78264 130 8

First edition 2014

A catalogue record for this book is available from the British Library

Printed and bound in the UK, October 2014, LH26

Keeping a secret is the first step
in becoming an individual.
Telling it is the second step.

Paul Tournier, *Secrets*

I
LONDON

PROLOGUE

When I was thirteen I lost myself. It was as if night fell and I didn't know where I was. People ask me: How can you not find yourself? How can you not know who you are? It must seem so dumb to them, not even to know who you are. But if they can't see it, I can't explain it. I just know that once you lose yourself, there's no easy way back. Kids sometimes pinch themselves to know if they're awake or dreaming. That should work for sure if you've lost yourself. You should be able to roll up your sleeve and slap your arm, squeeze the fat pink flesh of it and find out who you are. People who've never been lost imagine that would work – they think that something physical and real and maybe even painful should be enough to wake you. The point of a compass or a thumbtack, scratched across a knuckle until it bleeds and then goes deep; a tiny chasm opening up into the flesh. You're supposed to recoil in horror from the first pain, or if not, then at least from the blood and exposure of flesh. But what if you don't? What if you are watching the whole operation, fascinated by the effect of metal on flesh, following the lines of the canyons that have opened up in your skin, not even caring about the pain? At school I used blades from a pencil-sharpener. They made highways on my arms; ploughed fields; landing patterns for aeroplanes and passing spaceships. The problem with cutting yourself to find out if you're lost is that you do: you find out that you're even more lost than you thought. The lostness has depths you haven't even begun to explore. Your points and blades are just scratching the surface. It's like switching on a torch in the dark, thinking you will find your way by it, only to discover by its beam how lost you truly are.

CHAPTER ONE

*Rain is liquid water in the form of droplets that have
condensed from atmospheric water vapour and then
precipitated – that is, become heavy enough to fall
under gravity.*

"Rain", Wikipedia

Colom woke with a start, the dream slipping away like water
from a bath. Only the question, the puzzle, remained strong.
Once again he was at sea, trying to push himself towards a muddy
shoreline, where he might just find a grip and pull free. There
was nothing to push against. Every time he felt he was moving
closer, the drift took him further away. If he couldn't get to the
land he would surely drown when his tired limbs surrendered
at last to exhaustion. He knew that the ocean wanted him, had
claimed him. He knew that in the end he would not have the
power to resist. Nor would his sister, thrashing just as he was in
half-darkness at the edge of his peripheral vision. He couldn't get
to her, couldn't propel his body in her direction. And even if he
did, what use would he be? They could drown together, or they
could drown apart; either way they were both going to drown.

He woke up trying to solve the riddle, as if the question had
been set for today's exams: "My sister is drowning, and I can't
reach her. But I don't have a sister. How can I save my sister from
drowning when I don't have a sister?"

The room was dark, the house silent but for the noises he
already knew – his father's soft snoring seeping through the
wall. The central heating boiler, housed directly below his room,

clocking on for its pre-dawn duty. Was this what had woken him again? The creeping cold of his legs told him it wasn't. He swung them from the bed and shuffled barefoot to the drawers to find some fresh pyjamas.

Even with the broken night, he was up early, dressed and showered by the time his mother had put breakfast on the table. Neither spoke as he ate, the undulating rhythms of the *Today* programme filling the space they created. His father was already gone.

Fiona had dropped him at school, cleared away breakfast and folded a basket of dry linen by the time she found and washed the wet sheets from his room. The act of piling bedding yet again into the washing machine brought to light an unease that had been shadowing her for weeks. Her son's evident anxieties plagued her throughout the day. By the time she stood facing a heavily mascaraed and less than enthusiastic sales assistant across a counter cluttered with china, she could sense a shortness in her temper as sharp as hunger.

"Mrs Dryden. D – R – Y – D – E – N. They phoned and told me it would be ready today."

She followed the girl's eyes as she read slowly through the list on her clipboard. Even upside down Fiona saw her name two-thirds of the way down. She resisted the urge to point, checking her watch for the fourth time to slingshot a visual hint of her impatience.

"Here it is," she said at last, as if there had been some doubt. "Six side plates and one gravy boat in Blueberry Mist. I'll get them from the stock room."

Fiona shifted her feet to reinforce the urgency of the task, but the girl had already opened a half-hidden door behind the till and twirled herself into a backstage area. 2:45 p.m. If she made it back to the car by 3:00, there was still hope of being on time for Colom. She hated picking him up late in his first week back after such a long break. She regretted trying to collect the china this afternoon, but she came to town so rarely these days, and she had hoped it would be a quick task. In truth, the indulgence of ordering china filled her with horror. The pretentiousness of the shop grated against her. The smug superiority of the staff. Even in this cathedral-like glass shopping centre, the store retained its old-world snobbery. David, for his part, never tired of reminding her such things were now within their reach. Was there justice in such spending after so many years of privation?

She had also hoped lunch with Susie would not turn into an interrogation worthy of the Stasi, though she feared it would. Her troubles were travelling the church's rumour circuit like a dancing cat on YouTube. In the end, she left her friend with questions still hanging in the air. Susie wanted to gently let Fiona know that concern for the family was fast becoming a concern for her skills as wife and mother. Her sainted husband was above reproach and beyond criticism. It would be a sin to gossip about him, but Fiona enjoyed no such immunity. Those convinced she was no match for such a man were enjoying her struggles a little too much.

"So what will you do?" Susie's bluntness matched her dyed, cropped hair and grey executive suit. She was impeccably made up, her narrow designer glasses telegraphing the seriousness with which she expected to be treated. Fiona had made her own best stab at honesty, though neither her hair, three weeks past a missed appointment, nor her outfit, more randomly selected than strategically planned, cried out "managerial directness".

"I just don't know. We've discussed a few ideas – programmes we could follow; places we could send Colom – but I have no faith in any of them, to be honest. It takes all my energy most days just to keep David from blowing a gasket."

Susie's millefeuille pastry had been surgically sliced into eight well-ordered pieces, of which six now remained. They had both made the healthy choice of wholemeal open sandwiches, only Susie had partnered hers with an indulgent cake for dessert. Fiona wondered which poor soul would be on the receiving end of the calorie-burn when their boss got back to her office.

"Colom is back at school this week for the first time since before Christmas," she said. "I focus on getting us through each day. I've tried to think what might bring a longer-term change, but I really have no idea. I trust. I try to pray – though I've not had much success in that department lately. I press on: persuading; cajoling; caring for them both as best I can."

"What about the doctors?" Four pieces eaten, four left – a perfect square.

This was the question Susie had come to ask. By doctors she meant professionals outside the church: people who would struggle to understand their style of parenting. People you needed to explain yourself to. Avoiding such people – only ever having problems that could be resolved in-house – was one of the learned habits of their tribe. They weren't fundamentalists or cranks but they were a self-defined community with clear beliefs. It was so much easier to deal with people who understood this. And accepted it.

"We haven't seen anyone yet. David so wants to solve this our own way. I don't know if we can hold out much longer. We do need help with this."

At which point the waitress swept in to take away their plates, the conversation left spinning on the table like car wheels at an accident scene.

Fiona had taken the opportunity to pick up her coat.

"I mustn't be late for Colom," she said, "and I still have shopping to do." She caught from Susie a look that told her the interrogation would be resumed at the next available opportunity.

Susie had got through her defences and rattled her. She made a point of smiling when the girl returned with the china, hoping she had not been unduly impatient. She thanked her as she paid and quickly headed for the lift to the car park. The words she had never spoken out loud before were echoing in her mind. We do need help with this. Saying it didn't solve it, but by saying it to Susie she had said it to herself. Every step she took towards the car confirmed it. By the time she pulled out into the Hammersmith traffic she knew it to be an immovable truth, one that she would have to broach on the homefront before long. They needed help, and they needed it soon.

She clicked her mobile into the hands-free holder and pressed the first speed dial. All week they had played voicemail tag. Twice when he returned her calls she missed his. Their schedules were such that they could go for weeks without talking in depth. They were either in different places or in the same place with so many people around them that privacy was impossible. Or they were alone and so tired that sleep was an infinitely stronger attraction than communication of any sort.

His precise, clipped tones invited her again to leave a message or, if she needed urgent help, to call the Pastoral Helpline. "Me again," she said after the tone. "I really do need to talk to you this evening. Even if I'm asleep when you get in, will you wake me? Thanks." She rang off satisfied that she had forced herself into a corner. She didn't know what to do. They had made choices. They had commitments. She could see no way of breaking into his routines without breaking up his life's work. In the meantime she had Colom to think of. His flourishing meant more to her than even her marriage. Certainly more than the church.

She turned the last corner, leaving the shops and traffic of the Fulham Road behind her, and knew at once that something was wrong. There was a space beside the bus stop where Colom's shape was meant to be, his trousers sagging where they were too long for him; his dark curls full of movement and rhythm as if they made his head too heavy to keep still. No matter what the weather or the condition of Colom's health his hair bounced and caught the wind. She felt she could spot him across the O2 Arena. Today he was nowhere to be seen. Despite her efforts the traffic had made her late and the black-jacketed crowd, wheeling and diving like crows, was thinning. Colom's absence was unavoidable. Ignoring the hundred and one perfectly rational explanations for his non-appearance, Fiona felt panic rising in her chest.

CHAPTER TWO

I can feel the fire when it burns against my skin, the
rain when it caresses my face and the breeze as it
fingers my hair. I have all the senses that other people
do. I am just empty inside.

J. D. Stroube, *Caged in Darkness*

If you aren't extremely careful, slowing on just the right bend, it is all too easy to miss the turn for Caterham House. Overgrown hedges hide the opening and camouflage a sign that is, bizarrely, painted green-on-green. Like the secret access to the Batcave, a grand entrance is perfectly disguised as bramble. If you do catch it in time and turn through the gap in the jungle you will find yourself approaching one of the strangest stately homes in England. Once one of Surrey's finest, the manor house has gardens designed by Capability Brown. A single track curves elegantly through mature woods to cross a humped stone bridge over a kidney-shaped fishing lake, before perfectly bisecting the croquet-ready lawns. You might expect this picture to find completion in the elegant sweep of a Blenheim-like mansion, but something quite different now sits at the road's end: something small and squat and scarred with 1970s metal-framed windows.

The original splendour was lost when the manor fell into disrepair and whole sections were demolished. The upper storeys of the main house were removed and the ground floor capped with a flat asphalt roof. Three of the four wings were torn down, leaving the rump of the old house as just that – a remnant, the stump of what was once a spreading oak. The demolished wings were replaced by utilitarian extensions more like low-rent seaside bungalows than Edwardian jewels. You can almost hear the house sighing with regret and nostalgia. With lines designed to highlight the grandeur of the house, the surviving landscaped gardens serve now to draw attention to its poverty, like spotlights still trained on a stage long deserted.

Miriam had stayed twice before at Caterham, working alongside the resident convent community. Her own season as a nun had lasted less than five years, but her life since had been nun-like in many ways, including the one people were most puzzled by. It was thirty years since she had been under the narrow authority of an order but she had lived instead under the austere rule of her own free choice. She regretted neither the years she had given nor the years since. She wore her hair shorter now, trickles of white creeping into its auburn depths. Her habitual dress of trousers, blouse and cardigan had replaced the older, simpler uniform. She prayed more often in English than in French but at heart she remained the *bonne soeur* she had chosen in her youth to become, and she lived to fulfil the same vows. Apart from a brief season when the weight of loss and regret had all but crushed her, she had lived on balance a life of opportunity, not of disappointment.

The Great Hall of the manor was named for aspiration rather than history, the original no doubt taken by the wrecking ball. This had much more the feel of a breakfast room. The seventeen people spread around it made comfortable use of the available space. Floor-to-ceiling windows had been retained at this level and the late winter sun tumbled through them in angled shafts that set particles of the past dancing, dust rising from the rose-petal depths of an ancient carpet.

Miriam pressed play on her MP3 player and adjusted the volume of the portable speakers. The soft tones of John Tavener's "Ikon of Light" rose in the room like a slow tide. She held a well-thumbed paperback open to a familiar passage. A 300-year-old text from the letters of Jean-Pierre de Caussade. The words sat on the music like crows on a phone line as she read slowly, the pauses as important as the text. There were benefits, she had found, to working in a second language. First among them was the attention you had to give to the intonation of each word. Unfamiliarity made you careful, and care in reading was a prize worth working for.

She fell silent to let the sense of the words settle. For most of these young people this was the most important stage in the course. She had taken the morning and a large part of the afternoon to explain the exercise and its purpose; had encouraged each of them to process what they were hearing; had fielded questions and waited until she was sure they understood as clearly as they were ever going to.

"If you feel it is helpful to address your words to a specific person, please do so," she said. "You may choose to write them to yourself. I can't tell you what to write – only you know that. But whatever it is, write it all. Whatever has come to mind for you over these last days. Leave nothing out. This is an opportunity to let light shine in rooms that have lain in darkness. Use it well. We have time: there is no need to feel rushed. If you need to sit in silence for a while to gather your thoughts, please do. If you need to pray, please do. Either way, one hour from now, we will take what you have written and be done with it. God bless you as you write."

She turned the music up and watched them write, the Taverner a gentle counterpoint to the harshness of the events they were describing. Some occupied the eclectic mix of well-worn armchairs scattered across the room. Jake, tall and lean in denim dungarees, had squeezed himself instead into one of the window spaces, his long legs pulled up like an accordion into the sill's small breadth. Others sat on the floor, backs to the wall as if to occupy not the room itself but the border around it.

Miriam's eye was drawn to Jenny, pressed into a corner at the greatest possible distance from any other human presence. She was writing on a spiral-bound pad in a looping script, each page filled in no time at all. Flipping to the next page was a movement as fluid as a stroke of the pen. She was crying, but fought back the tears, such was her determination to get down what needed to be written. Miriam knew from earlier conversations what some of that might be, the rest she could surmise from similar days on a dozen or more courses. Page upon page in multiple languages, recording pain and anger; disappointment; anguish. All destined for destruction, as should have been the case long since. This was a day for release – release that you could see and touch and hear and even smell.

She sat in silence. Prayed. Leaned into the stillness of their concentration. Soon one and then another put down their pens, sitting quietly while others finished. Jenny was the last to stop. It looked as if she might have filled the whole notebook with her writings. She dropped it to the floor, pressed her back into the wall and closed her eyes. Waited.

"Thank you," Miriam said softly, fading out the volume of the music. "For being willing to write. For your trust in this process. To complete the exercise, we will need to move to the garden. Please bring with you the notes you have written."

She moved to the French windows; opened them; stepped through. A few metres into the garden on a cleared area of stone paving a cast-iron bowl had been set on a base of bricks to form a makeshift fire-pit. She took up her position beside it as the group gathered. The light was fading now, an early dusk sweeping in to claim the cluttered garden. She had heard no one speak since ending the writing exercise.

"I'm going to invite you to place the pages you have written into this bowl," she said. "There's very little wind today. I don't think we're in danger of losing any. If you want to say a prayer as you let them go, please do – but there are no set words to use. Please know that as you loose these notes from your hands, they will not come back to you. This is a moment of saying goodbye to that which has haunted you. Bid it *adieu*. Do not bid it *au revoir*."

Jenny was the first to break the stillness. She stepped forward to tear the pages from her notebook, letting them fall one by one into the bowl. Others followed until there was a crowd around the bowl tearing and releasing, some crumpling the pages into a ball for good measure. One man, small and bespectacled and so shy that he had barely spoken a word in the open sessions and Miriam was unexpectedly struggling to remember his name, took his three pages of close-packed, neat writing and tore them – once, twice, three times, more – until they were little more than a pile of tiny scraps. These he released into the bowl, like a child trying to manufacture snow.

Miriam held on to her own notebook. She had written just one sentence. She had first encountered the words as a song title and had feared them sentimental; trite, even. But they said what needed saying, and with use had taken on a weight all their own. Now she could not leave them unwritten. They were her liturgy. Her mantra. She tore out the page, folded it once, and stepped forward to commit it to the bowl, mouthing at the same time the words, "*Je t'aimais, je t'aime, et je t'aimerai.*" She stepped back and paused in silence.

As the last pages dropped into the bowl she again moved forward. The bottle of white spirit was where she had left it in preparation. She trickled it, waited for spirit to soak paper, held her breath in silent prayer, then dropped a single match. Two seconds of nothing, then a plume of smoke rising before the flames gripped, engulfed and ultimately consumed the papers. In time they were ash and charred scraps, curling and smouldering but inarguably destroyed. No one spoke. Like ancient worshippers before a sacrifice, they saw in the smoke itself the very meaning of their act.

"If you will permit me," Miriam said into the gathered silence, "I would like now to pray for us all." She recited Charles de Foucauld's prayer of abandonment, a prayer that had been, so many years ago, a source of equilibrium when all else was in turmoil. A mumbled "amen" rose from several people; a sigh from others – of relief? Of contentment? Of completion perhaps.

"This has been a good afternoon's work," Miriam continued. "You have been brave and strong, and though you may not feel it in this moment, this act will make a difference in your life. I want you to know that I am proud of each of you. Thank you for allowing me to share this moment with you. May God be with you."

A thinning wisp of smoke rose from the iron bowl as the tiny breeze began to play with the charred black fragments, their bulk at long last rendered light enough to fly.

CHAPTER THREE

In addition to graphical rainfall forecasts showing quantitative amounts, rainfall forecasts can be made describing the probabilities of certain rainfall amounts being met. This allows the forecaster to assign the degree of uncertainty to the forecast.

**"Probabilistic QPF for River Basins",
American Geophysical Union, 1995**

Fiona squeezed into the one space available in the car park – it didn't look as if any of the staff had left yet. She half-walked, half-ran into the school. Through the frosted glass window behind the reception area that shielded the office of the deputy head, she immediately spotted the blur of black curls that was Colom. The door was ajar and she went straight in. It took several seconds to make sense of the scene that greeted her.

She had expected that the head or deputy would be there with Colom. The three pairs of eyes that fixed on her belonged instead to Colom's art teacher, to a girl she hadn't seen before and to a woman sitting at an angle and closeness that suggested she might be her mother, though she seemed too old. The girl had been crying. She was holding a large handkerchief to her face. The mother looked as stressed as Fiona was beginning to feel. Colom looked much his usual self – detached, disengaged. Bored? Except that he had the beginnings of a magnificent black eye. Even without this Fiona would have known that there had been a fight. Both Colom and the mystery girl had completely lost any sense of grooming and the way they were sitting spoke volumes. They were as far apart as the room would allow, avoiding eye contact and drawing to themselves the awkward tension of the adults present.

Before anyone could speak, Mrs Grainger, a deputy head Fiona had met often but could not bring herself to like, came out from the head teacher's office. She wore a knitted dress in royal blue, matching shoes too good for school, a Ralph Lauren scarf held perfectly in place by a silver and mother-of-pearl brooch. Her hair was mid-length, blonde, and had been both cut and dyed recently, her make-up touched up more recently still. She extended a hand to Fiona, crossing the room in two determined strides.

"Mrs Dryden. Good to see you again. We did try to ring you. I'm not sure if we have the right mobile number?"

Fiona returned the handshake, caught out like a schoolgirl sleeping in class. "I'm so sorry," she said. "I have a new number. I completely forgot to give it to the office. Is there a problem?" The question was directed as much to Colom as anyone else.

"I'm rather afraid there is," Mrs Grainger said, urging Fiona to sit and taking her own place beside her. "You know Mr Gilby, Colom's art teacher?"

"Yes, we've met several times," Fiona replied, smiling hesitantly in his direction and trying to read his enigmatic expression. He wore a tweed jacket with leather elbow patches. Fiona didn't know such things still existed. She certainly didn't expect to see one worn by one so young. He looked seventeen, but she knew that couldn't be true. Perhaps the jacket was an affectation, a costume in which to impersonate a real art teacher. Everything about him was crumpled, as if his skin was three sizes too big and three weeks overdue for ironing. She reached across to shake the bony hand he offered. He nodded a silent greeting.

"This is Mrs Turner and her granddaughter Abigail," Mrs Grainger continued. "Abigail is in Colom's art group."

The girl was in school uniform, her skirt rolled at the waist to shorten the hemline. Fiona didn't want to stare but there was a redness to the tear-stained face that suggested she too might by evening have a black eye. The grandmother was square-jawed and large-chested, with the kind of masculine looks the Victorians would have attributed to a "handsome woman". She wore slacks, a blouse and cardigan in various shades of brown and cream. Fiona didn't know if she was supposed to shake hands. She had never been clear on protocol between parents whose only connection was their children's school. She held back and when no one else moved, she judged that she had made the right call. She wondered if Mrs Turner's silence was as portentous as it seemed. Nothing more than a glance passed between them; in the case of Abigail not even that. She was still sniffling, her eyes fixed on the handkerchief that now rested in her lap, as if she could read there the secrets of the universe.

"This is all very difficult," the deputy head pronounced in a tone fit for a funeral parlour. "As I've already told Mrs Turner, there was an incident this afternoon, in Mr Gilby's art class, that has rendered it essential that we all talk together. As I said, Mrs Dryden, we did try to phone you, so I do apologize for springing this on you. But we're here now, so..."

Fiona had sensed for days that this was coming. Her attempts to deny it had been wishful thinking, like hoping for a power cut to avoid paying the electricity bill. In her heart she sighed a deep, lost sigh but her body hid it. Resigned as she was to this reality, she had no intention of letting Mrs Grainger know she had been expecting it.

"Perhaps you could simply tell me what happened?" she said curtly, cutting off the speech she felt had been about to start.

It was Mrs Turner who broke her silence to respond. Her voice was deeper than Fiona had expected. There were traces of a smoker's cough and for reasons she had no time to fathom, Fiona found her respect for the older woman growing. She had a gravitas in speech that in silence had evaded her.

"What happened, Mrs Dryden," she said, "is that he, your son, attacked my Abigail. I mean physically attacked her. It's just not right."

Fiona caught her breath, stifling again a deep sigh that was trying hard to expose her. To be back here so soon after Colom's attempt to restart school was beyond disappointing. She looked to Mrs Grainger for clarification.

"Perhaps not the exact words I would have used, and there is more to it… but yes, that is the gist of what we have been told."

"Is this true, Colom?" Fiona asked directly, still not knowing what the full substance of "this" might be. Colom shrugged, unable or unwilling to answer.

Mr Gilby cleared his throat. "Perhaps I can explain?" he said nervously. In direct contrast to Mrs Turner, his voice was too thin for an adult male. Whatever shred of gravitas he might have had in silence evaporated the instant he spoke. "We were working in pairs, on portraiture," he chirped. "I assigned Colom and Abigail to the classroom next door to mine, where the light is good for sketching. I heard Abigail scream and ran into the room to find them fighting – I mean physically at each other, and both shouting at once. I separated them, but the shouting went on, until I told them both to follow me and brought them down to the office."

"When we got them calm enough to speak, Abigail made what amounts to a serious allegation against Colom of an unprovoked and violent attack," Mrs Grainger picked up, confirming that at some stage authority had been passed to her. "So we asked them to wait until we could speak to you both."

"Is this true, Colom?" Fiona repeated limply. She wondered if anyone else had bothered to ask him.

"Which part?" he asked innocently. They were the first words he had spoken since Fiona's arrival. Her heart leapt at his voice.

"Did you… attack Abigail?"

"I'm not sure," was the shrugged reply. Fiona knew this was all she would get. Not sure if he attacked her? Or not sure if he should have? Not sure, perhaps, what the fuss was about? She shrugged her shoulders in Mrs Grainger's direction.

"It isn't my intention to discuss this at length right now," the deputy said unexpectedly. "I simply needed you all here to establish that there has been an incident, and that we will be investigating it. The allegation Abigail has made is serious, and we will need to look into it further."

As she said this she looked not at Abigail but at Fiona. She had no intention of breaking a confidence in front of Mrs Turner, but there was a tacit acknowledgement of Colom's history. Perhaps in normal circumstances the incident would warrant a simple reprimand and a "shake hands and make up" moment – the bread and butter of a teacher's life. A child all but suspended from school twelve months ago, though, and then again just eight weeks since, saved from such a fate only by a voluntary temporary withdrawal, did not in any sense constitute normal. Mrs Grainger was banking on Abigail's grandmother knowing nothing of this, and she wouldn't raise it now, with its implication of liability for not having excluded Colom when she could have.

"Perhaps for now," she said, "it would be best for all of us to be in our own homes and with our own families. Abigail, would you come to see me tomorrow, straight after registration? I'll make sure you are excused from your first lesson."

Abigail looked up, sniffed, and may or may not have mumbled, "Yes, miss." It was difficult to tell.

"Colom, I'd also like to talk to you again tomorrow. I'll let Mr Cowell know when. You can both tell me what you think happened, and I will talk further with Mr Gilby." She didn't wait for a response from Colom, looked instead to Fiona and then to Mrs Turner. "I will inform both sets of parents as to what we believe happened and what is to be done about it. I am available to both of you next week should it be necessary to meet. Is this course of action acceptable?"

This last question was directed at Mrs Turner, an unspoken clause precluding any further claim or complaint. The grandmother either didn't see the catch or had no fight in her. She couldn't wait to leave the room, and agreed with a nod. Was she supportive of her granddaughter's accusations, or embarrassed by them? Perhaps, like most parents, she was both. The impromptu meeting was over as swiftly as it had begun, Fiona in no doubt that there would indeed be another next week. She wondered if it might be her last.

Mrs Turner avoided Fiona's eyes as she passed. Her granddaughter, skulking behind her, turned in a flash of unexpected animation to Colom. She part-spoke, part-hissed a single word, shuffling out before he could respond. The "weirdo" didn't rise to it. He had retreated, yet again, inside himself. The office might as well have been a fish-tank he was adrift in, for all the attention he was giving to its occupants.

Neither mother nor son spoke as they walked across the car park. Colom settled into his seat and locked his door, the loud clunk of the central locking system reinforcing his intention. Fiona paused before starting the engine.

"We don't have to talk about this now," she said softly, "but we will have to talk about it. Before tomorrow."

She took his silence as both a reply and an expression of preference, and said no more. A dirty rain was now falling. Drops like molten lead, thick with dust and fumes; the windscreen smeared where the wipers passed.

"I had that dream again last night," Colom said, his voice barely breaking a whisper.

"The drowning dream?" she asked, hoping the answer would be no, but knowing it wouldn't. He nodded, fighting tears.

"Oh Colom," she said. "I'm so sorry." Her anger had gone – a flame doused in ice-cold water. Taking its place the dull, unbearable weight of their impossible situation.

She looked at him, at the storm clouds passing over his face. Left space for him to say more, but he didn't. She wanted to speak, to form some words of consolation that weren't already overused. She had none.

She switched on Classic FM, and let Sibelius fill the space Colom wouldn't. They turned into traffic, heavier now. Fiona fought the urge to swear at the stop-start, brake-light-watching driving conditions that dogged their journey home.

CHAPTER FOUR

It was a rainy night. It was the myth of a
rainy night.

Jack Kerouac, *On the Road*

David Dryden passed under his own severe gaze as he crossed the thick-piled foyer carpet: ochre leaves swirling in a rich blue ocean. Up-lighters accented the mouldings of the pastel walls. The walnut panel doors and brass fittings had been preserved from the original cinema, the matching waste bins polished like exhibits in a cultural museum.

He still wasn't used to the giant posters, strung high in the atrium roof space. Richard had insisted on their usefulness, arguing that they were good for the brand. By stubborn determination David had stopped them from placing A4 versions in the toilets – but that had been the limit of his influence. Since their re-launch, branding had become their obsession. The words he had coined and used so often shone out at him in white Helvetica – the designer had been quite specific on the font – "Your family matters to God". Underneath, in red: "You matter to your family". Beneath this, the Parent Positive logo, the words set within the white outline of the original parish church, its tall steeple unambiguously declaring the religious nature of their work. Lower still, the inevitable web address. According to Richard, their growth was now fuelled by their web presence. At least half the interns were engaged in little else, spending their time designing and maintaining the sites; responding to enquiries; plugging the brand through the social networks. David understood none of it.

He had missed being an early adopter of the internet revolution, then resigned himself to not being an adopter at all. It all seemed so superfluous, so peripheral to the things that really mattered. In staff meetings there were times when he had no idea what his team were so animatedly talking about: his theological studies had somehow failed to explore Search Engine Optimisation. If it wasn't for Richard there would be no decisions made at all.

He passed through double swing doors into the darkened auditorium and turned sharp left to exit again, this time into the executive corridor. Here, in contrast to the deserted foyer and rows of empty seats beyond, there was life. All six interns were in the main communal office, each working at their own screen, music emanating from one of them.

"Afternoon, Pat," he said, cheerfully. "Richard in?"

Sixty-five but with the bright eyes of a teenager, Patricia Brigham's mid-length white hair was perfectly trimmed and her jacket just the right unobtrusive blue. Her glasses bore the tiny signature of a Paris designer. Perfume clung to her like a dust cloud. Pat's husband Jack had chosen Youth Dew by Estée Lauder as a fitting extravagance to mark their first anniversary and had repeated the gesture for thirty years. Widowhood had only confirmed the habit and the scent was now worn daily, in memory of that one great love. David wondered how long the fragrance would linger if she ever moved on or, God forbid, died. Hours? Days? Years, probably – a fragrant presence as much a part of the working environment as its desks and chairs. Pat had moved with him from the old parish office, had brought the same calm competence to this new one, despite the more demanding workload.

"Hello, David," she said, looking up from her workstation, a bright smile in an expensively made-up face. "He's at the *Chronicle* offices. Advertising review. He should be back before the meeting."

"Of course, I'd completely forgotten. Anything I need to be concerned about before tonight?"

"Not from me. We're all good here. Gwen Jones called, about next month's Deanery Synod, but she said she can wait until Monday – I've put a note on your desk. There are cheques for your signature. From Richard. No hurry."

She paused. He sensed there might be something more.

Pat looked towards the interns; looked to his office door. Hesitated. "There is one thing…"

He signalled her to go on in. Followed her. Pulled the door to.

"This came for you," she said. She opened the desk diary she had brought in with her and took from inside its cover a white envelope. It was addressed to him, as Mister not as Reverend, with a logo printed in the top left corner; "Private and Confidential" added with a stamp.

"I didn't want to leave it lying around," she said. "It seemed personal." For all her valued skills, her unquestioned integrity and loyalty, Pat's one abiding weakness was a curiosity as vigorous as weeds in an unkempt garden. David ignored her fishing. Took the envelope from her as if it hardly mattered. Slid it into his jacket pocket, where he could hear it already screaming to be taken out and sliced open.

"Thanks," he said. "I'll get on with preparing, then. Keep the wolves from the door, would you."

"Of course." She returned, her curiosity unsatisfied, to her desk. David closed his office door.

Shutting himself away on the afternoon of the first Thursday of the month was a ritual as established as Evensong. First Thursday was the keynote parenting event on which the church's ministry – and his career – were founded, even more than the Sunday preaching. The seminars had filled and then outgrown the parish rooms. Richard's bold plan to buy the old Embassy Cinema on Bishop's Road and transform it into a conference venue had catapulted them from being a little known church on the fringes of London's cultural scene to being a talked about and popular presence in the city. It was a long way from the traditional approach to ministry – David had been accused often of being "not very Anglican", but this didn't concern him. St Luke's was no ordinary church and he had always promised he would be no ordinary vicar. On a day early on in his training when he had refused to remove his three earrings, invoking the wrath of George Cole, his flamboyant college principal, they had both known his path would not be conventional. Filling a London church, by whatever means, was no small victory. Bishop Henry didn't approve of his techniques any more than George Cole had, but David knew that in secret both were proud of his success.

His office was narrow but long; one end occupied by his desk, the other by a pair of chairs and a wooden coffee table. The desk was a cheap knock-off but the red leather chair was something special, imported at ridiculous expense from Sweden, where rumour had it that backache had been all but eradicated from national life. Floor-to-ceiling books lined one wall, his own cowering in the shadow of the weighty collection inherited from his father-in-law. From the window he could see towards Dawes Road and Fulham Broadway beyond, or turn to overlook Bishop's Road, where a Victorian terrace led towards the vicarage and, out of sight, the parish church itself.

He was sorely tempted to open the envelope now, but he resisted. He needed focus for the evening ahead, and knew how easily the letter's contents, either way, could derail him. He couldn't take such a risk. He would wait. He sank into his Swedish chair and opened his laptop to make the last adjustments to his presentation.

* * *

Three hours and fifty-five minutes later, a packed auditorium hanging on his every word, and he was ready to bring his talk to a conclusion. They had laughed at his ice-breaker stories, held their breath in the high-spots of content. The visuals had flowed perfectly; the timings were just right. Everything just as he had planned, but appearing – just as he had planned – spontaneous.

Meticulously plotted but conversationally delivered, presentations were David's version of bed-hair.

He stepped forward, hands gripping the lectern at both sides. Fifteen minutes into the talk he had loosened his tie. Thirty minutes in he had taken his jacket off. Now he leaned into the light, as if he could make eye contact with every person in the room.

"Parents, it is your responsibility to set the agenda for your children. Couples, talk about this before it is too late. Future parents, make plans to give this role your all. Politicians, if you're listening, let's make policies that support parents in the vital work they do, instead of treating them as if they were the problem. Fathers – and I know you're listening – don't leave it to teachers and social workers to dictate your child's character and future. You are the sculptor – take up your tools. You are the artist – raise your brushes. It doesn't take a village to raise a child, it takes a vigilante: a courageous father who will watch over his family and will not rest until they are safe and established in their life's journey. Above all, don't be afraid. Parenting is yours for the taking. Will you take up the challenge? Let's take a moment's silence."

A slight rustling as people changed positions, put down notebooks. Some bowed their heads, closed their eyes. David let the silence deepen; pressed into it, felt its significance, its embrace. Broke it only with the softest of voices, his mouth close to the microphone now as he prayed.

A ripple of sound as the more habitually religious, or the plain nervous, tentatively echoed the "amen". David stepped back from the lectern. Marguerite, host for the evening, thanked him and made final announcements. People were already getting up to leave, putting coats on. He could see a trickle of the crowd moving, as ever, towards the space in front of the platform to his left, where a set of four steps meant it would be possible for them to get to him or him to them. Preferring the second option to the chaos of the first, he moved across and descended the steps. He didn't have to do this part. There was a whole counselling team set up for this, and he could see where others were going to them, at both sides of the auditorium. But this trickle were coming to him, and he couldn't bring himself to walk away. His foot came into contact with the thick matting of the auditorium floor just as the first young man reached the same spot, distress all over his tear-stained face.

Only as he moved to speak to him did David realize his phone was buzzing for the second time in the evening. The first had been the moment before speaking. Again he ignored it. Felt it stop. Felt, too, the subsequent buzz that told him that his caller had left a voicemail message. Made a mental note to check it as soon as he had finished with the trickle.

It was more than an hour later, leaving the building, the cold night rain a slap in the face, that he remembered the phone. He sheltered in the doorway to check his wife's texts and messages, turning his back to the wind-borne squall. Which was when he also remembered that Richard had left cheques for signature. That he had a letter from his publisher requiring an urgent response. That a full weekend of speaking engagements was not yet fully planned out.

And that the results of a lab test no one else knew he had taken were burning a hole in his pocket. He pulled open the heavy door. Headed back into the building, and to his office.

CHAPTER FIVE

*How much water vapour a parcel of air can contain
before it becomes saturated (100% relative humidity)
and forms into a cloud (a group of visible and tiny
water and ice particles suspended above the Earth's
surface) depends on its temperature.*

"Cloud", Glossary of Meteorology, American
Meteorological Society, June 2000

"What do you mean he won't tell you what happened?"
Exasperation simmered in David's voice. He had finally
come home at midnight after a tense exchange of texts. Colom
was long asleep. He had not left his room since returning from
school. Fiona had looked in to find him working through his
habitual cycle of activities: Xbox; sketchpad; laptop. She told
herself she was waiting for the right moment to talk to him, but
knew that she was putting it off. She didn't know what to say, or
how to say it, or what was expected of her. What words could she
use that had not been used already?

When she had finally, falteringly asked him what happened,
he had shrugged and said again, "I don't know." She pressed him.
Did you hit her first? Did she hit you first? Were you provoked? Did
something upset you? Every angle she tried met with variations
on the same response: "Maybe", "I'm not sure". Accompanied
by the all-encompassing shrug. She felt like the defence lawyer
who can't crack the prosecution's main witness. Didn't he even
care? She dreamed of the moment when Colom would collapse
in tears and confess what was troubling him, but didn't see it

coming any time soon. She wondered if he had any more clue of what was going on than she had. They were both in the fish-tank – underwater, unable to connect, both wondering what the lights and colours from the room beyond might mean. Fiona longed for someone who did know, someone to explain it to them both.

She had always thought it would be David. In many areas of life he was that someone, but around Colom he was clumsy and inept, stripped of his customary competence. He used his frequent absences – all in the worthy cause of the church's needs – as an excuse for not knowing what was happening. Colom's school life, he implied, was Fiona's business. She was the qualified teacher. She was the one who met frequently with staff at the school. He had the PCC; the staff team; the Deanery Synod to deal with. Where once he had tried to be at home an hour before his son was asleep, these days he had an uncanny ability to arrive just after Colom had gone up to his room. Tonight he was hours past even that. She didn't like the mood he had come home in – something at the church had set his teeth on edge.

"He won't tell me anything," she said, after recounting the meeting at the school and Colom's subsequent silence. "At some stage Mrs Grainger will let me know what she thinks happened, but Colom won't talk to her so it will be whatever this Abigail comes up with, which won't be the whole truth, by any means."

They were sitting at the kitchen table, a recent purchase along with the refreshed units and the new appliances – fruit of a legacy at last released from Fiona's father's estate. David had again taken off his jacket, had no tie. He had poured himself a glass of wine. He rubbed his temples. He had said little and had nothing to say now. She looked for the habitual signs of anger, but saw none. She knew that like her, he was as frustrated as he was angry. He wasn't used to problems that defied solutions. He was the repairman in so many people's lives. A kind of miracle-worker, some said – not in the sense of wheelchairs made redundant, more of finding a way out of problems they had thought intractable. Fiona saw him now as defeated, deflated. The man who couldn't solve his own son's problems.

"Do we send him tomorrow?" she asked.

"How can we not?" he sighed. "He's not sick. If we say he is they'll know we're lying. He's only just started back. If he does stay home, how long will it be for? A day? A week? The rest of the term? We've got to… we've got to break this thing."

"I know."

She paused, seeking the moment. Not finding it. Taking the plunge anyway.

"David, we need help with this. It's beyond us. He won't talk to me. I don't think he'll talk to you. Though you could try."

His eyes flicked towards her. She instantly regretted the barb, prayed silently that the moment would pass. Moved on.

"We need to talk to someone."

"Who do you suggest?"

"I don't know… a doctor?"

Now he looked fully at her, anger rising at last.

"No. I'm sorry, Fiona, but we've talked about this. I'm not taking our family troubles to someone who won't… who won't understand us. We can't do it. I won't do it."

"But we can't talk to anyone in the church. Can we?"

"Richard. I can talk to Richard."

There it was. The same answer as always. Richard. The fixer. The first and last port of call for every Gordian knot David came across. Except for two problems. The first was that Richard couldn't fix this. The chance that he would have a perspective they hadn't considered or an approach they hadn't tried was far enough below zero to freeze a lake. Have you really tried? he would ask. Have you been firm and consistent? Have you… (and here he would look not at David but at Fiona) have you set aside your own feelings and stood on the authority God has given you? All this Fiona knew with a rare and pure certainty. Richard was not the answer to their difficulties. But it made no difference, because she knew with equal conviction that David wouldn't talk to Richard. He would say he was going to; would make the appointment. He might even, under unrelenting pressure, go so far as to have a conversation. But when it came to it, he wouldn't talk about Colom. He wouldn't talk about himself in any useful way. David was incapable of telling Richard the kinds of truth that floated now above the kitchen table, an unspoken but unbroken reality hovering between husband and wife.

In Richard's presence, David the acknowledged leader became a cadet determined to impress an older brother. Richard was the only person around whom David took on, voluntarily, such a place of subservience. He didn't even know he was doing it most of the time, such was the depth of his assumption that others would acknowledge, as he did, the respect and honour the older man deserved. It was the one assumption Fiona couldn't bring David to question. Over the years of their marriage she had tackled David many times. To his credit he had responded with humility. He was no longer the sharp-tongued fundamentalist he had been well on the way to becoming when they met. She was not ashamed to take some credit for that change, though she tipped her hat skyward and thanked the heavens for their part. But onto the thin ice of his best friend's infallibility, she dared not skate.

Richard was the no-go zone of their marriage. The mention of his name was the bell that ended whatever round they were slugging through, breaking their contact and sending each to his or her own corner.

"I'll catch him in the morning," David was saying, "see if he's free for lunch."

She could see it already. A busy restaurant. No space to talk privately. David making some lame excuse for not having brought the subject up. She sighed deeply. Two roads before her. The one marked "conflict", the other "resignation". She cursed herself a coward.

"OK," she said. "Call him first thing. I'm sure he'll see you. But please, David, please do talk to him – I mean properly, about Colom. Not just boy's talk, eh."

The words were hollow, she knew. She wondered if he knew it, too, but he looked a little hurt and she thought perhaps not.

"I'll talk to him. Tomorrow. Maybe he knows someone we can meet with."

She put her hand on his arm. Consoled him, as she always did at such moments. It was strange, this lack of resolve in him. She knew that he felt overwhelmed by Colom's situation. And because she didn't know what to do any more than he did, she couldn't hate him for it. In a strange way, she loved him for it: loved that she was the only one who ever saw him this way. Loved that he let her.

"I'll get him to school in the morning," she said. "See if I can get him through a day without incident. I'll make an appointment to see Mrs Grainger on Monday – might help if I take the initiative instead of waiting for her to contact me. Maybe it will blow over. Maybe it wasn't as bad as it looked."

Though she knew it was. Feared it might be worse.

"Let's take this up to bed," she said, handing him a cup of tea and holding hers, ready to move. Restoring the familiarity of routine; the efficiency of a woman whose life was not out of control, whose marriage was radiant, whose son hadn't fallen into a bottomless pit of hopelessness and violence.

"Thanks, love." For the tea. For your understanding.

For not breaking the silence, she thought to herself. For keeping our conspiracy alive.

"I'll call Richard in the morning," David repeated, grasping at finality.

"OK," Fiona said, her voice almost a whisper, tears trying hard to get out. And I'll try to keep our son from hurting someone else's child. And from giving up entirely on the life we've made for him.

* * *

The thing about losing yourself is that you're supposed to sense it happening and do something about it. You're supposed to get scared when the shadows start to fall, and run home before the real dark comes. Or you can ask a stranger, someone approachable and kind who will put you back on the road home; maybe even take you there and tell your parents where he found you, not asking for any reward, just glad you are safe. But what if those instincts fail? What if you just keep walking, deep in thought, until it's too late and darkness has fallen and the road home is nowhere? What do you do then but carry on, knowing that every minute that passes, every step you take, every decision you make is taking you deeper into lostness and further from rescue? It's no good saying to someone who has lost themselves "Don't be so stupid", because to not be so stupid they would have to have found themselves, and then it wouldn't be an issue any more. "Who am I?" is only a question because it's a question – if it wasn't a question it wouldn't be a question any more. I don't suppose everybody loses themselves like this – maybe for some people they never need to ask. But everybody isn't me, and I am. And I did. And I do.

CHAPTER SIX

*Perhaps it was the result of evolution, he thought –
some adaptive gene that allowed the English to go
on making blithe outdoor plans in the face of almost
certain rain.*

Helen Simonson, *Major Pettigrew's Last Stand*

Fiona stripped the bed again, fetched fresh linen. Pressed his pillow to her face. To smell the smell of him.

His room was a monument to the childhood she had watched slip away. A high shelf ran along the two walls that formed the corner above his bed, filled with the photo frames that over the years they had bought for him. Colom as a baby, blanket-wrapped; as a toddler, chocolate-faced; the garden of the house in Canada, snow deep beneath a cloud-filled sky. Colom at the park, barely visible under hat and scarf. Colom shy with first-day nerves in his showroom-stiff school uniform. It was the pictures of Canada he loved most. For years his bedtimes stories had been drawn from them. He would select his favourite and Fiona would take it down and share its secrets. How she loved him as a toddler. His first steps across the garden of the house at Squires Avenue. His father, more blessed with enthusiasm than wisdom, breaking up a packing crate to build a tree house years before his son was old enough to climb into it.

She made the bed, tucking in Oscar, the rabbit he had kept from infancy and loved still – though he no longer admitted to the relationship in public. Oscar wasn't in many of the pictures on the shelf but he had found his way, in story, into all the worlds to which they served as portals.

Fiona rearranged the pictures. Nothing happened to them from one straightening to the next, but it was a habit. She moved along the row, taking down each frame to dust, the sleeve of her cardigan pulled down over the heel of her hand. She set each at the required angle to the next, spaced them perfectly, and all at once she found that she was crying. She couldn't hold the weight of her body. Such a grief rose up in her that she folded in two, twisting around to land, sitting, on the edge of his bed. She rocked as the sobs continued, her hands tight together, pressed between her knees. She didn't know how long she sat there before the storm passed.

For the thousandth time she asked herself how all this could have gone so wrong. They had done everything; had given him the best childhood their imaginations could offer. He was their only son, object of the full fervour of their affections. How could their bright, smiling son have become this passive-aggressive teen who slalomed daily between rage and indifference? His troubles starkly divided her life. Before was a time of happy memories interrupted by occasional showers. After was the reverse – rainy days, tornadoes; the rare moments of joy rendered all the more memorable by their infrequency; his nights disturbed by dreams of terror; hers by his cries. The frontier post between the two, their Checkpoint Charlie, was Colom's passage from the twelfth to the thirteenth year of life.

She remembered noticing, not long after his twelfth birthday, that one of the photographs was missing: the three of them on a beach in Cornwall. She found it in the drawer of Colom's desk, the frame empty, the image cut into about thirty pieces, corners sharp like shards of glass. She had stood for an age before the debris; hadn't known what to do. What to think. Should she clear it up, or close the drawer and pretend she hadn't seen it? Why would he do such a thing? What did it mean? Was she supposed to bring it up with him, or leave him be?

She thought of an evening meal more recently, the three of them in uneasy conversation. The daughter of a family friend had just left for university, and David asked, as he did from time to time, what Colom might like to study when his time came. There had never been any question that he would study – he had the intelligence for it, and David had already thought through the finances. This was a boy whose journey into adulthood had been planned and provided for. But where on other occasions he had been content to talk about his options – what he might want to study, what he might want to be – this time he was not. He was uninterested, detached. More shrugs again.

"Don't you want to even think about it?" David had asked, his temper beginning to rise. "You have choices, Colom. You could at least do us the honour of talking to us."

The boy had shrugged: the great shrug of indifference. Fiona had placed her hand, gently, on the soft red wool of her husband's arm. David had turned to her.

"But why shouldn't we talk about it?" he had said. "He's not mute. He can talk to us."

From the other side of the table a mumble. Low, but clear all the same. "I probably won't live that long."

Silence. Two forks hovering in mid-air. Two jaws dropping.

"Excuse me?" David had said.

"I probably won't live that long," Colom had repeated, calmly. "Not everybody does. I haven't decided yet."

And then there were the constant eruptions, anger blowing in like a storm and staying as an unwelcome lodger, a fourth member of the family. It didn't help that Fiona couldn't tell, at first, who it was that was angry. David's legendary pastoral patience, his capacity to listen calmly to the worst of confessions, didn't carry over into parenting. As Colom sank into a stew of shrugs and sulks – saying less; doing less; caring less – the temper David thought he had conquered proved itself alive and kicking. He would start with the best intentions, opening with a gentle word; making the authoritative stand that parenting required of him. But as Colom's responses moved further into indifference, David's words grew louder and harsher. Frustration pushed him back against the ropes, and the instinct of fight or flight took over. Fiona would hear an innocent question, "Have you tidied your room?" "Is your homework done?" and would know what was coming. Within a few minutes they would be shouting. Lashing out. Nothing physical, but words that packed a punch. And then the slamming door: David storming out of Colom's bedroom or Colom storming in.

Fiona would talk to Colom later, trying to see what damage had been done. But he would shrug it off. As if it didn't matter. As if he didn't care.

Before long she had discovered that it wasn't just David. There were conflicts at school; complaints about an argumentative attitude.

A year before this incident with Abigail, Fiona found herself in the first of many meetings with Mrs Grainger.

"I don't use it myself," the teacher said, a note of stern determination like an iron spine through her voice. "I don't know where people find the time. Facebook. Twitter. It's a mystery. But we do know that many of our children use both, and we try as far as possible to keep an eye out."

"I didn't know Colom had an account," Fiona replied lamely. What was it about these meetings that brought out the awkward schoolgirl in her? "He has his own computer. David, my husband, tries to keep an eye on him." Better. A lie, but better all the same.

"Well, apparently he does," Mrs Grainger explained. "The issue here though is another boy's account. Colom somehow found the password."

"And…"

"I thought it best that I show you. Daniel's father printed screenshots of the relevant postings. They cover several days."

She handed Fiona a slim pile of A4 pages. Daniel Tripp was the page owner, the majority of postings his own updates. On page two they changed in tone, a shift from "I hate homework" to "I hate myself". Then the reasons why: "I'm a tart"; "I fancy my mother"; "I am a faggot"; "I am queer". After that it got worse. Graphic. Anatomical. Humiliating. Fiona estimated about twenty abusive status updates, all purporting to come from Daniel himself. She realized that Mrs Grainger was waiting for her to respond. She looked up, and understood at once what was being suggested. But that couldn't be, surely? She couldn't connect the words she was reading with her fragile, curly haired son.

"Daniel had no idea, at first, how this could be happening," the older woman explained. "His father saw the updates and realized he had been hacked. They changed the password, and the abuse stopped."

"And you think this was Colom?"

"Daniel guessed it first. He had a hunch Colom knew his password, but more importantly, when the two next met at school, Colom asked if the password had been changed – something of a giveaway. Daniel spoke to his father and his father spoke to me. I felt I had grounds enough to talk with Colom, and when I did, he admitted that this was his doing."

Fiona could picture it. The shrug. The mumbled words, yes it was me. So what?

"Did he say why?" she asked. "It was just some kind of joke, surely. Don't they do this kind of thing all the time?"

"Not often in such a sustained manner, nor so vindictively. I asked Colom why he said such things, and his only response was, 'Because'."

"Had they fallen out over something?"

"That's the strange part. They don't know each other all that well. Daniel claims that until recently he had little or nothing to do with Colom, in or out of school. They were hardly more than Facebook friends, ironically."

"Well, thank you for bringing this to my attention. I'm glad it's stopped. I will speak to Colom this evening. I can assure you we will take action to make sure this kind of thing never happens again." She had bent down to pick up her handbag while gathering her coat around her, getting ready to leave. *Get me out of this room.*

"Thank you, I appreciate that. But I'm afraid it may not be quite that simple."

"How so?" She sat back down.

"We have taken a very strong stance as a school on bullying, Mrs Dryden, as I'm sure you know. There are policies in place which I know you will be aware of. Within those policies, we have been particularly clear on our zero-tolerance policy towards bullying of a racist or homophobic nature. The school will not tolerate young people being victimized for their sexual orientation, or for any confusions they express in that area."

"But what does that…" Fiona had begun to say, but stopped short. "Daniel's gay?"

"I don't know that to be the case, and he certainly hasn't told me so. But Daniel's father does believe that he has been the victim of a campaign of intolerance within the year group. We have been concerned for some time for his protection. And that is the suggestion these status updates make, and not in a remotely positive way."

"But you don't think… you don't believe that Colom means any of this, do you? Mrs Grainger, my son is not a bully. And I'm fairly sure he's not homophobic."

"That may well be true, but this behaviour," she pointed to the papers Fiona was still holding, "does constitute bullying. We know that Colom may not be the only boy involved, and he may not have intended the harm that has come from this, but intended or not, harm has been caused. If there had not been other instances of bullying and intimidation involving Daniel we might be in a different situation. But you can imagine how he must be feeling, and how concerned his parents are for him. Your son may well have been drawn into this by going along with the crowd, but I can't ignore the fact that he is now involved, and in the case of these Facebook incidents, he appears to have acted alone."

Fiona had sat in stunned silence. To have heard that her son was a victim of bullying would have disturbed her enough. But to hear him called a bully? It didn't add up. There must be something she was supposed to say at this moment. To leap to his defence? Or to denounce him and promise retribution? What was the parental obligation at such times? She had no script and had missed the rehearsal for this particular scene.

A weak "So what happens now?" was all she managed.

"I want time to look into this further, and I need to speak to staff to find out how Daniel is doing overall. Our first priority is to make the school a safe place for all our pupils. If this Facebook incident provokes further bullying against Daniel, I will have no choice but to hold Colom responsible."

"Which would mean?"

"Potentially a temporary suspension. In the worst-case scenario, removal from the school. I'm sorry, Mrs Dryden, but the policy is very clear, and we must apply it where it fits. Daniel's father would be within his rights to ask for Colom's exclusion from the school should he choose to."

"He was the one who brought this to your attention? The father?"

"He was, yes. He was very upset by what he read."

She shook her head. "When did this happen?"

"Last week – you have the dates on the printouts."

"I mean when did this happen to our schools – exclusion for a Facebook prank?"

Mrs Grainger ignored the question. Took it as a sign that the conversation was drawing to a close.

"It will be a governors' decision," she said. "I understand Mr Tripp has already spoken to our two parent governors. They meet next week."

Fiona had felt the room closing in on her. At home, the growing problem of Colom's behaviour; David's inability to deal with it. At school, a perfect storm brewing.

"So there's nothing I can do?"

"I would like you to speak to Colom, as you have suggested. And I am here if you need to pass on to me any information that might help us understand – if Colom was provoked in some way, for example, or if someone else put him up to it. Perhaps he himself felt intimidated by others? I don't want to assume that this was a deliberate act of bullying until we've eliminated every other possible explanation."

A lifeline, thrown late to a drowning woman.

* * *

Fiona finished with the pictures in Colom's room. Picked up clothes from the floor. Straightened books on shelves. Checked under the bed for old socks. Unusually, there were none. But there was a scrap of paper – a note that had slipped down the side of Colom's bed and was lying on the floor under it. Big letters, underlined, scrawled over several times – almost cutting through the paper in places: "I want to die."

She screwed it into a ball. Pushed it deep into her cardigan pocket. Touched, in the course of doing so, another note. This one she herself had scribbled from a few snatched moments on the internet. A visit she'd been intending to make, not knowing when she would. She went to find her keys. Kept the directions to hand. Reminded herself of the advice the site had given, to be careful not to miss the hidden entrance.

CHAPTER SEVEN

The truth is that the rain falls for ever and I am melting into it.

Edward Thomas, *The Icknield Way*

In the end Mrs Grainger's lifeline had not been needed. Daniel's father was distracted by other concerns; school life returned to some semblance of normality and, most surprisingly of all, Daniel and Colom became friends. Mrs Grainger had brought them together to give Colom the opportunity to apologize. He performed a sequence of shrugs and mumbles sufficient to be taken as remorse, and the two boys were sent to wait while their respective parents made peace.

The boys sat side by side on orange plastic chairs: Colom still, Daniel fidgeting in the silence. "How did you get my password?" he asked at last, a genuine curiosity overcoming the tension between them. A note of grudging admiration. A friend's Facebook page is not the American Missile Defence System, but all the same, a hacker is a hacker.

"You wrote it on the front of your exercise book," Colom said matter-of-factly. "It's the same word you've been doodling all year."

The hint of a smile from Daniel.

"How long you been on Facebook?" he asked.

"Since last year."

"What age did you give?"

"Sixteen. You?"

"Nineteen. I used my cousin's birthday. You got an iPhone?"

"Nope. Not allowed." He was going to return the question, but the phone was already in evidence.

"You ever played Angry Birds?"

A shrug. "Nope."

"You'll love this. Look..."

The iPhone tutorial ended with the exit of assorted parents: both in Daniel's case, only Fiona in Colom's. The meeting appeared to have gone well, with some kind of treaty being negotiated. To the evident surprise of all three adults, the boys said goodbye on tolerant, even friendly, terms.

Two days later they found themselves together in the lunch queue and got talking again, mostly about video games. Within a few days they were friends, all hostility forgotten.

For Colom, another bullet dodged.

How could Fiona have known then that the days of being called into Mrs Grainger's office would turn out to be the good old days? As the weeks passed it became clear that Colom's new friendship was not doing much to improve his emotional state. If anything, his dark moods deepened. She watched her son descend into a marshland of despondency. The only islands of solidity he could find to stand on were constructed of pure anger. He was either so switched off that nothing seemed to matter to him, or so livid that everything did. The truce established at school was soon broken. Not between Colom and Daniel – their bond was now unbreakable. But with others: more fights; angry scenes with teachers; and, on the homefront, with David. Work sometimes done and sometimes not; there was no rational or predictable pattern. Apart from his art, which he continued to pursue with a self-fuelled and independent passion, Colom showed little interest in education. Nor did he respond to the frustration of his teachers. He was intelligent and capable, they endlessly reminded him. He had a good home. Parents who loved him. He could do so much better, could make so much more of himself. But they needed him to do his part. They needed him to care, and he evidently didn't. Discerning why would require a capacity to interpret shrugs and grunts that entirely eluded the adults involved in Colom Dryden's life.

Each day presented the family with two possible weather systems – a mist of morose indifference or a lightning storm of unmediated rage. Fiona was still uncertain which she found more terrifying. Neither gave her room for hope. And all the time, a wall of silent fury from David; his refusal to talk to anyone outside the church; his constant promises to talk to Richard; the self-evident pointlessness of such a plan; the distance that she felt was growing between them. Two islands, pulled apart at exactly the time when they needed to pull together.

By the time Mrs Grainger threatened to suspend Colom, relenting at the last moment to accept instead a period of voluntary withdrawal, Fiona was relieved. She had fought so hard to keep him in school; to get him working; to hold him to his routine, but she was exhausted with the effort. She couldn't see how having him home for the last few weeks before Christmas could possibly be worse. She didn't know that he would snap back like a released elastic band, falling into a limp lethargy in which he slept half the day and hardly at all at night; in which he ate erratically at best. Having cared little about school, it seemed he now cared even less about life. He shuffled at a snail's pace through the work set for him by the school. He complained constantly of stomach aches. Headaches. Groin aches. Anything that could keep him in the undemanding isolation of his room. Only two activities seemed to spark any life or energy in him. He continued to communicate with Daniel on the internet, and he continued to draw. What had been intended as a two-week voluntary suspension became something much more, and on the 6 January Fiona had to phone the school to say that her son was too ill to return.

How she got him back, a month before Easter, she still couldn't fathom. It had been a mammoth effort of coaxing and cajoling.

Persuading him to eat. Doing his work with him; supervising sentence by sentence, sum by sum. Letting him sleep when he said that was what he needed. At the same time holding off David's anger. Keeping them apart. On top of that, negotiating with Mrs Grainger. Keeping the school place open; promising an imminent return; begging, time and time again, for patience. For grace.

Eventually they had offered a slow re-entry. A trial day, then two. Three days the following week. He wasn't asked to do a full week until all concerned felt he could handle it. But he did. One week. Two, and then three. Fiona was wading through treacle, but it was working. Until Abigail. Abigail was the sure sign that nothing had changed.

The girl's tear-stained face was clear in Fiona's mind as she made her way across the crowded dining room. It had taken a moment to identify the table she should be heading for, but the closer she got, the more confident she was that she had it right.

"Hello, Miriam," she said. "They told me I might find you here."

Miriam looked up from her fruit salad, spoon in hand, to greet her guest. She saw a middle-aged woman, smartly dressed in a knee-length grey skirt and a cream blouse with a relief of tiny yellow blooms. She held a raincoat over her arm, but extended the other to shake hands. Her fingers were thin. The skin dry.

"Forgive me," Miriam said, taking the proffered hand. She was often embarrassed by her inability to remember people she had met before. She knew too many, and the changing contexts threw her. "Have we met?"

"We have," her guest replied. "My name is Fiona Dryden. But that's my married name. When you knew me, I was Fiona Pascall."

The spoon clattered as it fell from Miriam's hand, bouncing off her china bowl before dropping to the floor. She scrambled to pick it up; straightened, red-faced.

"Fiona Pascall. *Mais c'est formidable.* How wonderful. It must be, what, twenty years?"

"Closer to twenty-five, I think. It's good to see you, too." Fiona was surprised by the familiarity she felt. She had not seen Miriam once in her adult life, and yet she felt she still knew her – like returning to a childhood home and remembering immediately how happy you had been there. Her friend had changed, of course. Mid-length, auburn hair had been cut short, and was flecked with white. She had filled out, the slim lines of youth long surrendered; her skin creased and lined where Fiona remembered it apple-fine. But the face was a map she knew well and instantly remembered.

"I didn't know you were in the area," Miriam said. "Didn't you move away? To Canada?"

"I did, but we've been back ten years now."

"How ever did you find me?"

"By accident, really," Fiona said. "We receive a newsletter that covers church activities in the South East, and events at Caterham Manor are sometimes covered. I'd seen your name mentioned before and had always meant to come and say hello but you know how these things are. There are so many things we promise ourselves we will do and never get done. I spotted last month that you would be here again and – well, here I am."

Miriam's physical memories of Fiona were blurred but her emotional memory was strong. She knew that she had been fond of the younger girl, that they had, indeed, been friends. The wide-eyed teenager had grown into a confident, articulate woman. Except that there was an edge to her confidence, a tension playing at the corners of her eyes.

"Is there somewhere we can talk?" Fiona said, the tremor in her voice betraying her.

The room the nuns found for them was compact and cluttered: a small sitting room across the hall from the dining area. A single large window, the daylight doubly blocked by heavy nets and partly closed curtains. Beige walls, a deep salmon carpet. Floral, unfashionable armchairs a touch too big for the setting.

"I've followed your work, a little," Fiona said as they settled.

"The courses you've run here at Caterham. I found some articles you'd written as well. It all seems… fascinating."

"It is," Miriam said, a ready response to a familiar conversation. "I decided a long time ago that I had the best job in the world, and I've not changed my opinion since. It's not everyone's cup of cocoa, but it is mine."

Fiona had a flash memory of the younger Miriam, the French accent stronger then, gleefully peppering her conversation with as many English idioms as she could. Not always getting them right. Storm in a teapot. Take it with a pinch of pepper.

"And your parents," her friend was asking. "Are they still with us?"

"My father died five years ago," Fiona replied flatly. "His heart."

"I didn't know. I'm so sorry."

"No need to be. It was sudden, and mercifully painless. We weren't close by the time he died. Did you know my mother had left him?"

"No, I hadn't heard that. Though much else, of course, is common knowledge."

"I'm sure it is. Even in Canada, I saw the headlines." She remembered them now, as fresh to her mind as if the ink was still wet. Senior Cleric Says Goodbye to God. Unlikely Atheist Declares "Here I Stand". Her least favourite, from the always reliable *Daily Mail*: Barmy Bishop Joins the Loony Left. "You followed the story?"

"From a distance, yes. Having known you I was of course interested. It must have been very hard for you."

"More so for my mother. She felt he had betrayed her; thrown away the life they'd built together. My brother left home before I did, and once I was gone there was nothing to hold them together. She went back to Wells; rejoined the cathedral; made her peace with the crowd he had so alienated. She's still there now. She has a small flat, works with the Mother's Union."

"Is that why you went to Canada – to escape the tensions at home?"

"It's not why I went, but it's what kept me there. I went as a volunteer with a church we had connections with. I met some people, made some friends. When I saw what was going on at home, I just stayed. Dropped the place I'd been offered at Newton Park and did my training out there instead. Dad footed the bill: for all his socialist rantings, he had always said he would pay my way through college. My first teaching job was in an elementary school in Newfoundland."

"So what about now?" Miriam prodded. "Are you still teaching? Are you married? Are there children?"

"No, yes and yes. I'm married to David, he's a vicar in Fulham." She ignored Miriam's raised eyebrow at this information. "I do volunteer work with the church – I haven't taught full-time since Canada." She hesitated for a second. "And we have one son, Colom."

"Which is why you're here."

"Yes, it is." Fiona was grateful for her friend's intuition.

"So, tell me."

CHAPTER EIGHT

*The summer sun was not meant for boys like me. Boys
like me belonged to the rain.*

**Benjamin Alire Sáenz, *Aristotle and Dante Discover the
Secrets of the Universe***

Fiona sat later that same evening with David in the kitchen
watching as, this time, he made the tea. There was an awkward
jerkiness to his movements. He was stooping, as if he felt two
sizes too big for the room. Colom's follow-up day to the Abigail
incident had passed without undue drama. He had grunted his
way through meetings with both Mr Cowell and Mrs Grainger.
No more was said for the time being: Fiona left to wait for the
promised conclusions.

David joined her at the table, sliding a mug across to her.

"Did you talk to Richard?" she asked nervously.

"Not today – he was tied up all morning, then I missed him
when he left the office." He shrugged. Silence simmered.

"What do we do?" she asked, depressed to realize how often
she had used the words. To no avail.

"I'll talk to Colom," David said, as if that answered the
question. "In the morning. There must be a reason for this. Or
maybe it was just a conflict that got out of hand. Maybe he was
just confused. It does happen."

"But what if it wasn't that?" she said. "What if he really
wanted to hurt her... what if this is who he really is?" Her hands
were wrapped around the mug, but shaking still; ripples tearing
up the surface of the tea. Her mind played back the Facebook

pages; the heartless cruelty. They both knew what it was she was asking; the abyss her question opened into.

"I'll talk to him," David repeated, and was going to say more but realized he had nothing more to say.

"But we have to get help," she said. "From someone."

"Richard," he said. "I'll talk to Richard. Tomorrow."

Fiona was so tired of hearing this that she pretended not to.

"We have to do something," she said. "We can't just ignore this."

When David spoke again his voice had dropped to a different register. He was measured; careful.

"Nor can we be held to ransom in this way. He's a child, Fiona. We can't allow our whole ministry – our whole life – to turn on his threats and moods. It's not right. It's not how it's meant to be. It's our responsibility to set the agenda, not his."

"Do you believe that?"

"Of course I believe it. What else is there to believe? You're not suggesting that the life of our family be directed by a fourteen-year-old? We're the parents here. I'm his father. I know where my responsibilities lie – hard as it may be. We know what we must do. We've talked about it enough times, and we've agreed. Other parents might crumble under this kind of pressure, but we won't. Will we?"

He was looking her in the eye. She knew that she was supposed to agree; to give in; to say that it will be all right if they just carry on. But she couldn't do it.

"Will we?" The voice firmer still, his hand on her arm.

She got up from the table. Busied herself with the dishes. "I don't know, David, truly I don't. Until today I thought I did. But I don't. But neither do I have a better idea just now, so for the moment, no, we won't. Do you want any more tea?"

"No. I'm fine. I have work to do. I'll be in my study."

And he was gone. Fiona pressed her hands deep into the sink of warm, soapy water. A tiny fragment of comfort in a life across whose plains a cold wind was blowing. Rain was hammering the windows and French doors; the big garden dripping. A wet darkness, pressing in. She pushed in deep, letting the water caress the soft skin of her arms. Holding them there. Still. Unable to move, because she didn't know where to move to.

She finished the clearing up; switched off the lights; went to bed, knowing that it would be an hour or more before he followed and that she would be asleep.

* * *

In a parallel universe two miles from the Dryden home, another husband dried the last of three dinner plates and hung a wet tea towel over the handle of the oven door. As he always did. As he had each evening for what seemed like the whole of recent life. His wife was working on her computer at the desk on the upstairs landing. His son had taken himself off to bed early.

The meal had not been the success he had hoped for. Not the cooking – that was beyond perfect. Tastes and textures, colours and concepts dancing in a symphonic ballet of culinary achievement. He had almost wished that Messrs Oliver and Ramsay, muse and inspiration both, could have popped in to see the triumph. And it was appreciated by both his wife and his son. As food. Not as an opportunity for conversation. Nothing he did, it seemed, could break the darkness of his only son's moods. Nor repair the breach that had opened up with his stepmother. He switched off the downstairs lights, willed his legs to push, step by step, up the stairs.

He looked in on his son to check that his reading light was off. Expected to find him asleep, his skinny limbs, as ever, tangled in mid-wrestle with his duvet. Didn't expect his heart to be run over by a truck.

They had noticed an increase in mood-swings; had witnessed deepening dramatic tantrums. They had seen how withdrawn he was becoming, but had put it down to adolescence: his further entry into the troubled waters of the teenage years. They had no idea it was more than that. Didn't know how desperate the boy felt.

Weeks later he would close his eyes and still see the boney body, hanging from the bar of the top bunk, the vicious edges of a leather belt pressing deep red weals into his neck. He saw it but for a moment did not believe it. He stood frozen in the doorway, then screamed for his wife so loud that she came running fast enough for their hands to reach the boy's body at the same moment. They took his weight, lifting him to break the pressure, the father fumbling with the belt to free him. He was unconscious. Was he breathing? They couldn't tell. He laid him on the bed, tried to take a pulse; leaned close to feel the breath if it was there. He heard his wife muttering over and over again, "What the hell happened? What the hell happened?", panic and anger meeting and mingling in her voice. As if he knew. As if he was responsible. As if he'd been in the room and had done nothing. As if it was he who had been playing some game of life and death that had gone so desperately wrong.

He, for his part, was less coherent. "Oh God, Oh God, Oh God, Oh God, Oh God," he mumbled. Touching the face, the hair, the mouth. Watching for the slightest movement in the chest. Willing it to rise and fall as if the power of thought alone could revive him.

She moved in to check the boy's pupils. Felt around his neck. A strange skill to have picked up over the years, but she was good with suicides. She had worked in secure youth units; had been the first on the scene of several attempts. And two successes. Now she was the head teacher; the competent boss; the better qualified of the two of them, in almost everything. He had gone through basic first-aid training but it was she who had learned, by sheer experience, to read the signs. She was competent in this.

But now she was as white as a sheet. "We need an ambulance!" she shouted, her voice breaking as if she was the adolescent in the room.

He forced himself to his feet; stumbled downstairs to the phone. Came back to see her alternating between CPR and mouth-to-mouth, her movements jerking and urgent; a cloud of desperation spreading around her. He knew then it was too late. Fell to his knees on the bedroom floor, a wild keening escaping from his lungs, as fierce and sharp as the wind he had felt on that day, two years ago: the last time he had walked with the boy and his birth mother across the desolate ridge of Scafell Pike.

* * *

That night Colom dreamed again. In his dream his sister is drowning. He has no sister, and in his dream he asks himself, how can my sister be drowning if I have no sister? In his dream he asks, why am I dreaming like this? She is being absorbed by a dark, brooding sea that laps against a rock-strewn, lifeless shore. He can see that she won't last much longer. The sea is claiming her, wearing down her resistance, waiting for the moment when, exhausted and limp, she will slide like a stone into the murky depths. He is looking for a place to dive in and save her, but the shore is slippery and he can't get his legs under control. Even if he can get in, he knows he will be too late. The timing is all wrong. His sister is slipping away. But it's OK, because he doesn't have a sister. So why is he dreaming this way? He wakes to the terrible, sickly feeling that a tragedy is unfolding and only he can avert it. Except he can't. *My sister is drowning. I have no sister. My sister is drowning and I cannot reach her.* He sees beyond the curtains that it is still dark outside, and wonders what has woken him. There is a sound, but it is not that of his alarm. It takes a moment to realize it is the phone ringing downstairs. He looks at his clock: 7:08 a.m. Why would the phone be ringing at 7:08 a.m.?

Fiona was asking herself the same question as she rubbed the sleep of an all-too-short night from her eyes. The ringing stopped and seconds later started again. This time she reached it.

"Hello, Fiona Dryden."

"I'm sorry to phone you so early, Mrs Dryden. It's Mrs Grainger, from the school. I'm at the hospital. I have some very bad news for you, I'm afraid. I wanted to let you know before you heard it from others."

How is it, in such times, our brains move faster than we ever think they could? When people speak of premonitions, of foreknowledge, is it this that they are referring to, this capacity of the human brain to know, when the phone rings at a time of day it shouldn't, just what's coming? The wave of horror that Fiona would experience like nausea in response to the news began before the news was delivered. Even as Mrs Grainger began to speak, she was reaching for the chair behind her, making sure she had a place to sit when her legs gave way, as she knew they would.

* * *

Someone showed me an animation on the internet once. It was of a woman dancing – a ballerina in a tutu. She was turning in circles in a pirouette: one leg drawn up into an arabesque, the other extended, en pointe. You were supposed to say whether you saw her turning en dehors or en dedans: in clockwise or anti-clockwise circles. But the thing was, you could only see her in silhouette, and the direction changed. To start with you were convinced she was turning clockwise, and you couldn't see how it could be different. Then something in your head flipped and you saw the opposite – she was turning anti-clockwise and it seemed impossible that it could ever have been otherwise. If you really concentrated, you could flip her back the other way. But whichever way she turned, it was impossible to imagine the opposite. Either can be right, but never both.

It made me mad, because you couldn't know which way was real. Whichever way you saw it, you felt sure that you were right, and the opposite was beyond imagination. But then you knew, if you saw it the other way, you'd feel the same. There was just no way of being sure.

It got passed around on the internet as if it was some kind of joke. But it's not a joke. It's not even funny, when you're the one who's spinning.

CHAPTER NINE

*I say to myself: it's raining today and it's going to
rain tomorrow and the next day, the next week and the
next century.*

Elie Wiesel, *Dawn*

Inspector Michaels introduced himself and his companion,
Sergeant White. He was as big in voice as in shoe size. Taller
than Fiona and David, and wider, she estimated, than both of
them together. A full beard outlined his ample chin like a lawn.
Wire-framed glasses perched on the sea of skin-tone that was his
face, their arms attached to a red string around his neck. Fiona
wondered how his weight played out in the life of a serving
policeman, but he seemed fit enough and carried himself without
self-consciousness. She opened the door to the living room and
stood aside to let them enter.

"I've made coffee," she said, following them in. "I hope that
suits."

"Perfect, thank you," Michaels boomed.

"Lovely," Sergeant White chimed. She was short, slim, blonde
– everything her boss was not. She wore a dark blue bomber
jacket, jeans and trainers, an FBI foil to his old-school Earnest of
the Yard.

"David will be here shortly." Fiona busied herself with the
Blueberry Mist cups and saucers. "He phoned to say that he was
about to leave the office." She didn't add that she had to persuade
him to be here at all. Didn't mention that even this afternoon he
had suggested that she meet with them alone. As if she wanted

the meeting any more than he did. As if she wasn't fearing with every fibre of her body that they were coming after Colom.

"Working late?" Michaels spooned sugar into his coffee. Took two biscuits from the plate, placing one in reserve on his saucer.

"Church work is never nine to five. Our life is probably not unlike your own, Inspector, responding day by day to the needs that arise around us." She offered the biscuits to the younger woman, who declined.

"I hadn't thought of it that way," Michaels said. "I'm not a church man myself. Sergeant White here could give you a run for your money: studied theology before she joined the force."

Fiona was intrigued by this idea. Inspector Michaels' glance at his colleague suggested that he wasn't.

"It's good of you to make time for us," he said. "There are just some things we need to follow up with you concerning the death of Daniel Tripp."

Fiona remembered where it was that she had seen him. He had been there at the funeral, a few rows in front of her. She had thought him a parent at the time. She wondered now why he would attend. Extending sympathy to the family? Or investigating Daniel's friends and relatives in the one place they were all certain to gather? He had seemed a giant among sparrows, a great island amidst the flapping of the uniformed flock.

"May I ask, Mrs Dryden, how your son is doing? Colom, isn't it?" he continued.

She nodded. "He's managing, I suppose. He alternates between morose apathy and raging anger. He spends a lot of time in his room. He hardly speaks to us. What more can I tell you?"

In truth, the ten days since Daniel's death had been a blur of shock and grief, Colom all but lost to them. Hardly a word from one day to the next. Did she really know how he was doing? How could she, with such distance between them?

"I understand. This whole affair has been very hard on Daniel's friends. They were close?"

"Close enough, in recent months. They had a falling out, about a year ago, but seemed to have become firm friends since. There were no signs of conflict. You're not suggesting...?"

He held up his hand. Did she imagine it, or was the gesture refined over years of directing traffic?

"I'm not suggesting anything at all. Is Colom here?"

"He's at Youth Group, at church. He doesn't enjoy it much these days, but he doesn't enjoy much else either, so he may as well be there as here."

"Does your son have his own computer?" Sergeant White asked, leaning forward.

"A MacBook," Fiona said hesitantly. "We bought it for schoolwork. He uses it for a lot more besides. They do, don't they."

The sergeant seemed about to answer, but stopped at the sound of the front door. David came straight through, extending a hand as he introduced himself. "I'm sorry to be late," he said. "Meetings running over all afternoon. It was a nightmare getting out of the office."

Michaels seemed unimpressed. He shook hands flatly. Once David had taken a seat he again took charge of proceedings. He had prepared a speech.

"A teen suicide would not always trigger a full-scale investigation," he began, looking first to Fiona, then to David, "but in Daniel Tripp's case we have found a connection with a number of websites that we have been looking into for some time. There have always been suicide sites on the net but we've seen a dramatic increase in recent years, particularly in those attracting young people. The sites are targeting younger and younger teens, effectively inciting them to suicide. Which is very much the stuff of a police investigation."

He paused. They nodded.

"As I think you may know," he went on, "we took Daniel's computer to see if it might help us to know why he chose to end his life, or whether anybody else was involved."

Fiona held her breath. Stared at the coffee table, avoiding eye contact as much with David as with the two officers. "Did you find anything?"

"We did," Sergeant White took over. "With teen suicides we often find evidence of visits to the same few sites," she explained. "There are people out there determined to help others kill themselves and the internet has given them a whole new audience to exploit. Some of the sites seem to almost be online youth clubs."

"And Daniel had visited these sites?" Fiona asked.

"For several months. He tried to hide his tracks but our techies have ways of uncovering old pathways. He'd spent a lot of time on one site in particular, where there were all kinds of opportunities for chat. It's easier to establish where he's been than to find out what he said when he was there, but we think he discussed the possibility of suicide extensively before he died."

"Do you know who with?"

"That's the concern we have, Mrs Dryden. Some of the conversations were with users we simply can't trace, but there are a number of names that come up more than once. There was one user with whom Daniel seemed to talk a lot – overwhelmingly more than others."

"And you know who this was?"

"We think so. His user name was 'Sparkout'."

"But that's…" Fiona began, stopping in mid-sentence as her hand went to her mouth.

Sergeant White cast a glance at her inspector. "Colom's username? We thought it might be. Were you aware, Mr and Mrs Dryden, that your son was visiting chat rooms?"

"No, not at all," Fiona said immediately. "David?"

"I'm a little lost in the world of computers, I'm afraid." Deadpan, a twinge of nervousness playing in his voice. "But isn't he likely to be hiding his tracks, in any case, as Daniel did?"

"It's possible. One of the first things they teach you on

these sites is to hide the fact you've visited them. Their goal is to become the only voice you trust: it suits them to make the whole thing secret."

Fiona looked at David, who was looking at the floor. She had no idea what to do or say. A dark hole was opening up in front of her and she was about to be sucked into it.

"Are you saying," she stammered, speaking to the carpet, "that Colom may also be contemplating suicide?" It was unthinkable. Unbearable. The crumpled note was still in her pocket – she hadn't dared throw it away.

"We can't be sure, Mrs Dryden, but it is possible. I'm sorry. We were able to recover some of the messages to and from Sparkout. Their tone and context led us to believe that this was a school friend. We are now fairly certain it was Colom. We need your permission to check his computer, to confirm this. But you do need to be aware that your son's life may also be in danger."

She left a space of silence for the gravity of this truth to settle.

"There is something else I need to ask you," Inspector Michaels broke in, authority in every fibre of his voice. "When we found evidence of these sites on the computer, we asked permission of Mr and Mrs Tripp to search Daniel's room again, in case there was anything we had missed the first time."

"And was there?" David, this time, finally acknowledging that the conversation was taking place, and that he had a part to play in it.

"There was: a letter. They give you a template on the site and you print it off. You fill in your name and some dates, and seal it with a thumbprint in blood. It's macabre, I know, but is in line with the overall tone of the site."

"And what does the letter say?"

"It says a lot about wanting to die and why suicide is a noble choice and so forth. But more importantly, it sets a target date. It's a pledge. Daniel had put the date of his sixteenth birthday. He committed to be dead before he reached it."

"And signed it in his own blood," Sergeant White added with unnecessary drama. Her superior shot her a look of caution.

"That's horrible," Fiona said. "When did he make this commitment?"

"A little under a year ago," Sergeant White volunteered. "May of last year."

Neurons were firing in Fiona's brain. The Facebook incident; the beginning of Colom and Daniel's surprising friendship. Spring of last year. Inspector Michaels looked directly at Fiona. Copper's instinct that a mother would know these things?

"Do you think there's any chance, Mrs Dryden, that Colom may have signed a similar letter?"

Fiona felt she was going to vomit. She stood up, hand over her mouth. Bolted for the door. It wasn't the bathroom she lurched towards, but the stairs. She scrambled up them; burst into Colom's room; started searching. Drawers, shelves. She took each book down to shake its pages loose. She was aware that someone else had come into the room. Sergeant White. But the young officer didn't try to stop her. She fell in behind her and calmly and systematically started searching too.

Fifteen minutes later they had checked the entire room. Relief was beginning to ease Fiona's tension. Her feet weren't back on the ground yet, but she was dropping out of orbit. Perhaps they had got the whole thing wrong. Perhaps "Sparkout" wasn't Colom at all and he had nothing to do with the suicide sites. Perhaps that was just Daniel's thing.

"Nothing," she said, certain that her search had been thorough.

"Nothing," Sergeant White confirmed as she got up from the floor where she had knelt to search under the bed.

Fiona replaced the last books on the shelf, and turned towards the door, catching sight as she did of Colom's favourite picture. A birthday gift from his Uncle Mark. A rectangular, framed print of Kandinsky's *Farbstudie Quadrate*. She remembered how angry David had been when he had seen it:

his irrational rejection of her brother's influence in Colom's life. She froze now. Sergeant White's eyes had been drawn to the same object. The younger woman stepped across the room to take the print down from the wall; turned it around; found a single page crudely folded and taped behind it. Unfolded it. Barely had time to notice the bloody thumbprint before she had to turn to catch Fiona as she fainted.

* * *

"But surely we should talk to him about it? Ask him why? Find out what he means by this?"

Fiona's frustration was evident in her garbled words. David's more evident still in his silence. He and Inspector Michaels had run up the stairs at the sound of Fiona's fall. Sergeant White had swapped places with them and found her way round the kitchen enough to locate the teapot. Fiona's cup was sweetened way beyond her normal taste, but she could feel it calming her. She sat on her son's bed, the big men a crowd in the small room.

"The best advice we have been given suggests not to," Inspector Michaels said kindly. "The suggestion is that exposing the secret can as much precipitate a crisis as end one. I don't claim to understand these matters, but this is what we have been told. This is a secret letter, and as such may turn out to be harmless. If your son believes no one knows of it, he is free to change his mind and no one need be any the wiser. There may come a time when you can raise it with him, but the advice we're given is that you should only do so with the support of a professional."

"You mean a psychiatrist?" Fiona's eyes were closed. Her voice weak.

"A specialist in this area, yes – used to working with teenagers. The school can make a referral, or your own GP can do so. Our practice in these situations is to encourage that such contact be made as soon as possible."

"That won't be necessary." David's first words since the cause of Fiona's faint had been revealed to him. The letter itself had been replaced where it was found. All part of the strategy, it seemed, of avoiding panic. "We have our own people for that sort of thing."

"I'm not sure what you mean, Mr Dryden," the inspector said. Politely, barely hiding the critical inflection to his voice.

"In the church," David said firmly. "We have a full counselling team, and specialists we can call in. They know what to do in this kind of situation." He looked at Fiona, urging her to silence.

"As you wish," the inspector said, his incredulity matched by that spreading across Fiona's face.

He turned to leave. "May we take the laptop?" he asked.

"Of course," Fiona said, pointing to the desk. "How long will you need to keep it for?"

"A few days. No more. Once we know what is on it that is of interest to us, we can copy that information and let you have it back. It's the websites we're trying to get to. Any of them that are held on UK servers, we hope to be able to shut down. Bring criminal charges if possible."

"Do I tell Colom you have it?"

"Best not to. Tell him you've dropped it in for an upgrade or something – if he's anything like my lad he'll be glad to have more ram."

"So we say nothing to him?"

"That's the advice we've been given. Until you speak to the doctors, or other specialists you know of," he looked directly at David. "We're told that it's better for the time being that Colom know nothing of our discoveries."

She nodded mutely.

"There is one other thing." He looked to his sergeant, held out his hand for the booklet she had taken from her inside jacket pocket. Plain, off-white paper; black print; some kind of illustration on the cover in sombre purple. Definitely not a holiday brochure.

"I know this is not easy for you. You want to be thinking about how your son's getting on with his football practice and whether he has a girlfriend. Not how to stop... Well, anyway, there's some advice here. Things to watch for. Things you can do to increase his chances, or decrease them, if you see what I mean."

In other circumstances Fiona would have smiled to see the inspector so flustered. This was a man she could picture pulling a bullet-ridden body from a skip without flinching. But talking about the emotions of children – that required a tougher constitution altogether.

"Thank you," she nodded, taking in the enormity of this responsibility. She dreaded the conversation that she knew would begin once officers Michaels and White were out of the door.

And begin it did, as soon as she walked into the kitchen, having seen them out.

"I knew we shouldn't have trusted that school," David blustered, releasing the anger he had so carefully suppressed in the presence of Inspector Michaels. "I knew it was a mistake to even send him there."

"You also know we had no choice. What does any of this have to do with the school, in any case?"

"That boy Daniel. Who knows what kind of family he comes from? He's filled Colom's head with these ideas, introduced him to these sites. We should never have let them become close."

You're impressive, Fiona thought. *I'll give you that. Not even a moment's reflection on whether it might have been Colom who had given Daniel these ideas; Colom who had found the sites and introduced his friend to them.* She shuddered at the implications of this if it were true; terrified at the thought that Inspector Michaels might find proof that it was. But she was staggered, too, at David's inability to see it. Though she hadn't shown him the Facebook printouts. Only she had seen in black and white the cruelty her son was capable of.

"That's not fair, David," she said weakly. "We don't know that Daniel was to blame, or his family."

"Well, somebody is," he fumed, the irony entirely lost on him.

Fiona fiddled with the suicide leaflet. Bent its corners over. Rolled, unrolled it. Felt time turning as if every clock in the house was amplified; movements of crystals and machinery marking history's passing like a roaring orchestral score. Her life was changing beyond recognition. She couldn't even remember what she had been planning to do tomorrow, before she knew what she would now be doing. Watching her son. Lying to him. Hiding knives. Emptying the medicine cabinet of every pill that might remotely be of use to him.

CHAPTER TEN

*The total amount of precipitation to fall to earth in one
year is 5,000 million million tonnes.*

"Rain", Wikipedia

"It's like he's hardly there. He goes through his routines but there's no life in him. I don't know what to do. I can't reach him. When I do speak to him, there's no sign that what I'm saying means anything to him."

"And David? Can he talk to him?"

"That's worse. They were already two ships drifting apart – they may as well be on different planets now." *Though on different planets,* her thoughts added, *with the vacuum of space between them, they might stop bothering each other and both be happy.*

She could hardly contain her gratitude for Miriam's willingness to see her. The days since their first meeting had filled with tragedy like rain barrels in a Newfoundland summer. Daniel's death. The sombre funeral: two hundred teenagers paying pale, shocked tribute to a brief but misunderstood life. Tearful. Hushed. Their shared confusion a cloud that hung like incense in the crematorium chapel. The visit of Inspector Michaels and Sergeant White. The discovery of Colom's blood-signed letter. The danger he was in. The chance he might share Daniel's fate. And Colom himself, slipping into the quicksands of emotional stasis. No ambiguity, this time, about her reason for seeing Miriam.

"You don't mind?" she asked nervously. "After all these years – I come to find you only because I need your advice?"

"Why would I mind?" her friend asked softly. "You need help. If I can offer it, I'm more than happy to. I'd love to catch up with you and hear all about the last twenty-five years. But it is evident that you have more pressing needs just now, and I am content to listen."

Tears filled Fiona's eyes. How long had it been since she had cried in the presence of another human being?

She had rehearsed a speech. Pictured the scene in advance. She would tell Miriam about Daniel and what was happening with Colom. Her old friend would instantly, instinctively understand, responding with advice as clear and sparkling as a crystal bowl. But now that she was here, now that Miriam was a real person, not a hologram projected from decades-old recollections, she was tongue-tied. Where do you start? How do you explain in a few moments a whirlwind you can't understand?

"Let's focus in on what it is that has brought you here today," Miriam said. On Fiona's first visit facts had tumbled out like toys tipped out on the nursery floor for sorting: a jumbled and jagged mess. There had been too much information. Miriam had struggled to build a coherent picture. She had suggested they meet again, with more time set aside, but this had been cancelled, falling on the day of Daniel's funeral. Two weeks had passed before Fiona could drive to Caterham again. Miriam was determined at least to find a place to start with helping Colom.

"Can you list for me what it is in Colom's life right now that concerns you?" she said calmly.

A bullet list arrived in Fiona's mind. These were things she knew. This was a list she had edited a hundred times, measuring the increase or decrease of each symptom. This was who she now was – the custodian of her son's evolving symptoms. She reeled it off, deadpan, objective.

"There's a temper problem. We thought it was just teenage sulks; tried to get him past it. It's more than that. When he gets angry he forgets who he is. Later he's so disengaged that you can hardly believe he is the same child. It feels like we're dealing with two different people..."

"And..."

"Fights at school; damage to property. We stopped a long time ago having friends for play-dates because they so often ended in tears, or worse."

Miriam could hear the strain of the telling of these truths. Fiona's breathing was shallow; her voice thin. She was twisting and intertwining her fingers as she spoke.

"What about the school?" she asked. "How have they responded to these incidents?"

"They've tried their best, but Colom has had two long spells at home in the past year. I'm not sure they can cope with much more."

"Have they not referred you – for more help?"

"Well… that's been part of our problem." Hesitant now. They were moving towards the thinner ice at the centre of the lake. "We have been referred, but we haven't followed through on the appointments…"

Miriam waited. Knowing there was more to be said. Knowing it was not her place to say it.

Fiona pressed on. "David is not keen on outside advice. He won't trust anyone outside the church…"

"But you can't trust anyone inside the church because he's in charge of it and Colom is his son."

"Exactly."

Miriam took this information in. Paused for a moment. Looked ready to ask more about it. To Fiona's immense relief she seemed to decide, for the time being, not to.

"So there's a problem with anger," she said. "What else?"

"He just seems so desperately unhappy. When he's not angry he's… morose, passive. I can't get him to care about anything…"

She stopped. Like a traveller at an unfamiliar junction, unsure which road to take. Miriam looked at her. Waited again.

"We found this," Fiona said at last. She had defied Inspector Michaels' recommendation. Had taken it from its hiding place. Would slip it back before Colom noticed. It had taken all her willpower to resist the urge to destroy it.

"What do you think?" Miriam asked, her eyes scanning the

letter. "Does he mean it?" Her flat tone belied the waves of emotion swirling like a magnetic field around the bloody thumbprint.

"I was hoping you might tell me," Fiona said, stress visible in her bloodshot eyes; in the lines around them. "I don't see him trying day after day to end his life. As far as we know he hasn't. But I'm not sure Daniel had tried either, until the day he succeeded. And I haven't seen Colom happy: not for two years or more now. It's like he doesn't care if he lives or dies."

She paused, rubbing the palm of one hand with the thumb of the other. Miriam said nothing; let the pause find its place. She could see that her friend was close to desperation – close, perhaps, to some kind of breakdown.

"I just don't know what to do," Fiona said.

"And you think I can help?"

"Can you? Would you?"

They talked for an hour more, Miriam probing, laying questions out like guard rails, Fiona lining up her facts as best she could. When she was exhausted with the effort, Miriam pulled back. Looked at her watch. One last question.

"Can we pray before you go?" she asked.

Fiona looked surprised, a little thrown.

"Yes, of course," she said, not meaning it.

Miriam prayed. Fiona couldn't. She wanted to, but couldn't force the words to come. They were there, somewhere, knocking around inside her, but she couldn't get them out through the doorway of her voice into the open air. She waited through the slow grind of an awkward silence. Miriam prayed again, her hand laid gently on her friend's arm. Fiona muttered agreement. In that moment, it was all the faith that she could muster.

* * *

"So you did talk to Richard today?" she asked later, when Colom was asleep and she and David were alone, back in the kitchen.

Back once more with the same tedious question. The letter had been surreptitiously returned to its hiding place.

"Yes." There was an unexpected edge to his voice, a note of uncertainty.

"What did he have to say?"

A pause. She turned to him.

"He wants to talk to you."

"To me? Why would he want to talk to me?"

He began to answer, fumbling for the words. She got there before him.

"Oh no, David. For God's sake, no. You can't be suggesting..."

"I tried to tell him. It's as much me as you. It's nothing you're doing, or not doing. But..."

"But he wouldn't let you say it. Wouldn't accept that it is anything other than the mother's fault. Because it always is, isn't it? The mother's fault. The only time the father is at fault is when he hasn't been firm enough in pointing out the mother's faults. The unending wisdom of the conspicuously single Richard."

"That's not fair. Richard has counselled hundreds of couples. You know he has. His own history has never got in the way of advising others. In fact, it helps. He knows how bad things can get. He's trying to help, Fiona."

His voice grew louder on the last words. Why did it always come to this – to Fiona's inability, or unwillingness, to accept his partnership with Richard?

"And he wants to talk to Colom."

Fiona had answered before she even knew how strongly she felt.

"That's not going to happen."

"It may have to."

"No. The last time Richard tried to help Colom was a disaster. I dread to think what damage he might do now. I won't allow it."

She regretted the words as soon as she had used them. David struggled to hold his temper. He was standing just a foot in front of her, his neck reddening, the telltale veins pulsing.

"It's not yours to allow or not, Fiona – you don't have that authority. It will be my de…"

She slammed to the floor the plate she had been drying.

"What is it with you and authority? It's an obsession. This has nothing to do with authority. He's not your employee, David. He's not in your army. Technically, he's not even a member of your church. He's your son."

"I know he's my son!" he exploded. "I don't need you or anyone to tell me that."

And then it happened. It was a relatively small movement; small enough to pretend she hadn't seen it. His left arm, raised across his chest. The body taut, poised. Transferring energy to the muscles of the arm, the back of the hand.

He caught himself. Dropped his arm. Not before she had flinched, her eyes catching the blur of movement then flicking to his. Momentarily making contact. All this in no more than three seconds. His inflamed intention. Her acknowledgement of it. His recognition that she had seen, knew how close he had come. Hers that he knew she knew.

He fell silent. Willing the echo of the moment to fade.

She spoke into the vacuum. Steeling herself. Fighting to keep the tremor from her voice. The tears from her eyes. Slowly she dried her hands. Hung the towel back on its hook.

"I'm going to my room." Her voice flat, controlled. "Please don't follow. The spare room is made up. I won't be talking to Richard."

He was mute. Wondered if there was something he should say. If there was, he didn't know what it might be. His anger betraying him. Nothing for it now but to wait out the storm.

"And neither will Colom," she added, and was gone.

David set to clearing up the broken crockery. Banned from the bedroom, he couldn't know that she would spend the night crying. Pacing. Turning over in her mind those three seconds. What they meant. What they changed.

CHAPTER ELEVEN

From where we stand the rain seems random.
If we could stand somewhere else, we would see the
order in it.

Tony Hillerman, *Coyote Waits*

The certainty of what she would do arrived in the early hours and refused to leave. By the time she fell into the shower to rouse herself from a cumulative total of maybe three hours' sleep, the idea was so familiar she could hardly remember what it had felt like not to live next door to it.

She occupied herself with getting Colom to school, relieved that David had already left for his breakfast meeting. It was after she had dropped Colom off, as she was heading back to the house, that she understood what her first step would be. And that it would be now. Her call went straight to voicemail.

"Miriam, it's Fiona. I was wondering if I could see you again today? I can make anytime before 3:30 this afternoon, if you're free. I hate to trouble you, but it is urgent. When you get this, can you call me back? Thanks so much."

As soon as she rang off, she wanted to phone back and say not to worry; it didn't matter; they could catch up next week. What was she thinking? Why should Miriam even give her time at such short notice? Mercifully, she had only been home ten minutes when her mobile rang.

Miriam had an hour free before lunch. The drive out to Caterham would take at least forty-five minutes. Allowing an extra fifteen minutes for traffic, she would have to leave at 11:00, a little over ninety minutes away. She needed half an hour to clear up the kitchen and leave the house in good order. That gave her a solid hour.

She went to Colom's room first. One suitcase, big enough for the combined load of his clothes and whatever books she thought he might need; his MP3 player; a few games and CDs. His drawing pads and pencil collection. A selection from the permanent display of photographs. The Kandinsky glared at her. Dared her to take it. Dared her not to. Eyes half-closed to it, she placed it in the suitcase, letter and all. She would tell Colom she had brought it for the sake of familiarity. Bitterly hated bringing it. Didn't want to even touch it. Knew she had to.

Then to her own room. What would she need? For how long? She had no idea, but started packing anyway; everything she could get into one large case. Make-up and toiletries. The Maeve Binchy she had started weeks ago but hardly touched. Hair dryer. Shoes, but only two pairs – one smart, one comfortable.

She congratulated herself on her packing skills as she forced the lid shut. She manhandled the suitcases to a position immediately inside the front door, ready to load into the car when the moment came. A soft bag for the items harvested from the tumble dryer, and she was ready. She went to the kitchen and immersed herself in tidying and cleaning.

At 10:45 she couldn't wait any longer. Doubt gripped her like a vice when she went to find Colom's passport. She took it from the desk in the study and slid it behind her own in the leather holder. It felt unworthy, conspiratorial. As though she were stealing it. Had David come in at that moment she had no idea what she would say. But it had to be done.

She pulled open the front door to find that there had been a break in the rain. A weak sun had found a gap in the clouds, was glinting off the passing cars even as their tyres slashed through puddles. The two cases slid neatly side by side into the back of the Volvo. She covered them with a picnic blanket.

She left only the briefest of notes.

* * *

"Are you sure this is what you want?" Miriam asked. They were in the small sitting room again, the urgency in the air belying its old-English cosiness.

"I don't think I have a choice," Fiona said, still struggling to talk through her tears. "It's not forever, and it's not the end. But it's what I need now. I don't know how I've got this far, to be honest. I need space; time to think. A chance to talk with Colom away from all the pressure."

"Where will you go? Is there somewhere you can stay?"

"That's the part I don't know yet. I could go to my mother's place in Wells, but I can't imagine how that's going to lower my stress levels. My brother Mark has a flat in London, but I don't want to turn up on him unannounced. I was thinking I might just book a holiday – one of those last-minute deals online. Head somewhere hot, just the two of us. A week, maybe two. I've packed for flying, just in case. But I don't know. For tonight I was wondering…"

Her courage failed her. Miriam read the question anyway.

"If you could stay here? Well, I think that might be possible for a night or two. They make a charge, but it's not very much. I can ask for you."

"Could you?" Relief washing over her. "Just for one night, two at most, while I decide what to do? We can share a room if need be. But…"

A second time her courage left her. It had been so long since she had asked for help. She had forgotten the words, or the order they came in.

Miriam waited, her hand on Fiona's. In time the words found their own way out.

"It's just that, after we talked yesterday, it came to me, and I wondered – if you could talk to Colom?"

"You mean see him professionally, as a counsellor?"

"You've been so helpful to me already, Miriam. Just to have someone to talk to who understands. But I was thinking, with the work you do… if he could talk to you himself…"

Again she ran out of words. There wasn't enough runway to get this plane into the air.

Miriam took charge, her voice measured, conscious of the minefield her friend was inviting her to cross. "I don't know if that would be the right thing or not: it would need to be his choice, more than yours, and I will need to meet him at least once in order to know. I can't even tell you right now how seriously you should take his threats of suicide. But I am willing to try, if he will allow me. You have to know, though, it won't be easy."

"It's not easy now. Can it be any harder?"

"Perhaps not. But if I spend time talking with Colom – if he'll allow me – there may be things he tells me that you don't know and I can't pass on to you. There may be things I do pass on to you that you'll wish I hadn't. I can't help Colom if I am not free to follow the conversation wherever it leads. It may not be a comfortable journey – for you, I mean."

"I do understand, Miriam. And I have thought about this. It's that very fear that's kept us for so long from facing this. But I have to do something. At the moment he isn't talking to anyone: we're just watching him crawl towards a sixteenth birthday he may never see."

"And you think he will agree to talk to me?"

"I think he might. I don't know for sure. Maybe he will need time to get used to the idea. That's why I need this space, with just him. I need to get him to the point where he will trust someone – or at the very least trust me again. When he's at home, with David in the house, it's… he just won't open up. I feel him slipping further and further away from me. And I can't let him. I won't let him slip away."

Miriam heard the desperation in her voice and, under it, something else. A steely courage. Just a little of the fire she remembered.

"I really do want to help you in whatever way I can, Fiona," she said. "I'm willing to speak with Colom and see what he wants. But there is a problem…" Could she cancel the trip? Put it off yet again? It was only three days ago she had finally booked the ferry. There were legal papers to sign; work to be done on the house. She had at last admitted to herself that she could put it off no longer.

"The thing is," she said tentatively, "I'm due to travel in a few days, and am planning to be gone for several weeks. I don't want to start a process with Colom that I am unable to see through to its end. Even at this stage I know that if we go ahead he will need more than a few days of my time. I don't know how we can do this. I won't be back here for at least five weeks, perhaps six. Can you wait that long?"

Fiona didn't answer. She didn't need to. Miriam wondered whether she could bear to wait a few hours, let alone six weeks. There was something boiling over in Colom that needed dealing with now, for his mother's sake if not for his own. Her decision to leave had already brought the crisis forward; increased its urgency. It was a wonder she had held on even this long.

"I understand. I shouldn't have troubled you. Forgive me," Fiona said, wiping her eyes and summoning the supernatural strength she would need to walk out of the room without collapsing. "I just didn't know who else I could talk to."

"I'm so sorry, Fiona. Perhaps I can find you someone in the area, someone who can be available to you for a longer period? I can help you set up an appointment for when you get back. I think you're absolutely right that right now what you need is space with Colom. It's going to take him days to come to a place where he can talk about his own feelings, and he needs to spend those days in a place of peace, away from the pressures he feels both at home and at school. It's such a shame you can't…"

She stopped in mid-sentence. It was like the bolt of a lock slipping perfectly into place; the last notes of a ballet matching with exquisite beauty the graceful movements of the dancers. She knew at once that it could work. The more she thought about it the more confident she became. Two worlds; two plans; two sets of priorities, coming together in unpredicted synchronicity. She waited for an objection to arise; a compelling reason why it couldn't work. None came. The best decisions often are those made in the moment, unburdened by extended analysis. The blink of an eye. Sometimes you just had to take the risk.

II

PORTIVY

CHAPTER TWELVE

It was raining in the small, mountainous country of Llamedos. It was always raining in Llamedos. Rain was the country's main export. It had rain mines.

Terry Pratchett, *Soul Music*

Thierry Delacourte stepped from his cottage with the rosy tint of the rising sun still gilding the clouds. He breathed deeply. The air was cold but pure, as stimulating to him of late as the first Gauloise of the day might once have been. Three years after quitting, the capacity was at last returning to his lungs. His head was clearer; his body stronger than for many years. He was eating well; walking more; rising and retiring early. To be older and yet fitter was an unexpected blessing. And he was producing his best work ever. The sales proved it, the canvases crated up and sent back to Seattle, but even without the buyers he would know. He had always known when the paintings of others were worth looking at, dismissing the dross with an unapologetic Gallic shrug. It was experience, not arrogance, that now told him his own work merited attention. It was a pleasure to be fifty-seven and no longer an impressionable fool.

The café wasn't open yet, but would be by the time he had completed his circuit of the outer roads of the village and worked his way back along the beach. Some days coffee was the stimulus that gave the walk its energy; today it would be the reward that gave it purpose. He took in his simple surroundings: the village of his birth and the community he had once fought so hard to escape. He thanked his stars once more that his health had been weak enough to force a return, and his will strong enough to deliver it.

There was no frost: it hadn't snowed all winter, but the wind blew cold here – colder still on onshore days when it bounced across the fridge-like waves before finding land. Neither was it dry. Was it ever? A breeze here was rarely balmy – more often a faceful of drizzle. He turned up his collar, pulled his scarf around his neck and headed up the hill, his hands thrust deep into his jacket pockets.

He had only one task to complete by way of interruption to his walk – to turn up the heating at the house in the Allée du Vivier. This would normally have been Sophia's job, but she was spending a week with her daughter in Paris and had recruited Thierry as a stand-in local agent. Later, when the shop opened, he would pick up fresh milk, some bread, maybe a few pastries. For now he just needed to make sure the heating was sufficient to render the house habitable. It had lain empty through the winter; shuttered against wind and rain, the last tourists gone by October. Its owner herself had not been back for five years. It was a feeling he knew well – to never have reason enough to return; to always have too many reasons not to. He remembered the last time he had seen her. She had not been slow to comment on the condition she found him in.

He walked up the gentle incline of the harbour approach, thrilled at his capacity to do so. Gratitude was the English word that best captured his condition these days. In French *reconnaissance* – literally to renew acquaintance. It was a perfect description of what he had been doing these past four years – renewing his acquaintance with the village of his birth. In late middle age he was in love all over again: not with a person but a place.

Cresting the hill, Miriam's heating duly turned up, shutters opened, the house breathing again after its long hibernation, he turned to survey the object of his affections, an artist considering the curves and contours of his muse. The pale sun was higher in the sky now, a full tide gently rocking a clutch of anchored boats. In his youth he would have known them all by name. The steady breeze stroked the skin of the water, massaging the dark seaweed floating just below the surface. His practised eye took in the details of the scene, from the etched white line of the horizon to the bobbing blue and yellow woodwork of the boats. He stood in stillness. Breathed the salt-damp air. *Reconnaissance*.

Portivy is the only harbour on the western side of Quiberon – a Breton peninsula extending fourteen kilometres into the Atlantic. Centuries ago this was an island, then a tidal island, until in the nineteenth century a rock causeway tied it to the world. This was now a fully surfaced road with a narrow point of entry, the sea a stone's throw to each side. The peninsula formed one boundary of the Gulf of Morbihan, holding in its calm embrace a rocky archipelago: islands big and small laid out like a sailor's playground. The curvature of this granite limb, cutting into the ocean like some prehistoric harbour wall, gives to the peninsula itself a unique dual climate. Gentle golden beaches run the length of the landward side making the "Côté Baie", in the language of the property developers, a paradise for holidaying families; for shell seekers; for couples in retirement seeking an environment of kindness. Across from these calm coves, on the island's seaward side, the cliffs and caves, the storms and surging waves of the Côte Sauvage, the Wild Coast, offer an altogether darker and more turbulent world. Between the two a hinterland of heath and forest; a sparsely populated area whose few small villages bear ancient Breton names and are linked by narrow, winding lanes – as if a neutral no-man's-land were needed to keep the warring sibling coasts apart.

Portivy had been one such hamlet, a small cluster of peasant cottages, until the 1870s when a harbour was created – the first and only such installation on the wild side of the island. From then it became a fishing port, a wild rival to Port Maria, the more sheltered harbour of Quiberon town itself. The cliff-shadowed waters of the Côte Sauvage were rich in fish, and those brave or foolish enough to head out each day into such seas found in Portivy a rewarding base from which to operate. These days only a handful of fishing boats huddle among the leisure craft. Families that for a century or more had lived by harvesting the sea have learned to survive by other means: summer crowds in search of a holiday let; weekend walkers; Parisians ready to pay over the odds for a seafood meal eaten within sight of the waters it was fished from.

Portivy is arranged around a single street that sweeps down a hillside to the harbour before looping around to climb again a hundred metres further on. Along and around the two arms of this loop lie the lanes, alleyways and courtyards of the old village: minuscule houses huddled together for warmth and shelter. Where the road meets the mud slopes and quayside at the heart of the village, half a dozen harbour-front houses face the full force of the sea. Two café-bars, a panoramic seafood restaurant and a small refurbished hotel surround the car park that serves equally for tourists, boat trailers and community events important enough to break out the bunting for. A diving school, a fresh-fish merchant, a new *crêperie*, and a small surf shop make up the remaining commercial interests of the village.

The oldest of Portivy's functioning businesses, the Café du Port, had been Thierry's home throughout his childhood, and for the first year after his return. Beside it was the odd cluster of Portivy's only municipal facilities: a bus shelter, public toilets, a village map and information panel. None of these were much used in the winter months. Their purpose was symbolic: to maintain a connection with the rest of Quiberon and by implication the world beyond. Thierry was no great fan of the world beyond, despite the visits he still made to it and the flow of money that came back, but he would never forget the feelings that had haunted his adolescence here. Of being cut off, a prisoner of this small world. Of longing for escape; hungering for the social interaction he was sure must be happening somewhere else. He was thirteen in 1968, listening daily with his father to the Paris radio reports: the student occupations; the marches and riots; the anarchic press conferences. He had pored over newspaper photographs of the huge crowds gathered along the Boul'Mich, the Boulevard St Michel, the *Police Nationale* preparing to meet them with a force that shocked the nation. He had known then that a new world was coming to birth; that he would have no part of it unless he had the strength to leave his island home. These days he would happily demolish the rock-pile road that had opened Quiberon to mainland traffic – to make of her an island once more – but he understood the desperation of those who needed that thin string of attachment.

Coming full circle, approaching the café, he saw up the hill that a white Volvo had parked beside the Allée du Vivier. He regretted that he hadn't had time to pick up the milk and pastries, but was relieved to see what looked like bags of shopping being unloaded from the boot. He wondered who Miriam had brought with her. He couldn't tell, at this distance and with the big coat flapping in the wind, whether it was a woman or a man.

About 150 metres up the hillside, the Allée du Vivier runs perpendicular to the main street. Car-wide at its opening, it quickly narrows to end as little more than a footpath. It is home to seven linked cottages, their styles and roof-heights varied, like a shelf of random pottery ornaments. A row of books in need of sorting.

Fiona pulled their cases out of the car while Miriam found her key and approached the largest property on the alley: a double-fronted, white-washed house with wide blue-shuttered windows either side of the canopied front door. Above this, at first-floor level, the windows of three more ample rooms. Higher still, attic roof lights.

They had seen no one as they came into the village. Apart from the one man she noticed now, looking towards them from further down the hill, the place might well be entirely unpopulated.

"We're not sure why they called it Allée du Vivier." Miriam was working the stiff front door open, twisting the key with one hand while throwing the opposite shoulder against it. "The actual *vivier* is down on the harbour-front, near the diving school. Probably the alley went down to it before it was cut in half by the newer access road."

Fiona looked blankly at her.

"It's how they keep the fish alive until the moment of sale," she explained, falling into the house as the door gave in to her persuasion. "Big tanks with sea water running constantly through them. Traditionally they were outdoors, re-filled by the tide, but ours is an indoor version, with water pumped up from the harbour."

"Maybe someone who worked there, or once owned it, lived here?"

"Could be. But not in this house. My grandfather built it in 1907 and it's been in our family ever since. Plenty of fishermen to keep the *vivier* stocked, but no one involved in running it."

Fiona ducked through the low door as she followed Miriam down three steps into the house. A single, open room covered the ground floor. The house was only around four metres deep, but it was long, perhaps fifteen metres. In one corner was a wooden staircase beside a simple kitchen, hardly more than a sideboard with taps. The floor had brown-and-white tiles, like an oversized chess board. There was a refectory-style table filling the kitchen end of the room, a long bench at each side. A settee and two non-matching armchairs occupied the far end, arranged around a stone fireplace, large and sooty and, to all appearances, available for use. On the stone shelf beside the fireplace and on the floor stretching into the corner of the room, logs had been neatly cut and piled, a promise of cosy days and comfortable nights. Fiona imagined the generations who had found security here – the shutters barred against the storms without, the fire fighting the chill within.

"This used to be three rooms," Miriam explained, the suitcases now piled as if in a hotel lobby. "We ripped it all out about ten years ago. Through there…" she pointed to an arch of stones set into the wall at the opposite end of the room to the fireplace, "used to be a scullery kitchen. We sealed off that end of the house and were able to sell it as a separate studio, with the room above. Then we took all the partitions out of what was left, to make this."

"It's lovely," Fiona said. "It all feels so… old." She didn't really mean old – lots of things were old. What did she mean? Rooted? Old like a tree is old, ringed with the memories of its passing years. Not old and tired, more old and satisfied. "It's been in your family all along?"

"Since the first bricks were laid. There were three much smaller homes on this same plot. My grandfather dismantled them stone by stone. He was quite prosperous by Portivy standards. It was a state-of-the-art home for its time. He was very proud of it."

"I'll bet he was. I was expecting something smaller. When you said a fisherman's cottage, I thought small and dark."

"Many of the older homes are, here in Portivy. I suppose my family were just fortunate enough to be able to afford something bigger, or perhaps my grandfather was gifted at making the most of what he had. He did most of the building work himself."

She pointed to a sepia photograph, hanging above the fireplace. It showed the house under construction. Bare-chested, both wearing caps, two men sat on a low, unfinished wall, wine and bread set out between them like an impromptu Eucharist. There was a fierce pride in their angular jawlines, visible even in the blurred and grainy photograph. They looked alike enough to be brothers, though it would need a good quality blow-up to prove it.

"Your grandfather?"

"And his brother, we think. There were several photographs from the rebuilding, but that's the only one I kept for myself. Let's get these bags upstairs, shall we?"

Colom had fallen asleep in the car and they had left him, a mumbling puppy curled up on the back seat. Fiona had picked him up from school; gone straight to Caterham; had explained her plan to take a few days away, just the two of them. She was pleased that he didn't throw a tantrum, but frightened to see him again so passive, so accepting, as if nothing registered on the screen of his emotions. His only sulk was reserved for the news that his laptop hadn't yet come back from being repaired.

"But I need it!" he shouted, the car filling with the tension in his voice.

"I couldn't get it in time," she said, working hard to keep her own exasperation at bay. "But you can read, draw. There'll be things for you to do, I'm sure."

Though she wasn't. She wasn't sure of anything. It made no difference in any case: he had turned from her and was staring out of the side window in silent process. "I hate this," she heard him mumble.

Passivity took hold of him in earnest through the two days at Caterham. Miriam offered to talk with him but he declined. He slept a lot; missed several meals. In the end Fiona focused on getting organized to go; put her hope in the trip itself breaking his foul mood.

They took the late ferry from Newhaven to Dieppe, arriving at 3:00 a.m. and carrying straight on into the five-hour drive. The boat had been shockingly uncomfortable. No possibility of sleeping on the crossing. They took turns at the wheel, stopping once to refuel and once at a deserted service station whose thin and tasteless vending machine coffee did little to shorten the night. A third stop, to post the letter Fiona had spent the ferry trip writing, lasted only seconds. Fiona was sleepy, but glad to have the journey behind her. There was nothing in her schedule for the coming days that suggested she would not soon catch up. It had taken her just seconds to agree to Miriam's invitation, and less than forty-eight hours to make the necessary arrangements. What else could she do? When you've fallen to the bottom of a well and someone throws you down a rope, you take it.

"I'll show you where your rooms will be," Miriam said cheerfully.

The first floor of the house was as straightforward and homely as below: three bedrooms, simply but comfortably furnished, and a worn but functional bathroom. Wooden floors were covered in a patchwork of old and unmatched rugs. The furniture was a random collection of pieces, all fifty years old or more.

Narrow steps had been added to the upstairs landing to give access to the attic. This was a huge room stretching the full length of the house. There was one original window, enabling one person at a time to see the sea above the rooftops of the cottages below. Three roof lights had more recently been added. Whoever slept in this room would be the first to know the day's weather: if there was sun, it would flood in here early; if rain, it would hammer like a drum. The windows let in a huge quantity of light. What might have been a dark attic of shadows and dingy corners was now an airy and spacious room.

Fiona knew at once that however long they stayed in Portivy, Colom would spend much of that time in this room. He would read here; he would draw here; he would sleep here, as often by day as by night; and for many hours he would just sit here, probably with the windows at least partly open, letting the distant rolling of the sea, the closer caress of the wind and even, at times, the chill of the rain take hold of him. All this she knew within a moment of climbing the stairs, though when in due course she roused him and coaxed him through the narrow climb, he looked around once, barely noticing his new surroundings, and fell heavily onto the bed. He was asleep again in seconds. She wasn't sure he'd even been awake in between.

She left him to sleep, wondering what this strange and foreign place would mean to them both. Wondering if she should have brought him here at all; if this would be for them a place of life, or of death.

CHAPTER THIRTEEN

*Back then, Billy imagined that drops of rain were
unanswered prayers falling back to earth.*

Jim Carroll, *The Petting Zoo*

The beach was deserted and thick with seaweed. Miriam had explained that the weed was cleared daily in the summer season but left to accumulate through the winter. She had been excusing the pungent smell that hung over the port; on some days taken away by the wind, on others left to hum like a brass band. Fiona counted twenty or more boats at anchor, a mixture of simple rowing boats and small fishing vessels. A compact, wind-screened wheelhouse was as sophisticated as things got around here. The rowing-boats were stashed with nets and buoys. This was no longer the working port it must have once been, but fishing remained the activity of choice.

A jetty pressed out some 200 metres into the bay, its seaward side a high stone wall, its sheltered side marked off at intervals by decaying metal ladders. Fiona felt the wind pick up as she moved away from the shore. There was damp in the air. Her coat was warm, but the wind burned her cheeks and a sharp cold was creeping into her fingertips. To her left she could hear a rhythmic booming: the muted thunder of the sea against the cliffs. Puddles mapped the uneven surface of the jetty. Rusted metal rings set into the stone bore testimony to the weather's power in this place.

She turned to survey the village, seeing it as if she were a sailor returning to port. She saw a cluster of grey-stone and white-painted houses, the blue of their shutters standing out even in winter. Behind them other rows, erratic and slanting, worked their way up the hillside. The impression was of a village that had unfolded over time, each new house clinging to the one before, a huddle of homes seeking shelter in togetherness. There was a glimpse of newer homes deeper inland, shielded from the worst of the weather by their braver, more rugged forebears. Beyond the uneven rooflines she saw clouds: rolls and layers folded like meringue to fill the sky. She saw grey and white; bands of pale purple; sinister accents in a dark, soot-like black. The village was a flat line against this turbulent ceiling, its buildings sandwiched between the power of the ocean and an immensity of sky. Beyond the village on both sides were small beaches: rock pools, sand and the ubiquitous weed. A thin coastal path followed the shore like a pencil line marking the edge of the world.

She turned back towards the open sea; let the wind meet her fully in the face. She couldn't tell if the tears creeping from the corners of her eyes were the wind's gift to her or the slow surfacing of her own desolation. She thought she should perhaps be praying, but no words came. What could she say? She didn't even know why she was here, let alone what she wanted from this place. Days ago she had stood in her neat London home not knowing what to do, and now she was here, among strangers, sleeping in a stranger's bed, foolish and exposed in a deserted holiday village that even in full summer she would probably never have chosen. And what of Colom, her son? The words rang hollow in her thoughts. What kind of mother was she being to him? With scant warning she had bundled him into the car and brought him far from home, with only her friend, a woman in her fifties, for company. Whatever this adventure was, it was not his choice. She wondered if this place would be a ladder for him to climb towards the light of day, or a chasm down which to fall.

She turned back to see a police car pulling into the car park. Her heart stopped. Already? So soon? Two *gendarmes* got out, both young and both women, the wind catching their hair as soon as they stood. They headed towards the café, its lights warm and welcoming in the winter half-light. Fiona started walking in that direction, saw as she approached that they were talking to someone across the bar. Too quickly, they turned to leave. She diverted her steps, mumbled a wind-muffled "*Bonjour*" and shuffled past them to huddle in the bus shelter. She had no idea if the busses even ran in the winter, let alone if one was due. She held her breath, waiting for them to approach her, but they headed to their car. One of them, on the driver's side, got straight in. The other hesitated for a moment, looking across the roof of the car towards Fiona. For an agonizing few seconds she looked as if she was going to say something or to come over. Fiona tried not to look at her, pretending to be rummaging for something in her handbag. She heard the engine start and looked up to see the car moving away.

Relief flooded her, but with it the sickly realization of what she had done. She let them move out of sight and crossed quickly to the notice board. A missing person's poster: a grainy, blown-up picture of a teenage boy; dark hair straight, not curled. Underneath, a brief paragraph. He was from the nearby town of Auray; had last been seen the previous weekend, hitch-hiking into Quiberon. She didn't know whether to laugh or cry; to feel joy at her own acquittal or agony on behalf of a mother who even now was imagining the worst for her son. And was this really an acquittal – or a warning of what was to come?

She heard her name and looked up to see Miriam and Colom heading down the hill. They had agreed to meet at the café for a drink once Colom woke, Miriam offering to wait and walk down with him so that Fiona could explore the village alone. Miriam was striding ahead, Colom struggling to keep up. His shoulders hunched against the cold; his hands deep in his pockets. His face communicating neither pleasure nor pain, fixed in its habitual grimace of disdainful indifference. Even at this distance, she could see that their short walk had not involved conversation. She took advantage of the few seconds afforded to her to compose herself, meeting Colom with a beaming smile.

"Hi, love. How did you sleep?"

He didn't answer her. Looked at her with the smallest of shrugs. Anger in his eyes. *Why have you brought me here? What right do you have to ask how well I slept?*

"Well, this is Portivy," she said, turning to take in the view of the sea, sweeping her hand across it like a tour guide. "It's a beautiful spot." This to Miriam, but also for Colom. Anything to speak life into him.

He still didn't respond. An awkward silence. Three wind-wrapped bodies, standing on a hillside. Saying nothing.

"Coffee?" Miriam asked, smiling hopefully. "Tea? Hot chocolate?"

The Café du Port was almost empty. At a corner table a middle-aged couple were just getting up to leave, zipping their cagoules, the woman strapping Nordic walking canes to her wrists. The only other customer in sight was a man who looked to be mid-fifties, with a white goatee beard, his long hair pulled back into a ponytail. He was wearing jeans and a US university sweatshirt, and sitting on a stool at one end of the bar, leaning forward on his elbows to read the paper. There was a coffee cup in front of him. He swung round as Miriam called his name.

"Thierry," she said loudly. "*Comment vas-tu?*" How are you?

He jumped down from the stool to embrace her: a kiss on each cheek and a hug for good measure.

"Miriam," he said. "*Ça fait du bien de te voir.*" It does me good to see you.

"I wondered if I might find you here," she said.

"Where else? This is where I work."

There was a half-smile as he said this, and Fiona wondered what the joke might be. She registered the look of disappointment on her friend's face. There was no time to find out what this might mean, as Thierry pushed past Miriam to extend his hand to her, saying in accented but confident English, "And who is this charming lady – I thought you always visited alone, Miriam?"

Miriam introduced Fiona and Colom, and nods of greeting were exchanged: in Colom's case a small shrug. Fiona and Thierry shook hands. Thierry asked what drinks might be required, and Miriam asked for coffee, Fiona hot chocolate for herself and Colom. Mother and son found a table and sat down. Colom immediately adopted a fixed stare out of the window. Miriam stayed at the bar talking to Thierry as he occupied himself with the espresso machine.

"I just didn't know if you would still be here," she said. "It's been more than five years since I was last home."

"Not still here. Back here," Thierry corrected her over the banging out of coffee grinds and the clatter of saucers onto the counter. "I too have been away."

Miriam was about to ask where when they were interrupted by a short, balding man who poked his head through the curtain that separated the bar area from the kitchens behind. He nodded ever so slightly to Miriam, but quickly turned to address Thierry.

"Thierry, don't forget you promised me a stock check this afternoon."

"Sure, boss, no problem," Thierry answered as the head withdrew behind the curtain. The same wry smile as he turned back to Miriam.

"Boss?" she asked, a puzzled look exaggerated on her face.

"I sold the place three years ago," Thierry said over his shoulder as he brushed past her to deliver Fiona and Colom's drinks. "Pierre is from Paris, used to be a professional weightlifter. Had to get out of the game for health reasons. He wanted to settle into a business here on the coast, and I wanted to leave one. We were each other's escape plan. I come in when I'm in town to work a few bar shifts. It helps Pierre out and gives me some much needed company."

"And when you're not in town…?"

"America: Seattle mostly, but also San Francisco, occasionally New York. I have galleries in all three cities that will take as much of my work as I can supply them with. And it sells. Very well, actually."

"So you are painting again?"

"Finish your coffee and I'll show you."

Miriam took her coffee to join Fiona and Colom at the table. Where her face had registered disappointment – perhaps disapproval – just moments before, she was now glowing with some deep satisfaction.

"Thierry is a very old friend," she explained to Fiona and Colom. "We grew up together here in Portivy. Last time I saw him this was his bar. I always hoped he would get free of it and paint again – and now it seems he has."

"Is he any good?" Fiona asked, looking past Miriam's shoulder to where Thierry was washing the cups and plates collected from the walkers' table.

"I think so," Miriam answered, looking directly at Colom, his eyes to the horizon. "He always dreamed of earning his living fully as an artist, and it sounds as if he might at last have got there."

They finished their drinks in the privacy of their own separate thoughts. As soon as they got up to leave, Thierry came over.

"Do you have time now?" he asked, looking to both Miriam and Fiona. "It's very close."

They looked at each other and shrugged. "Why not?" Fiona said for all three of them.

Thierry called back as he reached for the door to lead them out. "Pierre, I'm out for a few minutes." He waited to hear the grunt in reply, and was gone.

"It's just here," he said, moving in great strides to the property immediately beside the bar, the first of a short row of cottages facing the sea. The windows of the two upstairs rooms were framed in the curved stone arches so popular on Breton farm buildings. The contours of the roof and guttering followed the same curve, putting Fiona in mind of a hobbit's cottage. The ground floor appeared to boast two rooms – one each side of a large wooden door, topped by the same type of gently curving arch. Above the door the date – 1878 – etched deeply into the stone. The roof was sagging in the middle, but seemed to have been re-slated at least once this century. The paint on the exterior walls was flaking and worn but looked as if it might at one stage have been white.

Inside they were met with an explosion of light and colour. The internal walls had been taken out, leaving the ground floor an open, pillared space. Where the rear wall had once been, a glass-roofed extension had been added along the full width of the house. This flooded the room with light. Every other internal wall was painted white, bouncing the incoming light around. An easel was set up; a part-finished canvas still on it. Around the room other canvases were hung or stacked four or five deep against the walls. In one corner there seemed to be some hint of a kitchen, but it was clear that domestic normality took second place to the truly honoured occupants – the paintings. They were huge, bold compositions, but they had only one subject, in every part of the room, captured in a hundred different moods and seasons. In the day; at night; in calm weather; in storm. Scorched by the sun or caressed by the moon; green and wind-whipped; sky-blue and still; on fire with the oranges and purples of evening. The whole room was a sustained study in its one obsessive subject – the sea.

Fiona stood before a huge picture – at least two metres square. Tangled swathes of different blues crossed the canvas from one side to the other like a pile of crooked sticks ready for a bonfire. The composition was a slice of the sea; a fragment of an infinitely larger mystery, like a colour swatch promising so much more to come. There was an agitation in the deep blue waves. Moving closer she saw that there were other colours. White, of course, off-setting the waves, but mauve and black and aquamarine, too, even orange, in specks and flashes, hinting at a world of life and colour below the surface – of the painting, but also of the sea. Looking closer still she saw tiny objects: broken shell pieces; fragments of wood; the twisted threads of rope. All worked into the paint, submerged, as if by the ocean itself.

She imagined the canvas in a spacious dining room, spotlit against a stone wall. It would be impressive, and she guessed it would be priced accordingly. Large pictures are for people with large rooms, and people with large rooms have large wallets.

There was a stairway in one corner of the room but Thierry didn't seem inclined to show them upstairs. It was the paintings he had wanted them to see. He beamed at Miriam, anxious for her approval. She took in the room and all its paintings in a sweeping gaze.

"This is wonderful, Thierry," she said, almost breathless. "I'm so proud of you."

"Home at last," he said, the French more precise: "*Je suis enfin chez moi.*" She knew he wasn't talking about the house. He was looking at the paintings.

Fiona watched Colom as he moved around the room, stopping for a few moments before each canvas. He wasn't speaking, but his hands were no longer pressed into his pockets, and there was something in his expression, the tiniest spark of a change. She couldn't name it, didn't dare to call it hope. But she knew what it was not. It was not indifference.

CHAPTER FOURTEEN

Heavy rain is classified as being more than 0.30 inches of rain an hour. If droplets are very small they are typically known as drizzle.

"Rain", Wikipedia

The day after their arrival dawned with the pallor of a fevered child. They woke to rain, not hard and heavy but rolling in from the sea in layered curtains of drizzle. Where Monday's sky had been coloured and contoured with an orchestral mix of clouds, today it was monochrome: grey from the streets to the satellites. The houses were tiny boxes at the bottom of a vast, deep tank of greyness.

Fiona had some things she needed to buy and needed internet access so headed for town while Colom was asleep. She didn't expect him to wake before noon, but she was wrong. Miriam had only just finished clearing up from breakfast when she heard him on the stairs. He fell into the kitchen in a long-sleeve t-shirt and boxers, rubbing the sleep from his eyes.

"Good morning," she said cheerfully. "Did you sleep well?"

He ignored her question. "What time is it?" he mumbled.

"Just after 10:30," she said. "That's French time – 9:30 for your body clock."

He seemed a little confused by this. "Where's Mum?" he asked, coming to terms with his location and surroundings.

"She headed into town – some shopping to do. We were expecting you to sleep in longer."

"Couldn't sleep." Matter-of-fact. Indifferent again.

"Hungry?" she asked. "You hardly ate yesterday. I've got bread and there's a croissant left – or we have some of the cereals your mother brought."

He followed her gaze to the countertop where the cereal boxes stood guard. Walked over; checked one of the boxes; approved it; turned back with it towards the table to sit down.

She put out a hand to stop him, pointed to his boxers.

"You mind getting dressed first? I'd prefer it."

He looked up, confused again, but got the message. Shrugged and turned back to climb the stairs.

"I'll put some milk on for hot chocolate," she said to his back.

The milk was just coming to the boil when he re-emerged in jeans and a hoody. He sat down to pour Frosties from the family-sized box. She mixed the chocolate, placed the mug beside him. He looked. Grunted. She took a guess that this constituted thanks.

"It's sterilized milk, I'm afraid," she said as he flooded his small hillock of cereal. "UHT. We don't get much fresh milk here. We're used to the taste of this kind and it's much easier to buy in quantity and store."

He looked at her, barely registering a word she was speaking; dug his spoon into the bowl; took in a loaded mouthful; didn't seem to notice the difference. She turned back to her washing up, but was sitting at the table by the time the Frostie mountain was gone. He held his mug in both hands; sipped the chocolate slowly. She did the same with her coffee, though she'd poured it almost half an hour earlier and it was lukewarm.

"So what do you think of Portivy?"

He shrugged. She waited for words to follow but realized none were coming.

"Did you like Thierry's paintings?"

Another shrug, this time with the merest hint of a nod.

"Your mother tells me you've talked about killing yourself. Is that true?"

He lowered his almost-empty mug to the table. Turned to stare at her from under his curls. She said nothing more. Waited for him to decide. Fight or flight. Engagement or indifference. His choice. His face hardened. "Why shouldn't I? It's my life."

He'd made his choice, but their first stop-start conversation had begun. Having plunged in so directly, she reverted to more casual questions, about his childhood, his memories. There were several matters about which he had nothing to say, but over certain memories he surprised her by his willingness to talk. There were shrugs, of course, a front of indifference, but behind the defences he was not an entirely unwilling subject. She was treated unexpectedly to detail: colours and sounds; a picture painted in words. They sat at right angles to one another, the used mugs still on the table between them. She dared not move for fear of losing the opportunity that had opened up to her.

She asked him about Canada, his earliest years, how much he remembered of his time there. He was vague; odd details piled together like junk on a jumble sale table. A stream at the side of the house; trains passing not far away. Snow in the garden. He spoke of the house always being crowded; of there being other children around him. His mother had told him that there were always other church families around. He mentioned the pictures she had framed for him. He spoke quietly, not looking at her but at the table. Sliding his empty mug from side to side. His leg jumping, a constant movement.

"What's your earliest memory?"

Colom paused. A long, lingering silence; memories floating in front of his eyes like exotic fish in an aquarium: as soon as he tried to focus on one of them to examine it more closely, it would flit away – and then the rest would sense the movement and flee too. It was best not to try too hard. Let the memories float by; let them follow their course. If you were still enough, you never knew when one might swim close enough to show you its colours.

Miriam honoured the silence. If you wanted to help people remember you had to learn when to speak and when not to. Early on she had been impatient with silence. She had filled it with questions "to move things along", like a road mender filling potholes to ease the traffic. Then she'd learned that the potholes were her friends – it was the road that was the problem, burying everything under its dark cloak of asphalt. She learned to stay with the potholes; to look deeply into them. To meet silences with patience.

"There was a swing," Colom said at last. A single memory had presented itself for inspection. He left the others to swim on. His eyes had lifted from the table; he stared across the room, focused on nothing. He talked slowly, as much to himself as to her. "It was behind the house, around the corner from the downstairs bedroom window. I remember sitting on it on my own, when no one was around. There were two others but they were too high for me to climb onto. This one was mine because it was the only one I could reach. I must have been there at night at least once, because I remember leaning back and looking up at the stars."

Miriam saw a shadow pass over his eyes. A flicker across the screen he was remembering on.

"Were you supposed to be there?"

He paused, searching for an answer. "No one knew I was there. They were looking for me. They had torches and were calling my name, but I didn't answer. It was cold, but I stayed where I was, looking at the sky. Then someone spotted me and they came and told me to come in. They were pretty mad with me."

"They?"

He caught the meaning of the question and for a second was lost to a deep confusion.

"They… the… my parents, I guess."

The confusion was a rock thrown into the aquarium. Memories scattering like chickens from a fox. Miriam could see from Colom's expression that there would be no more of the saga of the swing today. His energy was waning. She had margin for only one more question. Had not expected to be asking it so soon.

"Colom, your mother asked if I would talk to you. Listen to you. About these things and others. Maybe let you explain to me how your life is; how you feel right now; if there's anything you're worried about. Would you be willing to do that?"

"Now?" It was his quickest response so far. Almost animated. A little defensive.

"Not now, no. Maybe tomorrow; the next day. Perhaps a little bit each day. I told her we'd only do it if you agreed to it. What do you think?"

He weighed the question.

"Like a counsellor, you mean? Like at school?"

"Something like that. But here, and when it suits you. And you can stop a conversation at any moment if it bothers you."

He thought some more, pushed the empty chocolate mug along an arc on the table, first with one finger, then back the other way with the other.

"Yeah, that'd be OK," he said. "Thanks for the hot chocolate."

And he was gone; back upstairs to the room that even in twenty-four hours had already become his sanctuary.

She marvelled at him. It had been hard to get him talking, but no harder than with most fourteen-year-olds she knew. And he had been polite. He'd thanked her for the drink. He'd made eye contact. He'd considered her proposition carefully and given it a reasoned response. What exactly was wrong with this picture?

She saw, or heard, some small part of the answer that same afternoon. Fiona came back from town with a loaf of decent wholemeal bread, a mixed bag of carrots and onions and a hand blender she'd found on the supermarket shelves. She called twice up to Colom – once when the soup was bubbling on the hob and again when it had been portioned out into three deep bowls. Both times she received an impatient "I'm coming!" in response, and nothing more.

The two women ate in silence, waiting for Colom to appear. He didn't, and Fiona left Miriam to clear their plates while she went up to talk to him. All was quiet for a few moments, before sounds of shouting made their way downstairs.

Colom's voice: "I told you I was coming, and I was coming!"

Something mumbled; Fiona trying not to raise her voice.

"I don't have to eat. I'll eat if I'm hungry. I don't always have to do what you say."

Fiona, louder this time, something indistinguishable, and then, "… being rude to Miriam. She's been very kind to let us come. And please stop shouting." This last request shouted.

"I didn't ask to come. This was your idea, not mine." Louder still, losing control. "I don't even want to be here. I don't want to be anywhere with you. I hate this place. And I hate you."

A door slamming. Then for several minutes nothing beyond the muffled sounds of continuing conversation. Fiona's steps coming sheepishly down the stairs.

"I'm really sorry, Miriam," she said the instant she stepped into the room.

"There's no need to be," Miriam assured her. "He's tired. He's had a lot to think about. Does this happen often?"

"Often enough. Not every day, but several times a week. He's crying now, lying on his bed. He won't let me near him." She stood hesitantly at the bottom of the stairs; wanting to go back up, but knowing it would be futile to do so.

"Come sit down," Miriam said gently. "Leave him to cool off."

"That's what I do, every time. It's all I can do – leave him to himself for an hour or more, and it will be as if nothing had happened. I'm not sure it's the most responsible way to deal with him, but it's the only one we've found that offers the slightest hope of peace. It's even worse with David. I can't leave the two of them alone without risking World War III. The tiniest thing – a comment, a request, the mildest of criticisms in either direction – and they're at it."

Miriam took the seat beside her, placed her hand on Fiona's arm.

"If it's not the nuclear holocaust, it's the zombie wars," Fiona said. "I don't know which frightens me more, his rage or his passivity."

"I know which should," Miriam said quietly. Fiona looked up at her. "At least he's expressing something," Miriam said. "Anger, rage, hatred: they're all preferable to indifference. He needs to let you know how he feels."

Fiona's head had fallen back into her hands. "We've had this so wrong," she mumbled through her fingers.

"Perhaps you have," Miriam said warmly. "But you're here now because you want to put it right, and you will get through this, Fiona. It will pass."

"I hope so," Fiona whispered. "It's been so long, I've forgotten what normal family life was like."

They sat for a while in silence; so much so that the distant sounds of the sea made their way into the room. A rhythm Miriam knew as well as she knew her own heartbeat. The rhythm she had listened to, in this very room, in the days of her own greatest darkness, when she had ceased to believe that she would ever know again her own kind of normal. Thierry had helped her then, and others. But it had been this place that had brought her through; the utter reliability of tides and seasons; the ocean's firm refusal to interrupt its cycles for the sake of any personal tragedy. She only hoped the same might prove true for Fiona. And for Colom.

They managed to coax him down for supper, which he ate with no great enthusiasm, expending only such energy as was needed to get the fork to his mouth. He left his plate half-full; turned down the offer of dessert.

"I'll tell you what," Miriam said to him, the effort at a convivial meal-time aborted, "why don't you and me do the washing up together while your mother puts her feet up?"

He looked up, a little confused, but shrugged agreement. Miriam ran a sink full of water, gave him the sponge, and stepped out of the way to stand ready with a tea towel. She watched as he gingerly washed each plate, taking items from the surface of the water without rolling up his sleeves. Until he couldn't do more without getting them wet.

He hesitated.

She moved in. "Don't soak your sleeves," she said, reaching across to push them up his arms. He went to turn away; resisted the temptation to run. She sensed his whole body stiffening. He stood like a statue, his arms against the edge of the sink. She worked the sleeves of first his right arm then his left away from his wrist. On his arms, for all his efforts to turn them from her, she saw the criss-cross of raw, puckered lines, a scratch pad from elbow to wrist. Some of the scars old, some evidently new.

From the shape of his body, arched away from his mother, the bare arms held inward to keep them out of sight, Miriam quickly concluded that Fiona knew nothing of this. She pulled the sleeves back down.

"Why don't I wash?" she said, loud enough to be heard across the room. "You can do the drying for me."

He took the tea towel from her, all the time looking at the floor. Dried each item numbly, mechanically.

"Thanks, Colom," she said, smiling, the last few items done. "I appreciate your help."

"Can I go now?" he said.

"Of course. It's pretty much bedtime anyway."

He turned to go. She caught his arm as he did so, until he looked at her. She held eye contact.

"It's good to have you here, Colom. It really is."

And again he was gone, back into his burrow; to the aloneness that was his safe house and his prison.

They were only two days into their trip but already Miriam was getting to know Colom. Better still, she was fast coming to like him. Her greater concern was that Fiona had told her so little. Did she really not know what her son was doing to himself? Or had she simply chosen not to speak of it? Whichever was the case, the end of a long and tiring day was not the time to find out.

* * *

Fiona sat in the half-dark, feeling the weight of all that hadn't been said; the tensions of their thrown-together household. She grabbed her coat from the hook by the door and stepped out into the night. A strong wind was blowing in from the sea. She felt it on her face; heard it in the trees around. Heard it, deeper still, in the distant waves. The sound had changed. The day's waves had been steady and rhythmic. Now they seemed wilder; more restless; wind-driven. Each new wave was cresting before the one before it had even found land. It was an endless, rolling roar; surging wave-caps stark in the bright moonlight. Little wonder these were called white horses: they had the urgency and energy of a cavalry in full charge.

She walked part way out along the jetty. A single, high light sent a pool of orange onto the waves and a few of the boats. Looking to the seaward side she could see the unremitting inward rush of the ocean. The tide was high. The deepest waves were breaking early, crashing against the harbour wall itself. Some bounced back out to collide with those still heading shorewards, spewing foam and spray. The sea was boiling. Even from behind the wall she felt an aching terror. She had never learned to swim. She watched the colliding waves and knew exactly how it would feel to drown in that cold cauldron. To be sucked down; nothing to hold on to; no one to call out for. And yet there was a fascination here, like standing at the guard rail of a ferry, staring at the green swirling mass she both loathed and feared and imagining herself thrown into it. Her legs, against her will, edging towards the climb, one foot already finding the first rung of the railings.

She turned to head towards the house. The wind was at her back, gently urging her away. There was more than water to be feared in this place. There was life itself. She wondered if that was why she found it so easy to imagine drowning: why the thought of being out of her depth seemed so familiar.

* * *

There's this dream I keep having. I am trying to stay afloat in the ocean. The water is cold and clammy and somehow I know there's no life in it. Sometimes another me is near me in the same sea – though even in my dream I know there is no other me. The water temperature is bearable: not so much a deathly chill as an absence of warmth, like when you fall asleep in the bath and it goes cold. I am treading water to stay afloat, but there is land close by; some kind of shore. I'm thinking maybe I'll be safe if I reach it. Sometimes I wake before reaching it, but sometimes I get there – only to find that the land is also cold and lifeless, a slippery clay I can't get a grip on. I try to climb out of the sea but I keep sliding back, and then somehow I know that even if I get onto the land it won't help, because I will be just as cold and exposed and unsafe as I am in the water. And whatever it is that haunts me – the shadow I feel so close in the water that it is breathing over me – will be just as able to find me on the land. I long for the other me, the me that is in the water with me, to reach out and help me. Just a hand, stretched out to me, its human warmth breaking the ocean's icy grip. But the other me is as lost as I am, and as scared. The currents are pulling us apart. And the shadow I'm afraid of even more than drowning is filling the space that has opened up between us.

CHAPTER FIFTEEN

It didn't rain for you, maybe, but it always rains for me. The sky shatters and rains shards of glass.

Tablo, *Pieces of You*

Colom didn't show the next morning. Fiona went out again to the internet café. Miriam had mentioned her surprise at getting the chance, so soon, to talk with him. They both felt it was worth trying to replicate the circumstances for a second day.

Pulling back into the Portivy car park, Fiona thought a second cup of coffee wouldn't kill her, and called into the Café du Port. Pierre, not Thierry, was behind the bar and greeted her politely. She took her *petit-crème* to a table by the window and watched clouds form and re-form over the distant industrial chimneys of Lorient. She was long back, and Miriam's book all but finished, before there was the least sign of her son.

She had bought lunch again: some ham cut fresh off the bone; salad; baguette. Even if she couldn't spark her son's enthusiasm, she could enjoy for herself the best of France.

After lunch Miriam suggested a walk. Much to her surprise, Colom agreed, though as ever he did so with the least number of words possible. They set out towards the headland where the shallow beaches and coves to the west of Portivy came to an end and the wildness of the Côte Sauvage began in earnest, running south all the way to Quiberon town. The day was dry but there was a chilling offshore wind. They wrapped up warm for walking.

They approached the only building on the headland itself: the ruin of a former customs officer's cottage. Roofless and windowless, the stark outline stood silhouetted against the vast expanse of the winter sky. A winding pathway led to the ruin, not by intention but by accident: the endless stream of walkers crushing the fragile clifftop grass. Graffitied walls, discarded bottles, and cigarette packets suggested that this had been more than once a teen party house.

The threesome headed south to pick up the cliff path, the village fast disappearing over their left shoulders. Further across the heath, part way between the old cottage and the beginning of the clifftop walk, stood the last remains of an ancient burial site. Two huge boulders laid horizontally across smaller rocks to form an altar. Around this structure, a circle of stones set into the ground. The whole assembly surrounded by a low wooden fence: a vain attempt to keep the curious from climbing. The site offered an extraordinary view across the heathlands and ocean, the ruined coastguard house the only man-made structure visible, tiny now against the broad canvas of sea and sky.

Skirting around the fence to head on, Miriam and Fiona were deep in conversation, Colom falling behind. They had been walking several minutes when Fiona suddenly interrupted her friend.

"Where's Colom?" she asked. "I thought he was behind us."

They turned around and shielded their eyes against the low angle of the winter sun.

"There's someone sitting on the stones," Miriam confirmed. "Looks like him." Fiona waved and shouted, but the black-coated figure on the rock didn't stir.

"I'll go back for him," Miriam said, launching off at a brisk pace. She too called out, but there was no response. Fiona stood and waited, wondering why she hadn't been the one to move first. She continued her futile shouting, adding great arcs of her arms, though she could make out, even from here, that the figure on the rock was looking out to sea and hadn't so much as glanced her way.

Miriam drew closer to the stone table. Colom was perfectly still but for the rise and fall of breathing. His knees were gathered to his chest, his arms around them; his eyes fixed on the ocean towards the horizon. The breeze was playing with his hair, teasing the curls back from his forehead. As she came closer she could see he had been crying. His lips were moving as though he was talking to himself, but he made no sound.

"It's so peaceful here," Miriam said, "even with the wind and the waves."

Colom said nothing for a long moment, then, "Maybe it's because of the wind and the waves."

Then another long pause – nothing expressed by either beyond breathing.

As Colom spoke again he swept his legs around, sliding off the rock and setting off towards the point at which he could now see Fiona, frantically waving. Miriam wasn't sure she had heard exactly what he said.

It was much later that evening that Fiona asked her what had happened at the rock. "Was Colom OK when you found him?"

"He was a little tense, distracted maybe. But he was OK." She paused for a moment. "He said it reminded him of his swing."

"What swing?" Fiona said, before she could stop herself.

Miriam looked at her for a moment, aware that something unsaid but significant was passing between them.

"It was something he told me about yesterday: a favourite swing he used to have in the back garden in Canada. He said it was the lowest of three – he was very young, and it was the only one he could even hope to climb onto. He didn't swing much, he said, but it was his favourite place to sit."

Fiona's face remained twisted into an expression of total puzzlement. "I don't... we didn't..." she stumbled.

"He remembered going out to it once at night. There was trouble because nobody knew where he was, and he was supposed to be indoors. It was a cold night, and he didn't have a coat on. Someone came looking for him – he said he thought it was you?"

Fiona regained her composure.

"Oh that. Of course. I'd forgotten all about it. I was quite cross with him because he was late for supper."

It was only later, thinking back, that Miriam found time to wonder why Fiona would choose to lie to her. The look that had come across her face, that had started as puzzlement – just for a second, before she had remembered the incident with the swing and Colom being late for supper – had morphed into something quite different. It wasn't puzzlement. It was panic.

Fiona struggled to sleep that night. She fell into a familiar vicious circle of anxiety and wakefulness in which she didn't know which was cause and which effect. She lay listening to Colom, the noises of his movements amplified in the stillness of the night. She had guessed back in London that his sleep was disturbed, but realized now that the carpeted house had muted her grasp on his condition. Here it was more obvious. She heard him moving about in his room for much of the night. At first light she thought he had perhaps come down the stairs, then silence fell and she fell with it into a restful sleep at last.

CHAPTER SIXTEEN

Very gently. Like there are eggshells on your pedals,
and you don't want to break them. That's how you
drive in the rain.

Garth Stein, **The Art of Racing in the Rain**

It took Colom twenty minutes to reach the ruined customs house. The tiny wheels of his suitcase jumped and bumped on the track, a world away from the marble airport floors they were designed for.

He had been sorting and packing for much of the night; piling his clothes onto the bed; choosing those he really needed as opposed to those he could do without. By the end of the process the suitcase was three quarters full. He pulled it tight to himself to tiptoe down the stairs without waking Miriam or his mother.

He couldn't see the sun for cloud, but a pale light was spreading across both sea and land. He sat for a moment on a fallen stone beside the ruined house looking out to sea, pleased to be at last ridding himself of encumbrances he didn't need. Wouldn't need for much longer, at least. This didn't constitute the deed itself, but it was a step in the right direction. A confirmation of intent. Rested and ready, he stood to his feet and moved towards the cliff's edge. He walked along until he found the right place. A tiny outcrop, the drop below it sheer and direct to waves: no hidden beach to thwart his purpose. He peered over the brink, fighting dizziness. Stepped back from the edge: one pace, then two.

The suitcase handle was fully extended and he gripped it in both hands. Swinging like a golfer, he pulled the case into the air, at the same time beginning to turn. He had once seen a video of a discus thrower, a Russian woman built like a bricklayer. He felt now what she must have felt in her spin, the promising momentum of an object held at a distance from the body. He spun twice around, then a third time before letting fly. The suitcase rose in a long arc, stopping for a microsecond before beginning its graceful descent. He was at the cliff-edge again, lying flat on his stomach, in time to see it hit the waves. Almost instantly, it was thrown against the rocks. He didn't wait to see it broken open, but he knew that it soon would be.

* * *

Fiona absented herself again after breakfast, in the hope that Miriam would once more get the chance to talk to Colom. There were things that she needed to say, and no doubt things she needed to hear, but for the moment Colom had priority. She set out once again for town, stopping at the Café du Port for the first *petit-crème* of the day. She got so caught up in conversation, the trip to town was almost forgotten. But not quite. She tore herself away, walked back to her car; headed south along the coast road.

Miriam had not long cleared away her own breakfast when Colom came in from the street. She had thought he was still sleeping.

"Been for a walk?" she asked cheerfully, only to be answered with a grunt.

She put the milk on to boil. He hung his coat beside the door; sat up to the table.

She knew that he was beginning tentatively to trust her. For her own part, she had begun to put together the pieces of a puzzle. The more she heard from Colom, the more she knew she wasn't hearing from Fiona.

"Fancy a drive?" she asked him, the Frosties once more demolished, the hot chocolate on its way to joining them. "I've got errands to run, and I thought I might show you the rest of the Côte Sauvage from the road?"

He shrugged, a kind of mimed "why not?". He drained his hot chocolate, getting up to put his mug and bowl beside the sink. She handed him his coat, buttoned up her own.

Miriam took a bunch of keys from a hook beside the coat rack. She led him down the alleyway to the road, then across it to a small car park. Tucked into the far corner was a low car shrouded by a grey canvas cover. Miriam pulled this off, folding it into the boot of the car itself. It was a scratched blue estate, short and squat with thin chrome bumpers and old-fashioned rounded lights. There were rear passenger doors – it seemed to be designed for a whole family – but it was small enough to be mistaken for a Mini. The whole body rocked when Miriam climbed into the driver's side.

A light rain was now falling, and she stretched quickly across to unlock the door on the passenger side for Colom. He climbed in, sinking into a thin, sprung upholstery of blue and red checks. His knees came up almost to the dashboard. There were black rubber mats on the floor; a fir-tree air freshener hanging from the rear-view mirror; a flat windscreen. The engine spluttered into life and Miriam switched on the wipers. They were no bigger than a bread knife and swished urgently, struggling to make more than a smudging impression on the rain-soaked glass. She manhandled a horizontal lever that came out from the dashboard and had a huge round knob at its end. The gears crunched as she found reverse. The car lurched back and then bounced forward onto the road, rocking and rolling with every dip in the worn asphalt surface.

"This was my mother's car," she said. "When she died it just stayed with the house. I have a friend here who uses it in the winter and looks after it to make sure it isn't going to kill anyone. She's away this week, so it's ours for the time being. What do you think?"

"It's OK," he said. Succinct, but she saw the faint hint of a smile.

They pulled away from the village and again towards the headland, the road following the contours of the coast, running fifty metres or so in from the cliff's edge. Once out of the shelter of buildings the wind picked up, buffeting the car. She drove carefully but saw Colom gripping the handle of his door, his other hand holding the seat edge. The suspension of a Renault 4 took some getting used to for a novice. She wondered how he'd feel a little further on, when the road came that much closer to the cliff.

She cut inland through the tiny, twisting village of Kerne, coming into the top end of Quiberon from the back road. Colom waited in the car while she dropped a letter into her *notaire* and ran to the post office. Jobs done, she headed back for the coast, this time picking up the Côte Sauvage at its town end, not far from Port Maria.

She pointed out to him the various landmarks; explained that the coast road continued all the way around the Côte Sauvage, running from Port Maria at this end to Portivy at the other. They passed the Vivier restaurant, the only building on the clifftop still in daily use. He acknowledged the information she offered with an array of affirmative shrugs. She was beginning to learn the code.

She dropped the commentary for a while and they drove in silence.

"Can we talk as we drive?" she asked at last.

He shrugged. Affirmative.

"Do you mind being here? Missing school – your friends?"

Another shrug. "I don't care," he said. No anger, just a bald statement. His unilateral declaration of non-engagement.

"Did your parents ever speak with you about your birth?" she asked. "Whether it was difficult for your mother; how it was in the first few days?"

"Not really."

She thought this would be all she was offered, but was surprised to find that more words followed. A fluency that caught her off guard; adult emotions leaking out from behind the adolescent facade.

"They've never talked about it much. They told me where I was born and when, but no more. She did used to sing that terrible song to me, about angels singing on the day of my birth, because they just wanted to be close to me. You know the one?"

"I'm afraid I do." She wasn't going to admit that she had the album, or explain that she had written a research paper on Karen Carpenter's battle with anorexia.

"She sang it every birthday. Each year she would make this little speech somewhere in the day. If she hadn't found space for it then it would come at night, when she was putting me to bed."

"What did she say?" She turned briefly to make eye contact, listening hard. Turned back to the road.

"That this day, above all others, was a day of celebration." His voice had switched into a kind of monotone, as if he was reciting from memory. "Because on this day so many years ago a miracle took place that changed the world forever. The birth of Colom David Dryden."

He paused for dramatic effect.

"It was pretty much the only time she used my full name – it made the speech seem more formal, somehow."

"And how did it make you feel?"

"Great, for a while. I thought I must be the luckiest boy on earth, to be so loved. I felt sorry for the other kids at school who didn't have my mum and dad for parents. She told me that seeing me for the first time was the single greatest moment of her life, and that no matter what happened, they could never take that away from her."

He paused. The mixed sounds of the wheels on the road, the rain on the roof and the wipers pursuing their futile battle for dry glass filled the car. Miriam watched the road, slowing into the steep curves where they so closely hugged the rolling pattern of coves and inlets. She wondered if the conversation was over. But Colom spoke again, a quiet murmur coalescing to form words.

"But it didn't stop the other thoughts coming back." His voice floating to fill the tiny tin cabin of the car.

Miriam turned briefly to see that he was looking out of the window, eyes fixed on the drops running down it.

"What thoughts?" she asked.

Another pause, then, "I thought she wanted to kill me."

They drove on in silence for a long time, each aware in their own way that they had crossed some invisible border. Miriam felt as if she were driving on the seabed, the car full of water. Above her was the weight of a million cubic metres. She had to work to keep the wheels on the road. The car wanted to float away, but she wouldn't, she couldn't, let it.

"Do you want to talk about that?" she asked, at last.

But he stayed where he was – turned away from her towards the window – and the shrug she could just make out in the movements of his shoulder blades was anything but affirmative. His brief mood of articulacy had passed; passivity returning like clouds across the face of the sun.

She decided this might be a good time to head home. Nothing more was said as she parked the car and they tumbled into the cottage, shaking the rain from their coats and hair. She was about to offer more hot chocolate, but his foot was already on the stairs.

Grateful for a moment's solitude, Miriam took her journal down from the shelf above the fireplace and sat up to the kitchen table. She prayed a silent prayer for Colom. She wrote his name on a blank page, around it a box, shaded to add definition. Not far from it, Fiona's name was added. Another box. More shading still. Then, unexpectedly, she found herself writing another name below the two of them. This one, too, boxed; shaded; darkly defined. She read it back, Miriam, and wondered what she was trying to tell herself. It wasn't Fiona's situation that most weighed on her mind, and it wasn't Colom's crisis she most feared. There was another, more dangerous explosion coming, one that had been building for much longer, and was more potent for being less expected. She sat to ponder for a moment, wondering how and when she would light the touch-paper. And whether any of them would survive the explosion that came.

For the first time in a very long time, Miriam found herself crying. In fear of the conversation she knew she must have. In deep regret for not having had it when she should have. She closed the journal, and her eyes. She let the deep unspoken prayer that only sobbing tears can utter rise from her, to be heard by the God she knew was listening. The God she knew to have orchestrated her journey into this cul-de-sac from which there was, truly, only one way out.

CHAPTER SEVENTEEN

The sound of rain needs no translation.
Alan Watts, In My Own Way

"The beach runs almost uninterrupted around to Port Louis, thirty kilometres away, and then it's just a jump across the estuary to Lorient."

Thierry pointed towards Penthièvre then took in the sweep of the coast in an arc that ended at Lorient. The proof was somewhere in the far distance, but mist and low cloud were masking all but the faintest of outlines. For today, Fiona took it on trust.

He led the way onto the beach path, moving away from Portivy towards the fort. Fiona picked up her pace to stay level with him so that they could talk as they walked. They followed a path squeezed onto a narrow band of grass between sandy and rocky coves on the one side and the walls and steps of the closest houses on the other: double-glazed new-builds nestling between blue-shuttered fishermen's cottages. A light drizzle was blowing across the bay, sweeping onto the beach in layered waves, a new invasion force with each gust of wind. Hunched against the rain, the sound of wind and waves filled their ears.

"So what brought you back to Portivy?" she asked, picking up a conversation that had begun over a series of morning coffees.

"Two people. My doctor in Seattle, and Miriam. My doctor told me the truth about my body. His news was not good. I needed rest, a severe detox and a complete change of lifestyle. Then when my father died I found myself back here – I had to see to the café and settle his affairs. Miriam came back to visit while

I was here. We talked, and she told me a different kind of truth about myself."

"Which was?"

"That whatever I was looking for would not be found there or here or any place in between, until I'd found it here."

He placed his hand over his heart.

"All my travelling, my drinking, my relationship disasters, were attempts to answer a question that only I could answer. She told me to listen to myself. So I did."

"What did you hear?"

"A longing for home. For Portivy. The sea. I realized that I had run away to elsewhere to find what had always been right here. It's more complex than that, but that's the gist. So I came home."

They stopped to look back in the direction they had walked from. She could see the dark grey rooftops of Portivy and, beyond them, the cliffs that marked the beginning in earnest of the Côte Sauvage. Even at this distance, with limited visibility, she could see the white of the foaming waves breaking on the rocks below the cliffs.

"*Je suis enfin chez moi,*" she said.

He looked at her, his eyebrows raised.

"You said it to Miriam, on that first morning, in your studio. I saw something pass between you. It was the first she knew, wasn't it – that you'd sold the café; taken up your art again?"

The wind was blowing her hair across her face. She reached up to pull it back; tucked it into the raised collar of her coat. He was looking out to sea now, eyes towards the horizon.

"She hasn't known until now how important to me our conversation was," he said. "She headed back to England, to her work, a few days after, and I returned to the USA – but I had already made the decision to come home."

"You didn't write to each other? Email?"

"No. We never have. It's a very Breton thing, I think. When you're here, you're here, and when you're not, you're elsewhere

128

and we simply wait for your return. Something from the days of fishing and sailing, I think. No expectation of contact when you're out at sea; communication squeezed into the time you're onshore."

He turned to her as he spoke, catching a smile on her lips.

"Do you find us a primitive people?"

"Not at all. I envy you your roots, this sense of belonging so completely to one place. I've never had that."

"Never? No place anywhere that you call home?"

"No. We moved around a lot when I was young. I'd been to twelve schools by the time I was eighteen. That was when I ran away and hit the road for myself. When I married David, the moving around just carried on. We've been in London for ten years now, while Colom has been growing up, but that's the longest I've ever lived anywhere, and even then we've moved house twice. I've never had a strong sense of belonging, or tribe."

"Well, if you'll permit me," he said, "I'd like to show you something of my own tribe's history."

She nodded assent. They turned to walk on.

The silhouette of the fort at Penthièvre grew as they walked, rising like an ancient temple from the surf. On the land side the fort was partly underground, visible as a series of grass-covered mounds like Teletubby houses. On the seaward side it boasted stone walls a good twenty metres high, rooted to the rocks at the very shoreline. When, as now, the tide was full, the waves broke directly onto the walls, splashing upwards in foam like a giant's spittle. The fort was not built for comfort but for war, watching outwards to sea and at the same time inwards, over the narrow road that offered the only landside access to the Quiberon peninsula.

Thierry led her off the beach path onto a narrow track that climbed the grassy hill towards the fort itself. At the crest of the hill an observation platform overlooked a street-wide dry moat that marked the limit of the inner complex, skirting the high, windowless walls. There was a stairway leading down from the platform's edge, and Thierry took it.

The moat was walled on one side by the high ramparts of the fort itself and on the other by a rocky cliff face. Thierry abruptly turned into the cliff. Fiona followed, to find herself in a narrow tunnel. It gave the impression of having been cut by hand from the rock, with barely room for one person at a time. There was a security lighting system, but its bulbs were old and weak, and gave little useful light.

Thierry stopped and said through the darkness, "Close your eyes. Keep them tight shut and count slowly to twenty, then open them again."

Fiona did as she was asked, and was surprised to find that she could see much better in the gloom. The jagged outlines of the walls were clear, and she saw that up ahead about thirty metres there was some kind of additional light source. As they continued through the tunnel, she saw more clearly what this was. A white cross, about a metre high, standing upright where the tunnel came to a stonewalled end. Protruding rocks around the cross had been commandeered as makeshift shelves for small floral arrangements and flickering votive candles. There was no plaque or inscription to indicate the monument's purpose, though it was well maintained. It clearly mattered to someone.

Thierry stood in silence before the shrine. Fiona followed suit. When at last he turned to leave, she asked, in her art-galleries-and-cathedrals whisper, "What's it for?"

"It's a memorial for those who are buried here," Thierry explained. "Come back outside and I'll show you why."

They worked their way back out through the tunnel: an easier task when walking towards the daylight. The phrase "there's light at the end of the tunnel" came into Fiona's mind and she wondered if perhaps there was.

On the cliff wall beyond the tunnel entrance, in a section sheltered by an overhang, a row of glass-fronted panels had been fixed, displaying documents and blow-ups of old black and white photographs. The unmistakable silhouette of a Nazi foot soldier told Fiona instantly when the photographs had been taken. They told the story of the fifty-nine bodies of local men discovered in May 1945, once the fort was no longer a makeshift German prison. Most of the photographs were of the mass funeral that was quickly arranged to give these men a decent burial, civic dignitaries and senior clerics hastily thrown together to perform their newly liberated duties.

Thierry moved along the displays, stopping before a particular panel, inviting Fiona to read it. It was a facsimile of a letter written by one of the prisoners the night before he was shot. Addressed to his young son, Robert, the letter had been hidden under the dirty mattress in the man's cell and was discovered after his death. It told of his determination to die courageously for France, just as his brother had, and urged his son to care for his mother and grandparents.

It was a moving plea to a son he knew he would never see again; an attempt to speak life and a future into him; to pour into a few short paragraphs a lifetime's worth of advice and encouragement. Fiona thought of David, struggling to overcome his own fear and guilt; unable to speak such a message of hope to Colom. She finished reading and guessed why she had been brought here.

"Your grandfather?" she asked.

He nodded. "My father was ten when my grandfather was shot; a few months older by the time they found the letter and brought it to him. The bodies had been thrown into a trench. They were discovered after the Germans had gone. The village was traumatized by the discovery – they had no idea the executions had been carried out. There was so much confusion at the war's end about where prisoners were; who had been deported to Germany; who had escaped or had stayed in hiding. Who had died in prison. All the time my grandmother was waiting for news, her husband was here; buried in a mass grave; five bullet wounds perforating his body. It was the worst kind of cruelty. My grandfather's letter became symbolic for many of the waste of such bright young lives, of their dignity in the face of death. The bodies were recovered and re-buried with a full military funeral – it was the village's first big civic event after the war.

"And your father grew up with only this to remember his father by."

He nodded. "He wasn't the only one, of course. There were thousands – here in France, in Britain, in Germany – pour souls whose lot it was to grow up fatherless."

"So what happened? How did your grandmother survive and raise your father?"

They turned away from the displays and began making their way back to the path.

"Some of the men who were shot here left families destitute, with neither income nor means to create it. Where there were no brothers or adult sons to take on the task of fishing, as was the case for my grandmother, the situation was critical: just weeks after the war had finally ended, any hope she had of re-building a future for her son was stolen from her. My father was too young at the time to work the boats, though he'd have done so if they'd let him. There was help from the government, but not much, and isolated villages like Portivy, where there was little visible war damage, received far less attention than disaster zones like Caen and Paris."

Fiona felt the crunch of gravel give way to the softness of sand underfoot as they left the fort behind and drifted slowly along the beach, heading back towards Portivy. The rain had not relented, and they were wet through.

"So the people of Portivy decided to pull together and took matters into their own hands," Thierry went on. "The families of those with no livelihood were adopted by those able to work. They established a committee and even years later were still making sure that the families of those who died were looked after. Miriam's father was the youngest man on the committee – he was a member of the Communist party and even then was known as a leader in this community."

"What about the café?" she asked. "I thought Miriam said it had been your grandmother's?"

"Not before the war, no. They lived entirely from fishing then. But the committee did everything they could to ensure the village's survival. The owner of the café, Madame Bodolec, lost her husband and both her sons to the Germans. She never really overcame her grief, and within months of the war's end was too sick to work. Somebody on the committee suggested that my grandmother be asked to take on the running of the café, and she moved in, with my father in tow. When Madame died five years later without an heir, she left the whole operation to my family. My father grew to be the heart and soul of the business. By the time I was born he was well on his way to being a chronic alcoholic. His drinking took his health, and eventually his life. When he left the bar to me I was in America, pursuing my own particular demons. I came back to see if I could do better as a barman than as a painter."

Fiona stopped walking and turned to him. "But you're painting again now. What changed?"

"I did. What's the phrase in English? I came to my senses. I realized that I'd left Portivy because I didn't want to be like my father, but I had become just like him. It didn't matter if I was there, or here, or some place in between – I was the one who had to change."

"So how does all this connect with the fort – the monument?" She had stopped, turned towards him. "I saw you in there – you looked as if you were visiting a temple. You never met your grandfather: why the reverence?"

"That's a good question. You ask good questions. I'll try to give a good answer. Miriam helped me to understand that everything I have I owe to these people. My father's success with the café; the thriving business I inherited from him, despite everything. My very life. At my lowest point, I realized that I had always imagined I would one day come back: to put something back into this village. I came to see it as a kind of debt, and I wanted to repay it before it was too late."

"How?"

"That's what I wanted to know. Initially I ran the café myself – I thought perhaps I would manage it, and that would be my life. But I soon found that this wasn't enough. There was something more I needed to do." He paused, as if reluctant to explain further.

"What?"

"Don't laugh at me."

"Of course I won't."

"Do you remember the film *Pay It Forward*?"

"Yes, I do."

"I saw it and came to the conclusion that that was what I should do. The café came to my father as a gift, and I thought I should pass it on in the same way. I thought that if I could find somebody to give it to, just as it was given to my father and his mother, then my debt would somehow be settled. Perhaps then I could leave for good; pursue my career as an artist and not feel that some part of me was always missing."

She could tell from his voice the Kevin Spacey plan hadn't worked.

"You couldn't find anyone?"

"No, no one that such a gift would be right for. The world has changed very much since those post-war years. Some echo of the old solidarity lives on in Portivy, but it is a sentiment, a memory – not a way of life as it was then. People here used to share gardens and courtyards – to hold land rights in common. Now everything is priced and measured and parcelled out. The meaning of property has changed. To give such a business away at random would simply not be right: for the café; for the village; even for the person receiving it. I couldn't find anyone who would understand the gift and receive it in the spirit in which it was given. I even thought of asking Miriam, you know. I thought I might write to her in England to tell her what an excellent café owner she would make. But I knew she wouldn't share my view. I never wrote the letter."

"So you decided to sell instead?"

"Not straight away. When I couldn't give the café away, I realized that I would have to change my thinking – that perhaps it would not be so easy to settle my debt to Portivy in one single grand gesture. Even such a wild and foolish generosity would not be enough. And then I understood something about my own motives: I was not trying to pay my debt but to escape it. There was and always had been only one way to repay."

"And that was?"

"To stay – to work out my debt in a million everyday decisions made right here over the remaining years of my life. How else could I honour the memory of those who died for their love of this place, and those who came after and by their solidarity and care saved my family? I remember the day I decided. I walked to the fort; to the monument, as we have just done. It was raining that day too, harder than today. I thought of my grandfather spending his last hours on earth inside those cold stone walls, and of my father, left with nothing – and that's when I knew that I would stay: that the gratitude I feel for every breath that fills my lungs would be expressed by breathing this air for the rest of my life. Once I had decided that I must stay, I realized that I wanted to: that this had always been my deepest intention."

"But not as a café owner?"

"At first I had no choice but to make the best of it. Then I got to know Pierre – he came here on holiday. He'd just come off the weightlifting circuit with a pocket full of cash and a heart condition. He kept coming into the café and saying how much he envied my life: living all year round in this beautiful place, serving drinks and food to locals and tourists. After two weeks, just before he was due to return to Paris, I called his bluff and offered to sell him the café. Not to give it to him – he would never have accepted it that way in any case – but to sell it for a fair price. I didn't know if he had taken my proposition seriously, but one month later he was back with a Paris friend who worked in property. They looked the place over, talked about the business, and two days later made me an offer, which I accepted without hesitation. Pierre moved down six months later, and I bought the house beside the café, which was vacant, in need of remodelling, and perfect for a studio and small gallery. Pierre made some good changes to the café, and hired a Swiss chef to cook for the main tourist months of the summer. He is making a profit, popular and, as far as I know, blissfully happy."

Without thinking about it, they had started walking again. They were approaching the village now, could smell the smoke from the lit fires of the few homes that were occupied all winter. They walked the last few metres into Portivy in silence. Reaching the point where they would go their separate ways, Fiona turned to him.

"Thank you," she said, "for sharing all that with me. It's fascinating, and helps me to understand why this place is so special to you."

"Thank *you*," he responded, "for your company, and your excellent questions." He gave a slight bow, the formal Frenchman peeking out from behind the bohemian artist's costume. "You'll come in for coffee tomorrow?"

"I'm sure I will," she said. "I'll see you then." She turned to walk up the hill. She didn't look back, but had she done so she would have seen that he didn't walk away but stayed, unmoving, watching her go.

Later that evening she took a shower before bed. As the hot water and shampoo caressed and soothed her, she thought about her body and how long it had been since anyone had touched her with anything beyond the most perfunctory intimacy.

136

CHAPTER EIGHTEEN

The amount of water held in the atmosphere at any time is sufficient to produce about 2.5 cm (1 inch) of rain over the surface of the earth.

"Rain", Wikipedia

Over the following days the rain came in earnest, filling the sky with billowing clouds of fridge-cold water. Fiona had never catalogued so many different kinds of rain in so short a space of time. If the Eskimos have fifty words for snow, Bretons must have a hundred for rain. Three types became particularly familiar. The first she would have previously called drizzle: a thin mist of tiny drops that hovered over land and sea, or drifted in currents and eddies, shaped by the changing winds. The surprise of this seemingly benign form, here in Portivy, was the sheer quantity of water it delivered: just a few minutes of exposure could lead to a soaking as deep as immersion, as if the sea itself were being picked up and dropped all over the village. The second form she was getting to know was heavier; vertical, with large individual drops. This seemed more familiar to her – she thought of it as Canadian rain – the weight of water expressed in the bulging waistline of each drop; the Jackson Pollock reach of each explosive landing.

The third type she'd last experienced in the outports of Newfoundland. Horizontal rain, driven by the wind like nails into a wall. When this type came out to play she kept herself behind closed doors, a timid child avoiding the school bully. Otherwise she braved both wind and rain to take her daily walks around the village.

The unusual household at 2 Allée du Vivier settled quietly into a makeshift routine. Fiona and Miriam would rise first and have breakfast together, leaving Colom to lie in. Then Fiona would take herself out: sometimes to town, sometimes to walk around the village, always to the Café du Port before or after, or both. Colom would come down mid-morning, never quite sure what time it was. Miriam would offer him breakfast, make hot chocolate. He would shrug his thanks; eat and drink in relative silence. At some stage he would start to talk – perhaps with Frosties demolished but chocolate only half gone. This would be Miriam's cue, and her gently probing questions would begin. She was building a picture, gathering the pieces she hoped in due course would make an image she would know what to do with. This wasn't psychoanalysis – such a practice was as far outside her capacity as it was beyond her intention. But if Colom did need analysis she wanted to know, to be able to refer him on. If there were things she had the skills to deal with herself, she would do what she could to be of help to him. Nothing was achievable without knowledge – and knowledge could only come from him.

As the days wore on Miriam felt frustration surfacing. Her own, but Colom's too. They were talking; becoming friends. Information was being shared. A picture was forming. But nothing in that picture accounted for the deep sadness that had come to dominate Colom's young life. It didn't make sense, and though Miriam could go on asking questions; go on taking notes; go on urging Colom to speak about his feelings and his memories, his words weren't adding up to a direction they could take together. How could she move him from information to action; from hurt to healing; from anger to forgiveness, if the root of his anxiety was unknown? She was eager to turn a corner, but the road they were on was too long, or too winding. Or the wrong road altogether.

Worse still, she sensed that Colom, too, was feeling this. He had opened up for her a window of trust. He had agreed to talk and was talking. But where was the return? Where were the outcomes, the clues as to where to go next? She saw a darkness encroaching on the edges of his moods; heard a strained exhaustion in his words. Found her own anxieties about him growing. Listened to the footfalls of his broken nights. They needed a breakthrough but they weren't finding it.

On Wednesday, just over a week after their arrival in Portivy, there was to be a midweek Mass, arranged for the Feast of St Joseph because a visiting Polish priest was available. Miriam asked Fiona to go with her. The single chapel bell was ringing as they walked up the hill, the winter sunlight sneaking through an unexpected gap in the rain. They found a dozen or so worshippers, their combined age probably touching a millennium. Fiona recognized the broad contours of the ritual but found the ageing priest's mumbled and heavily accented French hard to follow. She occupied herself with once more exploring the detail of the tiny stone chapel. She had been several times already, coming alone to pray, and each time found something new to ponder in the small, still space, its arched wooden ceiling painted blue and decorated with stars.

Above the altar a model boat was suspended from the ceiling. The families of fishermen had ample cause to breathe their faltering prayers into this air. The side wall was dominated by an inset statue of Our Lady of Lotivy, surrounded by marble plaques. The earliest was dated 1902, the most recent 1991. Many said simply "*merci*" but some gave a reason why – for the protection of our village; for my healing; for my survival through the war. The largest plaque, taking the central place, had been placed in 1945 and thanked Our Lady on behalf of the entire community. Fiona wondered how many of the families of the men shot at the fortress would have subscribed to the plaque. How many were grateful for their own survival when it came at such a cost? Were there some, she wondered, who refused to set foot in the church once the horror of their loss had gripped them; who chose instead to live inside their bitterness, to throw the spears of their anger at the God who had not, as it turned out, protected them at all?

Was the end of war the beginning of the end of faith for Portivy? She couldn't help but feel that it was so. The years from 1945 into the 1960s had been disastrous for the church throughout France. The exodus had not been fully noted until later – but it had surely begun in the aftermath of war.

The priest stood beneath the suspended frigate, his hands raised to the blue-painted sky. White-haired; well-fed; his words still unintelligible. He cast his eyes down to the book open on the altar before him and proclaimed the transformation of the elements.

Fiona had found the chapel open on her second day in the village. There were too many words in her head to make any kind of sensible prayer, but she lit a candle all the same. She found a printed card beside the altar that said, "Lord, I don't know how to pray. But I'm here, so I'll light this candle." It seemed as good a place as any to start. When she came back on her next day's walk, her candle was still burning. She lit another from it, amazed that there could be a place so still, so undisturbed, that even a single, fragile flame survived.

She had written in her journal later that same day, "It was like my own fragile faith. It was Colom's spirit fighting to survive. It was the tiny hope I still cling to that has long since shaken off the words once attached to it."

She had stopped by each day since to light another flame, dropping her daily euro into an otherwise empty box. Did she feel that a flame had the power to express the prayer she couldn't muster? She didn't know, in truth, if it was even a prayer at all. But there was something in her daily visits that had begun to calm her. Her journal again: "My hope is fragile, but it is still burning, and somehow this place, this Portivy, has become the sheltered harbour in which it will not be snuffed out."

She had said none of this to Miriam; had barely mentioned her visits to the chapel. She had no way of knowing how similar her friend's own journey had been. The candles she had lit across the years; the hours of silence; her inner raging at a God who had rejected her, or at the very least was sulking, his back turned to her. The time when the silent prayer of a candle flame had been her only option. She had thought at the time that she was doing it to spite her God: sitting in silence like a spoilt child to let him know she hated him. It was only later she realized she was running each day towards him, her silence expressing not anger but companionship: silence in the presence of the only one who would allow it, the only one who did not ask for explanations. Her childhood faith had taught her that God was always watching; recording sins; tracking failure; storing up offences for the film that he would one day show the world. It was her adult crisis; her failure; her fall into the pits of human frailty that taught her this was not so. Alone in the silence of this chapel, watching the flames she herself had lit in desperation, she had discovered God's outrageous amnesia; his unaccountable and irresponsible disinterest in her sins. Here she found at last that it was as a person, not as an acolyte, that God was welcoming her. As she, too, ignored the incoherent mumblings of the priest, she prayed silently that Fiona might also find such sweet acceptance here.

Walking back from the chapel she explained to Fiona the long history of the site. "There was a hermitage here as early as the sixth century," she said, "built by the monks who came over from the mainland to pray. This was a tidal island then, mostly forest – just the kind of wild place the early Christians sought out to imitate the hard lives of the Desert Fathers. A priory was built in the thirteenth century, but destroyed in the eighteenth by the British. Portivy became a fishing village, but it was a village without a church. It took a woman to put that right."

"How so?" Fiona broke off the end of the baguette they had bought, still warm. She offered it to Miriam, who declined, a little shocked. Fiona munched guiltily.

"Marie-Françoise Sonic. A local girl; uneducated; devout in her faith. She made it her habit to recite her prayers each day in the ruins of the old priory. One day she was saying her prayers, pleading for the blessings of the Queen of Heaven, when she heard her speak."

"Mary?"

"The very same – though she spoke in perfect Breton, which as far as I know is a unique occurrence. She gave a simple instruction: 'My daughter, go tell them to rebuild the chapel in my name.' So she did, and they did, and in 1845 the Chapelle de Notre Dame de Lotivy was opened, and the village had its own church."

"Was she recognized for her part in all this? I see no shrine."

"No, this never became a Lourdes or a Medjugorje. The message was too simple and too local for that, and it was given in Breton, which wouldn't have gone down at all well in Rome, or in Paris for that matter. But Marie-Françoise is honoured in local legend. She isn't forgotten. She is one in a long line of women whose shaping of the church goes unnoticed."

They turned into the Allée du Vivier, every house except their own still shuttered against the winter. Miriam's hand was already on the cottage door. "The chapel has always been one of my preferred places of prayer. I always think of it as sacred space."

Fiona followed her in, put the bread on the table and took off her coat.

"Do you believe in that – the sacredness of place?" she said. "Isn't it just because it is a very still chapel, with a painted blue ceiling and some nice statues?"

"Perhaps. But for me there is something deeper there. There was holy ground there long before the chapel was built; before even the priory took shape. There are some places that become holy because a church is built on them, I'm sure. But there are places where a church is built because they are holy. I don't think the monks who crossed the sands at low tide to spend time in prayer here much cared if there was a church or not. They cared that they had found a kind of 'thin' place. They marked the landscape as holy because the landscape had marked them."

"And the pagans before them?"

"Why not? If God is our creator, if he made all this, might there not be places where it is easier to sense his presence; where even pagans in their ancient emotions might find the Spirit brooding?"

Fiona did not reply, only smiled with a kind of suppressed laughter. Miriam looked confused.

"I'm sorry. I was just thinking what David would make of what you're saying if he were here."

"He wouldn't like it?"

"I think that would be an understatement. He's not good with Catholics as it is, worse still with prayers to Mary. And if you told him there was a pagan place of worship under the existing chapel, he'd probably recommend the building be demolished. He certainly wouldn't worship here until it had been cleared in some way."

"And you?"

"I don't know what I think, Miriam. Everything I've learned would urge me to stand with David, but I've been to that chapel every day to sit quietly and pray – though I've done more sitting than praying, to be honest. I didn't know any of these stories, but I can tell you I've come closer to finding personal peace there than anywhere. I wouldn't hesitate to call it a place of peace."

"And of holiness? A sacred place?"

Fiona didn't answer; shrugged as if to say she wasn't sure, didn't yet know.

"Well, I have to say I'm glad for you. Once you've found solid ground on which to stand and pray, you never know what else might fall into place."

Could it? Would it? Had it already? Fiona had no way of knowing. But the feeling she had named – of Portivy as a sheltered harbour, a safe place in which to seek long-needed solutions – stayed with her. A fragile hope; a shaft of light; the beginnings of possibility. This place had at least given her that.

CHAPTER NINETEEN

The rain of Madre de Dios is similar to that of the
Amazon, but there is a petrifying aspect to it, as if it
seeks to wound rather than to nurture.

Tahir Shah, *House of the Tiger King*

As if to compound Miriam's growing anxiety, the next days proved difficult for Colom. He was awake through Wednesday night and didn't get up on Thursday morning. When he emerged at lunchtime he was surly and non-communicative, the shrugs returning in earnest. Miriam would have loved to have been free to check his arms, but to do so would have shattered completely the fragile trust they had begun to build. She had little doubt of the condition she would find them in. It wasn't rocket science.

Fiona asked cheerfully if he had slept OK, though she was sure he hadn't.

"What do you care?" he said with an unaccountable edge of anger. Fiona retreated, an uncomfortable silence establishing itself.

While Colom sniffed and shrugged his way through lunch, Fiona slipped upstairs; came down not long after with a pile of sheets for the wash.

He couldn't wait to get back to his room. Offers of afternoon activities, even of a trip to the mainland where movies were occasionally shown in English, were all rejected, not a word spoken in thanks or response. He was gone the whole afternoon; didn't come even when called for supper. When Fiona went to check on him she found him asleep, on his bed but fully dressed. Drawings lay all around him. They were cartoon-like, in harsh,

145

dark lines. Images of violence; of injury. She chose not to look too closely. She tried to wake him gently but made no progress. Decided to leave him. Wondered if again tonight, as twice earlier in the week, she would be at his side when nightmares woke him, crying. She went back down to Miriam, who had cleared the supper plates and was working on her journal.

Fiona took a seat, but wasn't relaxed. Miriam could sense her fidgeting movements from across the room. "He's asleep," Fiona said, finally. "I expect he might well sleep through now. I'm not sure what's got into him today, but he could probably do with the rest."

Miriam looked up, but didn't speak.

"I thought I might pop over to the café," Fiona said. "Maybe play some cards or something?"

"Of course," Miriam answered, leaving silent the question as to which of the locals Fiona had got to know well enough to play cards with on a Thursday night. "I won't join you; I'll be glad of an evening to catch up with my journal."

"OK," Fiona said, a forced cheerfulness raising the pitch of her voice a semi-tone. "See you later."

And she was gone, leaving Miriam to her journal, and her questions. She opened her notebook to review her conversations with Colom. At times she took notes as he was speaking – but these were snatched sentences; phrases; questions. The fuller paragraphs were written after each session, when she was alone. Her habit, picked up over many such conversations, was to underline important words and phrases. When they surfaced more than once, she would box them. Where, on the other hand, something didn't seem to fit; didn't make sense; raised more questions than it answered, she would place, in the margin, a question mark. Should the same question, the same doubt, surface later, she would use a boxed question mark. It was not a foolproof system, but it gave her a way to track visually the progress she was making.

In Colom's case she was struggling. A brief review of the notes, covering some five or six conversations, confirmed the suspicion that had been growing in her. There were too many question marks. It wasn't that she doubted Colom's word. She trusted him. The memories he was sharing with her were true, or he believed them to be true, but they didn't make sense. They didn't fit together. She couldn't make the image work – it was as if the pieces of two different puzzles had been shaken up and thrown into one box. To get at the truth she would need to push harder, to break open long-held secrets, but there would be a cost to this. It would require her to break her own long-held silence. She could hardly expect transparency of others and run from it herself. She owed it to Fiona to speak the truth. She took some time to pray; committed her decision to God; set her journal aside and picked up her book – to read while she waited up for her friend.

* * *

Negotiating the cottage's stiff front door just after one in the morning, Fiona felt like a giddy schoolgirl out after curfew. Doubtless the Bordeaux contributed to the giddiness, and she wondered if she would regret it come the morning, but there was more than that. There was a feeling of justified irresponsibility, of being let off the leash for the first time in months. Years even. On the walk home she had stopped to look into the night sky; had let her eyesight adjust until the few dozen visible stars became hundreds and then thousands. She had felt the energy of those distant suns, the sheer hugeness of their presence and power. It flowed into her, as if the universe itself were confirming her existence; offering its nurture and support. It was not that she suddenly knew why she was alive – knowing "why" was a complexity whose inaccessibility she had long since accepted – but she did all at once know that she was alive, and that the cosmos knew it too.

There was a light on in the downstairs living room, and Fiona was brought back to the here and now by the sight of Miriam lightly snoring on the settee. There had been a fire in the grate at some stage, but it had lost its flame and was lazily pushing up a last thin wisp of smoke. The chill of the night was slowly creeping from the walls and windows of the room to its centre – the heating would have switched itself off already, would not come on again before dawn. Miriam's book had fallen, face down, to her chest and sat now like a tiny tent, moving up and down with the rhythm of her breathing.

Fiona walked over and gently touched Miriam's shoulder. She stirred, shook her head slightly and sat up, knocking the book to the floor.

"Oh, sorry," she said, momentarily unsure where she was. "I must have fallen asleep reading. What time is it?"

"Just gone one," Fiona said, somewhat guiltily.

"No wonder it's so cold in here. I need to get into my warm bed. Did you have a nice evening?"

"I did," Fiona replied honestly. "I had a really nice time. Thierry is..." But she couldn't finish the sentence. She couldn't make her words fit the situation.

"Thierry is a very good man," Miriam filled in. "He's been more of a brother to me than my own brother was, even when he was alive. Had I thought about it I would have guessed that you two would get on."

There was a pause, an intersection in conversation at which it was impossible to proceed without making choices. Fiona jumped the lights.

"Miriam," she said awkwardly, "I..." But again she stalled. She didn't know how to finish the sentence. Miriam rescued her, gently pressing a hand against Fiona's arm.

"Fiona," she said, "you don't have to explain anything to me. I'm not here to judge you. I care very much for you as a friend, and I don't want to see you hurt, either of you, and of course I am concerned for Colom just now – but none of this changes the fact that you face your own choices. I don't want you to feel that you are in some way accountable to me."

"I know, and I appreciate your friendship, thank you." She wanted to go on, to explain that nothing had happened between her and Thierry; that they had talked, were enjoying each other's company, and that yes, she was facing thoughts and choices she never thought she would even consider; that it did frighten her; that, for now, there was nothing more – but none of the words would come. Instead of her fumbling explanation, an awkward silence filled the night-time air between them.

Until Fiona realized that she wasn't the most tongue-tied person in the room. It hadn't occurred to her that Miriam might have been waiting up for her deliberately, but it did now. Her friend had never struggled to make eye contact with her: the directness of her gaze being the trademark of her confidence. But she was struggling now.

"Can we talk?" she said nervously, as if it were she who had played the giddy schoolgirl.

"Of course," Fiona said, taking a seat beside her, suddenly sober, and a little afraid. "What is it?"

"I've not been truthful with you, Fiona, and I feel the time has come to put that right." She looked pale, her hair dishevelled from its impromptu nap on the cushion. Fiona saw lines around her eyes she'd never noticed. Saw her fifty-something years as never before.

"I have something to tell you, and I want to help you to understand it, so I need to start with telling you about my brother. Have I ever told you about Jean-Pierre?"

Fiona shook her head.

"I grew up here with my mother and my brother," Miriam said. "My father died of cancer when I was a child. Jean-Pierre was ten years older than me, so in some ways he stepped into the breach; but he drank heavily, even as a teenager, and by the time he was old enough to know better, he was hooked. He kept working but his behaviour both on and off the boats was dominated by drinking. He was always either drunk or in a foul mood for being sober."

"He died?" She had kept her coat on. Miriam, for her part, had wrapped her shoulders in the blanket that had been across her knees where she lay.

"In the early 1970s. He was killed on his motorbike. He had this habit of racing the train. If he had to wait at the level crossing at Penthièvre for the train to pass, he would then try to get to St Pierre before it. Then he would wait for it again before racing it to the crossing at St Julien. It was a stupid game and he was the only one who played it. I think he was often drunk when he did it – drink had never stopped him from getting on his bike. On the night he died it was raining, and either he was a few seconds slower than usual or the train was a few seconds faster, because as he approached St Julien it was clear he wasn't going to make it. They say he tried to brake but he skidded on the wet road and lost control. He went under the wheels of the train and was dragged for around thirty metres before the wreckage brought the whole thing to a halt. He didn't stand a chance – they called an ambulance from Auray, but everyone knew he was dead long before it got there."

"That must have been awful for you – to lose your father and your brother."

"It was worse for my mother. Jean-Pierre was her world. She couldn't see his faults, though others saw them clearly enough. When he died she insisted on blaming the train driver – though the police reports completely absolved him of all blame. There was nothing he could have done in the face of such stupidity. My mother was not one for such a rational response. As far as she was concerned the train had taken her beloved son from her. From that day to her death, she never again used the SNCF. She turned this house into a shrine to Jean-Pierre's memory: she sat here in the dark surrounded by photos of him, waiting to die so that she could join him. That's one of the reasons I packed up all the old photographs and gave so many of them away. I couldn't bear the sense that the house was a museum for the dead."

"Did you not miss him yourself?"

"I was fourteen when he died, so I was upset of course and cried my way through the funeral. But we had not been close. I mostly remembered him being either out on the boat or out at a bar with his friends. Now I remember him more for the effect he had on my mother. When he was here she fussed over him; when he wasn't here she talked endlessly about him. She had no time for me. She was so obsessed with him, even after he died, I felt as if I didn't even exist for her. But here's the thing..." At this point she looked very directly at Fiona, turning slightly in her position on the settee. "I didn't realize it at the time, but in a very real sense I never got over his death. I never recovered any relationship with my mother. I don't think I ever filled the empty space that was created inside me."

Fiona caught a hint of something more; something hidden.

"Why are you telling me all this, Miriam?"

Miriam looked up. "I remember you at sixteen," she said. "You had such an energy for life. I loved your questions. Whenever there was a discussion about religion or politics or something in the news, you would ask the most intelligent questions. I looked forward to hearing them, to be honest. I didn't want to let you down. I didn't want to leave so abruptly. I so wanted to stay and tell you why."

"I turned seventeen two days after you left," Fiona said. "Why did you?"

Miriam pinched the bridge of her nose between her thumb and forefinger, as if she were nursing a headache. A deep sigh escaped from somewhere within her like steam breaking the surface of boiling tar. Their eyes met. The information arrived in Fiona's mind before Miriam could voice it, like the falling of some huge, newly cut tree. The thud resounded so loudly that Fiona couldn't tell if it existed only inside her head, or could be heard echoing around the ancient room. She spoke at the same moment as thinking.

"You were pregnant."

CHAPTER TWENTY

*The only noise now was the rain, pattering softly with
the magnificent indifference of nature for the tangled
passions of humans.*

Sherwood Smith, *Crown Duel*

Miriam's eyes were closed now. Her head moved with the
faintest of nods. When she began to speak her voice was
deep, distant, as if she was dredging up words from some place so
buried that she had to hold her breath to dive for them.

"Russ. He was older than me. I don't think you knew him.
He was a musician and an artist; had travelled in Tibet, India.
Told the most outrageous stories. I didn't even realize I had
fallen in love with him until it was too late to escape it. To say I
was naive in matters of the heart would be an understatement.
We only slept together once but it was, of course, enough. I felt
wretched with guilt. It's hard for those who have never taken a
vow of celibacy to understand how devastating breaking it can
be. It wasn't that he didn't love me; I think in his own way he
did. But it was me. I couldn't be loved in that way. I had broken
it off – for all I know, broken his heart – by the time I found out
I was pregnant."

"What did you do?"

This part seemed the hardest for Miriam. Fiona felt a flood
of compassion for her. She had known this woman to help
others; could guess that in the years in which they had been out
of contact those others might have run to hundreds. Now here
she was, wracked by the same human tragedies and doubts with

which those "others" had doubtless been bruised. She waited for her friend to find the words.

"I can tell you what I didn't do. I didn't come back here. To have told my mother, to have faced her bitterness, was just too much. I left the order, of course. That was the first decision, and in many ways the easiest. But I still took refuge in a convent, near Worcester. I lived in relative seclusion through the pregnancy with just a handful of other expectant mothers. And I had a baby. I had a son, Fiona, and I held him for a precious, perfect forty-eight hours."

"Until…"

"Until he was taken for adoption. I haven't once seen him since."

Fiona saw the tears forming in her friend's eyes. She was thinking of Miriam's work; her compassion for young people; her specialism in matters of adoption. Her confidence with Colom.

"I am so sorry, Miriam. I didn't know…"

"And I'm sorry I didn't tell you – that I never came back to explain." She looked her full in the face now, seeking absolution through a curtain of tears.

"It was so long ago," Fiona said, returning her friend's gaze, "but it's one of the feelings I most clearly remember from those days; discovering that you had left. I missed you terribly."

"Can you forgive me?"

"Of course I can, Miriam. I already have – a thousand times over. I knew even then that you must have had good cause to leave. I never held it against you."

Silence settled between them. Fiona was the one to break it; her question born of compassion, not cruelty.

"You've never found him?"

"I wanted to, so many times. But that wasn't the arrangement I was offered. It was to be total separation; I gave up the right to even know him. I sometimes wonder if he is looking for me; if he even knows of my existence. I promised that any search would not be initiated from my side, and I've held to that promise for almost thirty years."

"But you regret it."

"Every day. The world has changed so much in those years. Back then I had no idea that any other path was possible. I thought that I had forfeited any right to know my son, and by the time I'd realized that it could be any different, I knew it was too late. For me, at least."

"Did you ever tell her? Your mother?"

"I did, yes." The memory was as vivid in her mind as this morning's news. Her attempt to break through the bitterness; to find a place of human commonality. Mother and daughter, women together. How badly it had turned out.

"It was not long before she died. She had terrible arthritis – her wrists and ankles. She hardly left the house. I came back to care for her as best I could. Her hands were twisted over on themselves. She was in constant pain. Did you know that there is a traditional name for arthritis – 'creeping resentment'? Some suggest it is linked to unforgiveness, as if the mental blockage is somehow transferred to the body. Living with her those few months, the connection was written over her like subtitles. She would say, 'I'm in pain today,' and I would read, 'I'm still angry. I can't let go.' I thought if I told her my own sad truth, I might find in her some tenderness; awaken the mother in her; help her towards a more peaceful death."

"It didn't work?"

"Far from it. It still gives me a chill to think of it. She was standing at the foot of the stairs, ready to begin her painful nightly climb. She listened as I spoke; said nothing as I poured out my story. Then as I finished she asked only one question. Do you know what it was?"

Fiona shook her head.

"'Was it a boy?' I can hear it now, echoing off the walls of this very room." In her head her mother's voice; the harsh Breton intonation; bitterness in every syllable, "*C'etait un garçon?*"

"She turned away and climbed the stairs, complaining of the pain in every step. I knew then that I had been foolish to tell her. To her, through the filter of Jean-Pierre, my actions in giving up my child were cruel. I thought she'd be angry at my sexual indiscretion. Instead, she was angry that I'd stolen yet another man from her. My actions confirmed to her that the universe was determined to rob her of joy. I should have known that she would see it that way, but it didn't occur to me. Not once."

"And neither should it have. This is your story, Miriam, not hers."

"I know that now. But I didn't see it then. It drove me into the darkest season of my life. I know now that I was depressed, and in time I did get through it. But at the time I thought my life was over. In the end I realized why it was she had never overcome her grief. She had made it her friend. It had become her companion, her identity, like a woman who takes her husband's name. She couldn't bear to let it go, even so close to her life's end. I cried at her funeral because I loved her and in the end I really did miss her; but also because I saw that the larger part of her life had been wasted, poured away in the name of this so-precious grief. She kept Jean-Pierre alive, and my father before him, in the shape of her own anger. To let it go – to forgive and move on – would have felt for her like killing them all over again. It taught me so much. About dealing with grief and anger. About telling the truth."

She didn't want to do this. It was clever but cruel to turn this tender conversation back on Fiona. She had to tell her friend, in the kindest possible way, that the lies must end. For her own sake; for that of her son. Fiona heard the switch in inflection. Knew what it meant; what was coming. Had known, in reality, for days. Miriam looked her full in the face. The same eye contact, except that the polarity had switched. Miriam's eyes were clear now. Penetrating. It was in Fiona's that a tide of tears was rising.

"I'm sorry about keeping this secret from you all these years, Fiona. I'm sorry that I let it break our friendship instead of cementing it. I'm sorry that I never got back in touch. But I would be lying even now if I let you believe that this was the only reason for sharing this with you now. I had to tell you because I didn't feel we could go any further in our friendship if there were secrets between us. And someone had to start."

She paused. Fiona said nothing; nodded slightly; pushed back the tears.

"I didn't feel I could ask you to tell me the truth – the whole truth – unless I was prepared to do the same for you." She felt wretched, but knew she could not waste this moment. A clear space had opened up between them; an airstrip ready for incoming flights. She had looked for it for days; knew it might not come again for several more. Tired as they both were, this was the time.

Another pause. Still no words from Fiona. She was catching her breath, eye contact abandoned. As if her body was deciding whether it should cry, breathe or talk, unable to do all three at once.

"You have to tell me, Fiona. Everything that Colom has told me points to something. It's like the outline of a story at the centre of his life. He can only sketch its boundaries. He can't tell me what's missing from the centre, because he doesn't know. Did you know that he was self-harming?"

Fiona looked up, shock registering on her face; confusion; guilt.

"He cuts himself. I don't know what with – a craft knife perhaps; the blade of a pencil sharpener. He's been doing it for some time. And my best guess is he's still doing it – even here. Have you noticed that he won't let you see his arms?"

She had, of course. Had assumed it was some odd expression of teenage modesty. Had never thought…

She could hardly form words, but managed, "What does it mean?" Her eyes pleading for mercy.

"It means different things for different people. For Colom, I think it means that there is a pain in him that he cannot put into words. Something so deeply buried that even he can't understand it. He's cut off from the world around him – even from you, I'm sorry to say – and in his isolation he articulates pain by feeling pain. Perhaps he feels it's what he deserves. I'm not sure."

Fiona was nodding. Still struggling to speak, her movements implicitly acknowledging the truth of Miriam's words.

"But there's more here…" Miriam was saying. Fiona looked up again, let her friend see her face.

"Fiona, I have been trying very hard to put this together. For Colom's sake, and for yours, I wanted to find out what the source of this pain was."

Fiona was listening intently now, her breathing both amplified and accelerated. Miriam's voice by contrast calm, measured, circling a truth she was very close to naming.

"I've spoken to you about Colom's childhood, and I've spoken to him about his memories. I've pieced together everything I can about his early years. I've asked you about his birth; about your early experience of caring for him. I've asked all the questions my training has taught me to. And a good, clear picture has emerged. Can I tell you what it is?"

Fiona nodded. Panic etched into the very creases of her eyes.

"It's a picture of the happiest child on earth. The perfect childhood. Everything where it should be. Nothing to disturb the lake's calm surface. Nothing to account for the darkness Colom is fighting to be free of."

Fiona's eyes were closed now. She swallowed hard.

"The only explanation left lies in the things you've chosen not to tell me. I didn't want to come to this conclusion, Fiona. But there is no other."

She opened her eyes. The moment before drowning. The clarity and calm of knowing that you face at last your ultimate fear.

"Will you tell me? All of it?" Miriam asked, a gentleness returning to her voice. She felt guilty for the trick she had played, and was once more flooded with sympathy for her friend.

Fiona tried to speak. "Miriam, I…" She couldn't do it. Tried again, came at it from a different angle. "We… Colom…"

But nothing could coax the words out from their hiding place. They were holed up in the shack of her brain, with furniture piled against the door; shotguns at the windows. Fugitives ready to make their last stand. Miriam, her sheriff's uniform clean and pressed, waiting silently: red lights, blue lights flashing all around her. The words had been on the run for so long. They had no intention of surrendering now.

Fiona had run out of options. Run out of road. Run out of air to fill her lungs.

"I'm sorry," she half-spoke, half-retched.

She rose from her seat, knocked over a cup Miriam had left on the arm of the settee and caught it just before it fell; placed it on the table; moved out from where she had been sitting and lurched across the room towards the stairs. She was part way up when the tears came, in sobs that so possessed her every muscle that she had to fight to remain conscious. She stumbled through her bedroom door; slammed it behind her; fell to her knees beside her bed and howled like a woman caught in the agonies of birth.

Miriam let her go; would not press her now. Knew she would, in time, speak her secrets; would open at last the safe that she had chained shut.

Fiona climbed onto her bed. Pulled her body tight into a foetal posture. Cried her way into a fitful, aching sleep.

CHAPTER TWENTY-ONE

The rain fluctuates between drizzle and torrential. It messes with your mind. It makes you think things will always be like this, never getting better, always letting you down right when you thought the worst was over.

Susane Colasanti, *Waiting For You*

It seemed that only minutes had passed when she was woken by an urgent knocking at her door. Miriam came in without waiting for a response.

"Wake up, Fiona," she said breathlessly. "Colom's gone. He's not in his room."

It took her a moment to remember where she was.

"What did you say?"

"Colom. He's nowhere in the house and it's past three in the morning. We'll need to go and look for him."

By the time Fiona came to properly and descended the staircase, Miriam already had a pot of coffee brewing.

"We may well need it," she explained. "It's cold out there, and black as pitch, and this is not an easy place to find a wanderer. Has he done this before?"

"Done what?"

"Taken off, in the night. On his own."

"I don't think so. You know he's often up at night. But I don't think he's ever left the house."

"Well, he has now. I heard him on the stairs about an hour ago – I thought he must have come down to get a glass of water or something to eat – he ate hardly a thing yesterday. It seemed strangely quiet when I woke again, so I came down to check. No sign of him, and the door is unlocked – I locked it before going up to bed. Where do you think he might have gone?"

"Where? I have no idea. What does he think… No, Miriam, please. Not the police. Please."

Miriam had her mobile phone in her hand and was about to dial.

"I'm calling Thierry – he won't mind and he knows this village like the back of his hand. He and Colom have spent some time together; he might have some idea of where he's gone. Why not the police?"

"It's complicated. I can explain everything, and I will, I promise. But please – they mustn't know we're here."

Miriam hesitated. She wanted to know more but right now had other priorities. "OK," she said reluctantly. "But Fiona, if we haven't found him in an hour, we have to call. This is a dangerous place."

Thierry picked up. Miriam explained to him in short, sharp bursts of French, then turned once more to Fiona.

"He'll meet us in the car park in five minutes. Torches. We need torches – under the sink in the kitchen."

Fiona rummaged as instructed and found two good torches in working order.

"Do you have spare batteries?" she asked, without turning around.

"The drawer next to the oven – there should be a new pack."

Miriam was by this time wrapped up to the neck in her raincoat and two scarves; a woollen hat pulled low. Fiona followed suit, though had no hat, and regretted it as soon as they headed out into the night, the wind howling. They found Thierry in the car park, torch in hand. The night was cold and fresh, the tang of salt slapping at their skin like an exfoliant. Small clusters of cloud, wind-driven, passed across a bright three-quarter moon, toggling the night between total darkness and a wash of thin, pale light. Beneath the sound of the wind, the deeper roaring of the sea.

"What do we do?" Fiona asked as they huddled in the deserted car park. "Should we split up?"

"There's no point in you going alone, Fiona," Thierry said. "You're as likely to get lost yourself as to find Colom. Before anything else we need to check the coastal paths – we may as well be on foot for the time being. I think the coast is his most likely choice. That's what everyone does around here, and by moonlight it's the most obvious path. I'll take the track towards the fort. You two stick together and head out towards the Côte Sauvage. Go as far as the customs house and then head back if you don't see him – further than that we can use the car. I have my mobile, Miriam: call me as soon as you know anything. I'll do the same. Let's be back here within the hour if we've seen nothing, then we can try the roads out towards St Pierre."

He switched into French and spoke quietly to Miriam, though Fiona heard enough to know what he was asking. She heard the word "police"; saw that he was unconvinced by Miriam's response. Saw, too, the look from her friend that silenced his questions.

They headed off, Fiona feeling helpless and foolish and entirely out of place. She followed Miriam along the harbour front, past the Café du Port and Thierry's house to the right of it, to where the coastal path began. The torches were useful for finding the path in the dark but no help for their search. For this they relied on the further reach of the intermittent moonlight. They said little, focusing their energies on scanning inland to the higher ground and seaward to the line of the beach. Neither direction offered any sign of hope.

"I know Thierry suggested going only as far as the customs house," Miriam said as she climbed a bank where the path left the beach-side and began to ascend the heath, "but let's keep going as far as the stone table. Colom was there the other afternoon – he may just have headed back."

Fiona's answer was little more than a grunt of assent, barely audible over the wind and waves.

"You OK?"

"I think so. I just need to find him, Miriam. If anything happens to him I…"

Miriam stopped in her tracks; turned to face her friend.

"Don't even think about it," she said. "He's out here somewhere, and the most likely thing is that we'll find him and he'll tell us he just went for a walk. It can be dangerous out here, Fiona, but it doesn't have to be. If he can see the paths, he'll be safe."

"Unless he doesn't want to be. What if he was trying…"

Miriam put her hand on Fiona's arm. "We need to find him," she said. "That's all we need to be thinking about for the moment."

She looked as though she was about to turn and move on, but she stopped again. Saw the fear in her friend's eyes. Didn't move. "Fiona, I want to call the police," she said, reaching once more for her phone. "They have a search protocol for this whole area, with volunteers they can rally within thirty minutes. Let me call them."

The phone in her hand now.

Fiona said nothing. Stared into the waves. Lines of confusion forming on her forehead, the wind turning circles in her hair.

"I can't, Miriam." Speaking not directly to her friend, but into the middle distance. "I can't involve the police. They can't know he's here."

"But why not?" Miriam shouted; the wind, the waves and her growing frustration driving the volume of her voice. "Your son is missing, possibly in danger. They are trained and ready to help. Why not ask them?"

"I can't."

"But you're being ridiculous. Let me call them." Her patience was evaporating. She was poised to dial.

"I can't because he's not my son."

"What do you mean?"

"He's not my son, Miriam. Colom is adopted."

Miriam stared. Neurons firing. In her mind's eye the puzzle falling into place, but an anger rising in her. So much time that could have been saved. Even the events of this night avoided, perhaps.

"Why didn't you tell me?"

"I couldn't… I wanted to… it's complicated."

"Not as complicated as all that, Fiona. You're not the first adoptive parent in the world. You asked me to help you; to speak to him. How could you not tell me?"

"I'm sorry. It's just… I'm not." She was perfectly still, her pale skin cold in the moon's light, speaking to the void between the sky and the sea. "I'm not his adoptive parent. I'm not his mother. I'm not anything."

"I don't understand." Gentler now, her anger subsiding. Concern taking its place. "If you and David adopted him, that makes you his mother under law, no matter how you feel."

"No. David adopted him. As a single man," Fiona said, and once the words were out, more followed. A torrent of words, her secrets, ripped from her by the fierce clifftop winds. "We weren't married until six months later. It was… complicated. We knew we wanted to adopt Colom, but I have a police record. About a year after you left England, I got into the drug scene. I was naive and stupid, and luckily for me I got caught early. It scared me so much I was out almost as quickly as I went in. But it put an arrest on my record for possession, and for the Canadian government, drugs are drugs – it doesn't matter how minor the charge. I was lucky to get into the country at all – adoption would have been impossible. When we discovered that David would be eligible to adopt as a single man, it seemed the perfect solution. He was ordained already, and had been a youth pastor in Canada for years. His background and situation were unblemished. We found out that he could be accepted as an unmarried man and would have the right later to move, with Colom, to the UK if he wanted to. So he adopted Colom alone. I became his mother in every sense that mattered. But we never had the papers changed.

165

David altered his will to appoint me as legal guardian at his death, and we left it at that. It never occurred to us that I would need full guardianship while David was alive."

She stopped, guilt reddening in her wind-whipped eyes.

"Which means that you are here with Colom illegally," Miriam said, struggling to hide her anger, "and should David choose to pursue it, you can be accused of kidnapping."

"Or worse, if something happens to Colom. Miriam, we have to find him. We have to find him ourselves."

Miriam reflected quickly. Blinked. Made two clear choices: one for now, one for later.

"OK. We go on looking," she said, slipping the phone back into her pocket. "But tomorrow we talk about this. All of it. There is too much here that you haven't told me, Fiona. I need to know your situation. I can't help Colom if there are things you won't tell me. You tell me everything, or we end this. Tomorrow. I'm sorry. And if we don't find him in the next thirty minutes or so, we call the police anyway, whatever the consequences. We can't take risks with his life."

This was an ultimatum, not a negotiation. She had turned and taken her first step before the last word was spoken. Fiona had never seen Miriam angry. She had nothing to say in response. There was no alternative proposal. She moved quickly to walk a stride or two behind Miriam. *Find Colom*, she said to herself. *The rest we'll deal with afterwards*.

Just let him be safe, she said to whoever was listening to her thoughts.

There was no one at the customs house, nor anywhere around it. They looked towards the stone table but it too was deserted. Miriam called Thierry. She spoke in French, shouting over the noise of the waves and the jet-like effect of the wind blowing past the phone's mouthpiece.

"Thierry. Miriam. We're close to the customs house but we've seen nothing. As far as we can see from here there's no one on the coastal path, and no one on the inland path either. Have you seen anything?"

His voice was clearer than she expected, until she realized he was in the car.

"No. I ran as far as the fort, but no sign. No one on the beaches; no one on the path. I'm in the car now, out towards St Pierre. I've seen no one. I don't know what speed this boy is walking at, but if it's been an hour since he set off, he could be halfway to Plouharnel by now, or already in Quiberon."

"I know. But let's keep looking. I'm sure we'll find him. We'll carry on checking the coast; you cover as many of the roads around as you can. We'll talk again in half an hour. *D'accord*?"

"*D'accord.*"

Fiona had heard much of Miriam's side of the conversation, and knew that whatever Thierry had reported, it was not good news.

They headed further along the coast, retracing the route they had taken on their walk to the stone table. The path was as white as a dry bone in the moonlight, but to its right dark shadows loomed, masking a drop that meant certain death. As much by sound as by sight, they kept their distance from the edge.

Fiona had been focusing her energy on the search, on her conversations with Miriam. Now she felt hope drain from her, swallowed by this night and its winds and the unending roaring of waves. She knew there were a hundred dangers here: a hundred ways to die. A hundred different ways to taste defeat, the enemy always the same: this coast; this ocean; this relentless weight of water. The uncontested triumph of nature over humanity. She should never have come here.

She knew she was crying because the wind chilled her tears as they hit her cheeks. Miriam was circling the stones, looking into the night all around; moving as close as she could to the cliff's edge to look down; experiencing with each new discovery of nothing the twin tastes of frustration and relief. Praying she would see Colom upright and alive. Praying more fervently still she would not see him broken on the shoreline, or floating facedown in the sea.

Fiona climbed, as Colom had, onto the stone table. To look for him, or to see what he had seen? To invoke his presence, somehow. She stood upright at the very centre of the monument, her clothing rippling with the currents of the wind. She looked back down the path they had come along, the silhouette of the customs house sharp against the clouds where they caught the moon's weak beams. Keeping her neck rigid so that the arc of her field of vision would be smooth, she moved her feet inch by inch, a security camera in slow rotation. Looking inland, she scanned the grass-covered hillside, sweeping top to bottom before twisting through another inch. Sweeping again. Twisting. All the time straining her vision to catch the least sign of movement or of human presence. Nothing: just darkness and the brooding hill and bushes shaken by the wind. She came around through 180 degrees and saw the coast path stretching into the distance – the route she had walked with Miriam when Colom had stayed here, on the rock. She imagined she was him, watching the backs of his mother and her friend disappearing into the distance. Between the coastal path and the open sea her arc took in the view across the coast's next cove. She saw the darkness of a sea inlet, beyond it the shadow of the hill's next outcrop, smooth and curved like the elbow of a sleeping giant. The main path ignored the detour, cutting straight across the outcrop at its top, but a smaller path followed its contours, looping out along the line of the sea.

There was a break in the clouds. It couldn't have been for more than three seconds. The change in light was far from spectacular, but change it did, and Fiona knew she had seen something. A shadow moving against darker shadows. The night had swallowed it before she had time to look closer, but her brain held it like a photograph. The faintest of movements. A ripple in the texture of the night. A tiny cloud of something? It could have been a sheep, if there were sheep here. It could have been a plastic bag blown by the wind. It could have been nothing. Or it could have been her son's wild hair: visible at a hundred metres, the hair she had never once lost in a crowd.

"Miriam," she called. "I see something."

She slid down from the rock. Scratched her leg on the stone slab. Ignored it. Fixed her gaze where it needed to be fixed. Nothing visible there now, but she held the line. Her feet back on the ground, she lifted her arm, straight as an arrow, to take a bearing on the dark patch she had seen.

"I saw something moving," she said urgently to Miriam. "Over on that next hill – there's a path there that breaks away from the main coastal walk. We didn't take it the other day. It could be nothing. But it could be Colom."

She set off, walking as fast as she could, not daring to run for fear of tripping, her eyes on the prize. Miriam was right behind her.

Later, thinking back, Fiona realized that as she slid from the rock she had seen Miriam getting up from the ground, as if she had been kneeling. It was later still that she had the chance to ask, and Miriam confessed she had been praying.

CHAPTER TWENTY-TWO

*The wind has shifted to the East. A storm isn't far off. I
can smell the moisture in the air, a fetid, living thing.*

Libba Bray, *A Great and Terrible Beauty*

Moving onto the smaller track was difficult and dangerous.
The path clung to the side of the hill, hugging the slope
precariously close to its edge. By daylight on a calm day it was a
route parents would forbid their children to follow, or allow them
only with hands tightly held. By night it was lethal. The only
compensation was an onshore wind that pressed them into the cliff
instead of tearing them away from it. Fiona and Miriam picked their
way slowly. They could see no one ahead of them. If Colom was on
this path he must have already rounded the bend at the head of
the outcrop. They shouted, but the wind and waves swallowed his
name as quickly as it was spoken. They pressed on, leaning close
into the path's landward side, their hands finding rock-holds where
they could. Fiona wanted to close her eyes to the drop just metres
to her right, but she couldn't risk blindness: she needed every scrap
of sight her eyes could muster to keep her feet from slipping.

They found him at the very end of the outcrop. He had
stopped where a large rock made a kind of pulpit overlooking the
sea. He was sitting on it, motionless. Fiona imagined it might by
day offer a fine view. By night it offered only death and danger.
Waves of relief and anxiety met in her and fought for tenancy.
He hadn't seen or heard them coming. She didn't want to startle
him. When she was close enough to guarantee his hearing her,
she spoke as calmly as the drumming of her heart would let her.

"Colom."

He turned slowly and spoke dreamily. "Hello, Mum."

She had the fleeting thought he could be sleep-walking. The thought passed, in its place a seething, burning anger. She wanted to shake him; to shout; to make him feel just a tenth of the anguish he had put her through. It was bubbling up like milk at the boil, touching the top of the pan. Exhausted for lack of sleep, it took every ounce of energy she had to force it down and speak calmly.

"Colom, you need to come down from there. Please. Just turn around slowly and walk back up the path with me, will you?"

She saw a tiny inflection in his face, as if he hadn't noticed where he was until she spoke. He got up slowly, looked at the waves far below him, and stepped off the rock.

She wanted to lead him back to safety, but she also wanted him in front of her, where she could see him. There was a place where a circle of ground offered a kind of lay-by for the narrow path. She stepped into it to let him pass. As he came level he turned to face her. She saw he had been crying. As instantly as it had come to the boil, her anger went; a wave retreating from the beach. "Oh Colom," she cried, reaching for him. He fell into her embrace to press his head against her chest.

"It's OK," she said. "It's all going to be OK."

She held him there – against the wind, the cold; against the ocean's dark power. She gripped tighter, willing her arms to communicate the love and safety her voice could not find words for.

Miriam phoned Thierry as soon as she saw that Colom was safe. By the time they climbed back to the road the sweep of his headlights was already on the horizon. They were home within minutes, by which time Colom was already asleep on the back seat of the car. Fiona went to open his door, but Miriam stopped her, a hand on her arm.

"We need to talk, Fiona," she said.

The wind was still playing chase with bursts of cloud, the cold of the night matched by Miriam's seething anger.

"Do you know why Thierry was able to find us so quickly tonight?" she asked.

"No." Sheepish, hesitant.

"The place we found Colom is well known," Miriam explained. "There's a monument there in honour of two men who died on the cliffs. They were locals – a volunteer fireman and a *gendarme*. They had gone to the rescue of a child who foolishly climbed down and couldn't make his way back up before the tide came in. They succeeded in reaching him and he was winched to safety, but before they could climb back up one was caught by a wave. The other dived in to save him and both were lost. Thierry knows the place well because the fireman was a friend of ours. These are dangerous cliffs, Fiona. People die every year. Colom could so easily have become a statistic tonight."

"I know, and I'm more than grateful for your help in finding him. I don't know what I'd have done without you and Thierry tonight. But I really don't think… I don't think he intended to harm himself."

"It makes no difference."

"It does to me."

"Of course. I understand that, but it doesn't to him. You know he could have died out there tonight, and I know it, but he showed no sign of knowing it. When we drove him home he was unaware of the danger he had been in. Even without wanting to kill himself, he almost did. He may not be trying to take his own life, but he's not fighting to save it either. The danger to his survival is just as real."

"Because he's not afraid of death?"

"Because he doesn't care. Living, dying; sleeping, waking; loving, ignoring – they are all the same to him. Children who have been hurt desensitize themselves to dull the pain until they find they have no senses left. Things that should matter to them – love and loss and how to know the difference – don't any more.

All the colours blend into one dull grey, and they live without motivation or passion."

"And what happens to such children?"

"Sooner or later, they self-destruct. Either because they self-harm and don't know how to stop, or because they allow themselves to be drawn into destructive behaviours and relationships, because nothing matters any more. It's how you would be if you'd never learned to be afraid of fire. Sooner or later, you would burn yourself."

Fiona sighed deeply. Like a plane coming in to land, where you first hear the engines, then see the shadow, and all at once it is upon you, she knew that something was landing in this moment – a choice; an intersection; a truth she could no longer avoid. Colom had almost died. The stakes were too high now for pride. She leaned against the car, her head on her hands. Quietly, almost whispering, she said, "What should I do?"

"You have to tell the truth. Everything else just medicates the pain. Only the truth can expose its root and give us hope of healing it. We can't be brutal with him, and we certainly can't be cruel, but we need to start telling Colom the truth about himself." She paused, before adding, "All of it."

Fiona caught the tone of voice and looked up, terrified.

"I know there's more, and I don't want to hurt you, but I can only help you if you will tell me. If you can't trust me with the truth, then I don't think there's much point in you being here. I'm sorry, Fiona, but either you start telling me the truth, or I will have to ask you to leave."

With this she turned, walked to the house and was gone. Her message delivered. Her anger expressed. Fiona was shaking, tiny ripples and shudders passing through her like earth tremors. The wind was shaking her clothes, but this was something else, a rumbling from the inside. She felt nauseous, wondered if she might even be sick. There was a dryness spreading across her palate and onto her lips.

She stood, her breath coming in short, desperate gasps. A sea of grief and panic was breaking over her. It would surely drown her. She forced herself to open the car door; shook Colom into sufficient wakefulness to make it into the house. Saw him to his room. Headed towards hers, but sensed suddenly that captivity lurked even there. The roof of the house was too low, the walls closing in. She turned full circle, headed back downstairs. Picked up her scarf from the chair-back she had draped it on; took her coat from the hook. Pulled at the door. Fell forward into the mercy of the dark and sky-wide night.

Already in her bed, Miriam heard the car start. Knew that whatever secret Fiona was struggling to tell, it was she who must face it, and decide. This was a battle only she could fight.

CHAPTER TWENTY-THREE

Once the rain starts falling it's hard to tell it to stop...
Samantha Young, *On Dublin Street*

Fiona let the car steer itself, her only decision the firm choice not to take the coastal road along the Côte Sauvage. She bumped across the level crossing and found herself approaching the main road. The light turned green as she approached. She turned instinctively right, towards Quiberon town.

She felt like a ghost as she drove through what felt like a ghost town. Shops and houses shuttered tight. She didn't know where she was headed, but spotted a sign for the aerodrome and followed that. This too was silent, lightless – the windows shuttered; such planes as there were canvas-covered; tied by their wingtips to anchors in the ground. Past the aerodrome she caught a sign for the Pointe du Conguel, Quiberon's most southerly outcrop. The lanes were dark now as she left streetlights behind. She drove as far as was possible, coming to a halt in the car park, car nose towards the sea.

She got out, pulled her coat and scarf around her. Locked the car without thinking, though there was no one here to steal it. She was struck by the loudness of the bleep; the brightness of the indicators telling her it was now secure. She watched the courtesy light fade a few seconds later until all man-made sounds and radiance were gone; the car and its driver alike swallowed by the night.

Beyond the end of the car park, a pathway followed the contours of the point. The sea was shallow here, the waves small. The wind that earlier had pressed them against the cliff was offshore here, travelling across the land before heading out once more to sea: less violent; the arrogance knocked out of it. It was hard to believe she was on the same peninsula. She walked awhile, growing accustomed to the moon's pale shining until it seemed to her as strong as daylight. The clouds were clearing and she began to see stars; a great richness of them, deep as a barrel of diamonds. She stopped to look, seeing more and more of them; knowing she had never watched such stars at home. Light pollution, they call it – the glow that stops our eyes from seeing stars. Life pollution, she thought – the distractions that had stopped her eyes from even looking.

Questions flooded her mind. What was she to do? Could she do it: alone, without David? Did she have the right? Was this even her door to open? Could she make that choice – for Colom, for all of them?

She kept walking. She wasn't sure how long, because she hadn't checked her watch since leaving the house. She focused on the ground in front of her; on the shadows of the trees; on the sea's soft rhythms. At least the night was real; was not a pattern of thought that ran away from her as soon as she tried to think it. This at least – these rocks; this wind; this moon – she could believe in. In due course she turned, made her way back to the car park of which she was the sole occupant. Once in the car she called David's mobile; left a message when he didn't pick up. Texted. Called again. Did the same on the home number. Wondered if he would call her right back. What she would tell him when he did.

There were still two blankets in the back of the car. She pulled them forward and rolled her scarf into a makeshift pillow, pressed against the window. Waited for his call. To the extent that she could pray as she drifted into shallow sleep, she asked for courage. For a breakthrough. For a miracle.

She woke stiff and cold. She didn't know how long she'd slept, but a thin, pale light was breaking the horizon. The wind had died down, the sea was calm. She checked her phone – no call; no text; no message. She texted again; pressed her head into the scarf; found that she could sleep a little longer.

The fullness of morning woke her to an unexpected break in the weather. There were clouds in the sky but they were white, whisper-thin; between them patches of blue, a pale denim to herald spring. The thick grey lid had lifted and where the sun found gaps between clouds, it teased both land and sea with longed-for warmth. Fiona climbed out of the car and walked onto the beach. The tide was low; the sea flat. She could see in the distance the thin line of houses that was Carnac. David still hadn't responded. She splashed her face with a palmful of cold seawater, went back to the car and took to the road again, heading north along the coastal route that skirted the peninsula's bay side. This was the mirror opposite of the road they had taken in their desperate search for Colom. A flat, still landscape in place of the restless ravings of its wilder twin. Dune grass at the side of the road, a smattering of thin, wiry weeds. This was a summer coast, a place kind to small children, gentle on lazily moored boats. A place of sandcastles, not shipwrecks; of snorkellers, not storms. Here was Esau to the Jacob of the Côte Sauvage. As calm and lazy as the other was driven and grasping. Which twin she was, which she was supposed to be, she didn't know.

In the thin morning light the road was all but deserted. She saw a lone dog walker, the beaches otherwise naked; left to the Sabbath rest of their winter season. It was like walking the aisles of a department store long after closing, like wandering an airport evacuated in a bomb scare.

She found herself in Port Haliguen, a vast marina whose long pontoons rattled with boats but were empty of people. She pulled into the car park at the centre of the harbour. There was a large hotel that seemed to be shut up for the winter, but opposite it a tired old café that looked open. Bare stone walls, a deserted terrace, chairs and tables piled and folded, threaded through with a locked steel cable. A single wooden door stood ajar. She entered a narrow and poorly lit corridor. This gave onto two rooms, both in shadow. The first was laid up for restaurant service and when she tried its door she found it locked. The second was a bar area, the room divided by an L-shaped wooden counter. Behind one leg of this, a ceiling-high display of cigarettes, cigars and tobacco. Beside this a rack of magazines. On the counter a pile of the day's papers.

Behind the other longer leg were the necessary effects of a café and bar. An espresso machine old enough to pre-date Starbucks by half a century. Bottles and glasses dusty enough to suggest a similar age. Shuffling between the stations in slow movements that were agony to watch was a woman who looked old enough to have received the espresso machine as a retirement gift. She was wearing a loose-fitting dress in a blue floral pattern and over it both an apron and a full-length housecoat. Her frame was so stooped that a customer seeking eye contact would need to approach the counter on their knees. Only children and wheelchair users would be afforded the unique pleasure of a full-face perspective.

The woman heard, rather than saw, Fiona come in. There were no other customers. She approached the counter, and to the tired but polite "Madame?" replied, "*Un grand crème, s'il vous plaît.*" She needed caffeine this morning, and she needed it in quantity.

The coffee was made in a series of the same shuffling movements; a ballet in stop-motion. It arrived on the counter beside a wrinkled, outstretched claw, accompanied by a gruff and unadorned, "*Deux soixante.*"

Fiona paid up and took her drink to a Formica-topped table. On the wall closest to her were old photographs of Port Haliguen, some from the 1950s and 1960s in fading colours, others in black and white from twenty or thirty years earlier. On all of them, the sea coming almost to the doorsteps of the small cluster of buildings. The last of these, even in the oldest of shots, bore the name that even now adorned its bare stone wall. The Café du Midi had been resisting change longer than Fiona had been alive.

She was alone and grateful for it. She checked to make sure she had a signal and that her battery would last the call. It was almost eight French time – just before seven UK. Surely she could catch him now?

She pressed the familiar speed-dial button, waited just a few seconds for the call to go through, but heard again, to her immense frustration, his voicemail greeting. Tempted to hang up, she pulled her temper into check and waited.

"Hello, David. It's me again," she said, an edge of exasperation pulling at the tiredness of her voice. She pressed her forehead against the upturned palm of her hand, her elbow jammed against the table. "I was hoping to catch you at last. I just need to talk to you. There is so much I need to tell you; to ask you. Please call me when you get this. As soon as possible. For what it's worth, I'm sorry."

She hung up. Foolish. Flustered. Embarrassed by her own message. Angry that she had had to leave it at all. It was the fourth she'd left since late last night. She wondered if David's phone was switched off, or if he'd seen her number and refused the calls.

She still didn't know what she should do.

CHAPTER TWENTY-FOUR

… I don't just wish you rain, Beloved – I wish you the beauty of storms…

John Geddes, A Familiar Rain

Discouraged, unsettled, confused, Fiona drove back to Portivy. She couldn't yet find the courage to face Miriam; was certain Colom wouldn't surface before lunch. She parked and went to the Café du Port, and was surprised to find Thierry there so early, after last night's heroics.

"You look as tired as I feel," he said as she came in. "How is he?"

"Sleeping, I think. No permanent damage done." She didn't want to say that she had not been to bed. Could he guess from her crumpled appearance?

"To him, no. But what about you? How are you?" He was already busy with her coffee. No need to ask.

"Tired." She smiled weakly. "Afraid. Confused." The coffee arrived on the counter, Thierry sliding it across to her.

She freed two sugar lumps from their neat, individual wrappings. Dropped them in; stirred absently.

"Do you believe in God, Thierry?" she asked.

He raised his eyebrows. "The God of my childhood, of the church, no, I'm not sure that I do. But I don't think that makes me altogether an unbeliever." He paused, thoughtful. Looked up suddenly. "Can you wait here a moment?" he said.

She nodded yes, confused. He lifted the hatch that released him from behind the counter and was out of the door. He came back after less than five minutes with a book: heavy, colourful. Turned it towards her on the countertop.

"I've been meaning to show you this in any case. But with your question... well, you'll see." Reading upside down, he turned the pages for her; past blocks of text to the place where the paintings began. Full-page, full colour. The sea in all her moods.

"I discovered Aivazovsky when I was studying in Paris," he said, as she took over the page-turning. She turned to the very back of the book and began to work back towards the beginning, letting each plate drop for the few moments of attention she felt able to give it. "He was Armenian by birth and is now a great hero of that nation. At the time I only thought of him as Russian. My course tutors didn't like him – they had little interest in much that happened before 1900 anyway, and he was too figurative for their tastes. I had to do my own research to find out much about him. There was this one painting I discovered – it's one of his most famous and is called *The Ninth Wave* – and it really haunted me. The image stayed with me for years. Much later when I was struggling to know how I really wanted to paint, I remembered the energy of that picture; the way colour was used to underline the emotion of the scene; the way the light became a messenger somehow between sky and sea and back again, and I wondered if he might have something to teach me. So I began to study him in more depth. In 1999 I had the opportunity to visit St Petersburg, and I found some of his paintings at the Tretyakov museum. I went back day after day just to study these pictures, and then suddenly – it was my fourth visit – the light came on. I realized that it was not how to paint that I was searching for, but what."

The book was open at a wide, double-page plate. A shipwreck, the struggling vessel dwarfed by enormous waves. A battle with the elements, the elements winning. In the foreground one wave had risen above those around it and caught the light to become translucent; radiant almost. Somehow the artist had succeeded in telling her that the light was shining through the water. She thought of Thierry's more contemporary works. A different style altogether, but the same subject always.

"The sea, you mean?"

"It was Aivazovsky's most frequent subject – you could say his obsession. He loved the moods of the sea, particularly the anger of the storm. As I got to know his work, I realized that the feeling he was able to convey in his paintings, this atmosphere he caught and reproduced, was the feeling I had grown up with here in Portivy. It is the feeling of knowing the sea. Sometimes a friend; sometimes an enemy; never a stranger. I looked for hours at the paintings at the Tretyakov. It was like meeting a man who had fallen in love with the same woman as I had. I felt that I knew him; knew why he painted. I knew then that I would paint the sea, and apart from one or two minor detours, that is all I have done ever since. It took a little longer to find my way back here, as you know, but I have never gone back on my decision. I paint the sea and the sky in their perpetual embrace, and if the land strays into the frame, it is only as a prop on which to display the majesty of the other two."

She felt sure the last words were rehearsed; that he had used them before; published them in exhibition catalogues. She was moved by them, but she was tired: more tired than she remembered ever being. Had her original question even been acknowledged?

"And God?" she said, trying not to sound impatient.

"Keep looking," he said, his eyes falling to the book.

She leafed through it further still. Plate after plate of Aivazovsky's seascapes. She could see what it was that had inspired Thierry so; could feel the passion that connected the two painters even though their styles were so different. She was almost back at the beginning of the book, where the text Thierry had passed over had first given way to the images. She let fall the last picture. He looked at her; his expression urging a response.

The picture was called *Chaos (Creation of the World)*. The caption dated it 1841. It was of a darkened, storm-tossed ocean; the waves like small mountain ranges, peaking sharply between shadow and light. Above them layered clouds rising like the tiers of an opera house towards a pale yellow radiance that filled the upper sky. And there at the centre of the canvas, breaking through the cloudscape, presiding over the waves, a single figure. God, or an angel he had sent, sculpted in light, arms outstretched over the sea, measuring out the ocean's very boundaries. The image pierced her heart. Shook her. Reached out to her.

"Sometimes when you view an artist's early work," Thierry said, "when he is still young, still looking for his style, you see traces of a statement of intent: a message telling you of works that are to come."

Aivazovsky would have been just twenty-five when he completed this work. She saw in its rawness a primitive belief. To witness the sea in full storm is to see the energy by which the world was made. The power of the ocean is the power of God. Before he became a lifelong painter of the sea Aivazovsky told the world, in this one picture, that he would spend his life attempting to paint God.

Thierry tapped his finger on the page where the book lay open. "In this God," he said, "I think I can believe."

All at once she understood. A key was turning. She all but heard the tumblers falling. Thierry's desire to stay in this place. Miriam's need to return. Her own fragile but growing peace here. It was the ocean, this brooding presence; constant in its tides and yet different every day. It was the sea that had made of this shoreline a thin place, as if the curtain of spray that hovered in the sky was a veil between heaven and earth. As if at will she could reach out to breach it, to touch the realm beyond: the reality that had until this day, for all her faith, eluded her. Something was happening: in this connection that Thierry had made between himself and Aivazovsky; in his own quest, bound up so closely with this place. Something that she needed to grasp, to embrace. It lay just beyond her reach; coming into focus; drawing closer; calling to her. If she could only touch its hem, would she be healed?

She mouthed a "thank you" to Thierry as she closed the book and gave it to him, turning immediately to leave the café. She headed across the harbour mouth, towards the shoreline. For all her chronic lack of sleep there was an energy surging through her, moving her forward. There was a small tidal island: a wedge of rock and grass the size of a football pitch a few dozen metres offshore. She had spotted it before but paid it no attention. She saw it now in a new light. With the tide at its halfway point, the tiny island was again surrounded by water, the stone-piled causeway that linked it to the beach just visible above the waves. She thought of Quiberon itself, of the monks of ages past who picked their way across the low-tide pathways to find in this micro-world of wave and rock some sense of the sacred. She pictured them, alone with the sea, pressed into the onshore breeze, pouring their prayers into the ever-present immensity that was the ocean and had become, for them, God's very presence.

She crossed the narrow beach to work her way across the wet stones, taking off her shoes part way when bare feet seemed a better choice. Reaching the island, she climbed a slight incline and walked to the vantage point of the far shore. From here she could see a vast expanse of sea; other islands; rock clusters disclosed in the half-tide. The sun had found a gap through which to peer: the waters glistened with it, the white towers and chimneys of Lorient visible at last. She stood, salt-sprayed, and counted; looking for the pattern in the waves. Did the ninth rise higher, or was that all in her imagination? Perhaps every wave mattered. Every curving, crashing fall of water, the ocean's arms outstretched to her. She remembered where she had heard the phrase before: in Celtic writings, the ninth wave marking the boundary between our earthly experience and the world beyond. She linked it, in her mind, to St Brendan. Thoughts tumbled in on her as freely as the waves themselves; a new awareness breaking on the shores of faith; washing over rocks too long kept dry. An old fisherman's prayer came to her. "Lord, be good to me – the sea is so wide and my boat is so small."

What was it she was experiencing in this moment? What had she found in this place? She tried to find words. A wider sea. No. A bigger God. She hesitated with the word God, not because it was too strong a word, but because it seemed, quite suddenly, too weak. It was too familiar a concept; too often abused. Too often, if she was honest, disappointing. She had mixed and mingled with "God" people for so long that the word had become a possession; a badge of office; a fashion accessory they owned that others did not. Here, now, she was remembering what the word "God" had once meant to her: the power and personality at the centre of all things, a being too big to be contained by dogma; too wild to be controlled by religion. How could the ground of all being ever be the captive possession of her few friends? How could she have believed it so? Her desire had never been to own this God, possessing him as an antique collector might possess a Chesterfield settee. It had been to be owned by him: caught up in an adventure so much larger than herself that it would never cease to draw her onward. David too had wanted such a life. When had he become the curator of his own religious museum, a grave-keeper in the cemetery of faith? When had either of them, thrown together by adventure, become so tame?

She could no more trace the moment than know when being young had morphed into being old. But she knew that it had happened. And she felt for the first time in years that here on this wild shoreline, in this thin place Miriam had brought her to, there was some hope of putting right what had gone wrong. She spoke into the void – to the universe; to her maker; to the adventure that was calling her. To this being she knew so well but was afraid to name, for fear of taming him, she spoke one word. "Yes." And again, for certainty, "Yes."

As she spoke it, she knew what she was allowing. What she was accepting, after all these years. Doors that would be opened. Secrets told. Accounted for. What it was that she was no longer holding captive. Being held by.

She imagined the sea itself laid bare; its every rock and secret channel uncovered. Formations of stone and sand submerged for centuries, caressed by the ocean's currents, hidden from view by a dark weight of water: brought now to the light, laid open for all to see. A single fork of lightning; a wind like the very breath of God. Secret things, exposed at last.

"Yes," she said, knowing that her world, in that one word, would be unravelled.

She turned back to the village, sensing, in some deep place, that something real had moved. She had heard the key-change; had felt the time-shift; was even now hearing new music.

She understood how deep and real this change had been when, walking back across the car park, she almost tripped over the day's second miracle.

CHAPTER TWENTY-FIVE

He turned to look just in time to see the rain start
falling out as if the storm had finally decided to weep
with shame for what it had done to them.

James Dashner, *The Scorch Trials*

The few cars in the harbour-front car park were local ones Fiona was already beginning to recognize. Except one. A red Espace. A car whose dented bumper and rear window stickers she knew like she knew her own skin.

He was sitting on the bench on the quayside, looking out to sea. A low chain marked off a pedestrian area, the wooden bench set beyond it, at the centre of the harbour's span. His jacket was buttoned to the collar, but he was wearing sunglasses – an odd and uncharacteristic concession to fashion.

She sat beside him.

"Hello, David."

"Hello, Fiona. I've missed you."

She wanted to reciprocate, but couldn't force the words to come. She smiled weakly. Held back tears.

"Thank you for coming. I didn't think you would."

"Thank you for inviting me. I didn't think you would."

"You didn't answer your phone." The tears still threatening her, rattling the gate she was holding them behind.

"Sorry. Driving. I had no signal on the boat last night, then I saw that all the messages had come in when I was in the car this morning. Figured I was on my way in any case. I did send an email, to say that I would be coming. Yesterday."

"Sorry. I haven't managed to get online these past two days. It's been hectic here. Are you angry with me, David?" she asked.

"Angry? Yes. And worried. Confused. Upset. Lonely. Take your pick – I've been through all of them these past few days. You've fair unravelled me."

"I'm sorry. I truly am. I didn't mean to hurt you. I just knew I had to…"

"Fiona, let's not do this now. I've been beside myself with worry these past days, but I think I know why you've done what you've done, and I've never stopped trusting you. I know you want what's best for Colom, and I know you've known what's best for him a hundred times more often than I have. What do you say we set our own needs aside just now and see if we can work on his?"

"Really? You mean it?"

"Yes, I mean it. That lad's in trouble, and we're the cause of it. The least we can do is join ranks to help him. God knows we've put other needs before his often enough, but we've been wrong, and it's time to stop."

She turned to face him, twisting her body on the bench so she could see him clearly. Disbelief flowed through her, the speed of its onset matched only by the relief that followed close behind.

"He threw away his clothes," she said. He looked at her, puzzled. "When I asked him where his suitcase was, he said he'd thrown it in the sea. He'd kept a few things, but most of his clothes were gone. I asked him why he'd done such a thing, and he said, 'I won't be needing them.'"

He said nothing.

"You do know what he meant by that?"

He turned to her. Took his sunglasses off.

"I'm sorry, I didn't mean to imply… I just didn't expect you to accept such behaviour so calmly."

Glasses off now, he was looking out to the ocean; seeking the horizon.

"I think I've known for months that we've done wrong by Colom," he said. "I just haven't known how to put it right. It was like a knot I couldn't untie – like trying to find the end of a roll of tape. I don't know if what you've done here is find an end, but maybe it is. I know it's worth a try."

Fiona wondered where this David had been these past months. These past years. She recognized him now; remembered him. Was it her fault that she had lost sight of him? Had he been this same David all along? There was no way of knowing, nor of saying where things would go from here.

"How long can you stay?" she asked.

"I'm just here for today," he said. "I didn't want to presume on staying. I just needed to see you – and Colom. I'm not sure how he'll take me. Our last conversation was not the best we've ever had."

The sheer scale of his deflation was a shock to her. After months of rising anger with his son, this was a new emotion: to be afraid of him.

"I think Colom will be glad to see you," she reassured him. "The one thing I've never known him to do is bear a grudge – he's probably forgotten your last words completely."

"I hope so. But I'll apologize, all the same. I spoke unkindly, and none of what I said was true, nor needed saying."

Really? Was he moving on from vicaring to make a bid for Father of the Year?

"When I read your letter, Fiona, I was so angry," he said. "I went over and over in my head all the questions I would ask you. How you could presume to know what was best for Colom. How you could dare to take him from me. How you could be so dismissive of decisions I had made – we had made together. I read it again and I was angrier still. I was raging against you."

"I'm sorry, David, I really am. I didn't know how else to tell you all that had happened. I..."

"No, please don't. I need to explain. I was angry all that day, and the next day I took that anger to the office. I can't tell you the things I imagined saying to you. I rehearsed them in my head like a play. Richard took me aside in the afternoon and all but told me to get my act together – I'd been pretty foul to everyone all day. But it didn't make any difference. That evening I read your letter again, and I was still angry. I wanted to phone you, but I didn't because I knew you could so easily hang up on me, and that would make me madder still – I wanted to see you face-to-face, to get you in a room where I could tell you everything you had done wrong and you couldn't walk away from it. All the frustrations I'd felt since you took Colom and left – all the hurt I'd allowed myself to nurse – boiled over. I'd have torn the letter up except I wanted it for evidence: I wanted to wave it at you and make you acknowledge its stupidity."

"So what happened?"

"I saw myself."

She looked at him, her question posed in silence.

"I mean literally. I saw myself in the dining room mirror. I turned around, and there I was: red-faced, fuming. I saw the vein on the side of my neck pulsing – the way you always told me it did when I was angry with someone in the church. I saw an angry man, out of control, lost in his own rage. And I knew that something was wrong. I was angry in the way an addict gets angry when you take his drug away. I've talked so many people down from their anger – I never thought it would be me I had to talk to."

He paused. She joined him. Left him space to tell his tale.

"I've learned a few things about anger over the years, Fiona. I know that a man whose anger is out of control is a man whose life is out of control. I've seen others as angry as I was that evening and I have always counselled them to ask if this really is anger speaking, or hurt in a clever disguise. So I asked myself the same. I read your letter again, and then again. I forced myself to look differently at what you were saying, to ask honestly why it made me rage so. And then I understood. I wasn't angry with you, or

Colom. I wasn't angry with your Miriam. I wasn't angry about any of the things you said in your letter, or the things you'd done."

Another pause. She could feel, faintly, the warmth of the mid-morning sun.

"You were angry with yourself," she said.

"I couldn't believe that I had made such a mistake – not a one-off error, a small loss of judgment, but a huge mistake, made deliberately and sustained over twelve long years. I couldn't believe that I was capable of such stupidity; to so damage the people I love. I've been so careful, Fiona, not to make mistakes. I've protected myself, us, our family, the church. I've worked to get things right. But I got this – we got this – so wrong. We've been living a lie for twelve years, and forcing Colom to live it with us."

"We have. We did. I don't know, either, how we came to it. But we did."

"Well, no more," he said. "No more lies."

She saw fear again, as if he was the insecure teenager in the relationship. But there was something else, a change in his tone of voice. She looked at him. His eyes were shut. He was rubbing his temples with both hands. He sighed.

"David, what is it?" she asked, panic rising.

CHAPTER TWENTY-SIX

The battle of the next day was also succeeded in the night by a fearful storm which, in this case, consisted of rain, hail and sleet.

Edward Powers, *War and the Weather: Or, The Artificial Production of Rain*

He said nothing for a moment. Seemed to be having trouble breathing. When he spoke it was barely a whisper. She wasn't even sure she had heard him right.

"I've never told you, Fiona. The truth about why I fought so hard to adopt Colom."

She assumed there was more. But nothing came.

"David, what's wrong?"

He found his courage.

"I thought he might really be my son."

"But how? When? David?" She was drowning now; losing her grip; reality as she knew it slipping from her.

He was somewhere else. Not talking to her but to some invisible audience. Answering questions she wasn't asking. Eyes still closed. Barely making sense.

"There was no way of knowing for certain. I didn't know if I could believe her. It could have been a lie, for money. Extortion. But it could have been true."

"David, what are you saying?" she heard herself shout. Didn't know how loud it was. Was struggling to get a purchase on the words she was hearing.

At last he opened his eyes. Looked at her.

"Colom might have been my son, Fiona. His mother was a client. An addict. We had a relationship. It was only a matter of weeks. It was long over when you and I met. I couldn't tell you. I haven't told anyone, ever. I was ashamed. Scared."

"And you knew she was pregnant?"

"Not at the time. She disappeared from the project. We lost track of her for almost a year. Then she came back, asking for money. She told me there was a baby, that it was mine, and that he'd been taken for adoption. She said she'd expose me if I didn't pay her."

"And did you?"

"Three times. Five hundred dollars each time. I knew she could so easily be lying, but I couldn't risk it."

Three times, Fiona was thinking, three payments. "Why not more?" she said quietly. "Why only three payments?"

He had stopped speaking. Had looked away again.

"Why not more, David? What happened?" There was a weight on her chest; some force bearing down on her. There didn't seem to be enough air in the world for them both to keep breathing.

His eyes were closed again. The fingers working the temples once more. Rehearsing words he had spoken to himself a hundred times, but never to her.

"Three days after the last payment, they found her at her squat, with her boyfriend. He was also her dealer. They had both overdosed. Had been dead for at least two days. The police came to see us because she was known to have been registered at the project. They told us that she had scored one massive hit: way too much for the state she was in. They wondered where she might have got the money. I had to say I didn't know."

"It was your money – the money you had given her?"

She was watching the image of her husband collapse. An edifice she had taken for granted in all the years she had known him. His strength. His right-thinking. His superhuman capacity to resist temptation. Crumbling now. Because he hadn't.

He didn't answer immediately. Nodded faintly, his eyes tightening. "I don't know. No one does. But yes, it could have been."

"And Colom? Where was Colom all this time? Didn't you try to find him?"

This was the worst part, it seemed. Again the eyes. The temples. "I did find him. Traced him to the foster home. I thought he was being well looked after. I thought he would be better off. I kept an eye from a distance. Hoped he would find a good family."

"My God, David, you knew he was there, and you did nothing?"

"Of course not. I mean I didn't know what was happening. None of us did. Any of it. We had no idea. It was when it all came out that I pressed for adoption. Well, you know that – you were there by then."

"But I didn't know why. I didn't know you had... You might be his father!"

He took a letter from his pocket. Passed it to her. It was from a lab of some sort – Gentech. There were details, identifying him, identifying Colom. At the end of a long list of information a single word – NEGATIVE.

"When did you do this? How?"

"Last month. I used one of Colom's baby teeth."

She was numb. There was only so much stress her brain could manage, and the last twenty-four hours had delivered her a year's worth. At a loss for what to say, she took the easy option. Let her anger do the talking.

"And you're trying to prove something to me now with this? As if this lets you off the hook?"

"No, it's nothing like that. I just needed to know. And I wanted you to know. I don't want these secrets to be there between us any more." Fingers again to his temples. The eyes closing. A deep breath. "I want to put things right. If I can."

"But why, David? Why now, after all these years?" And then she realized. Remembered. A puzzle was coming together in her mind. Pieces she had never seen as connected were assembling. She knew why Colom had changed. What had changed him. She spoke it as she thought it. "Cornwall."

"Fistral. You remember?"

"I remember it's when you changed. I wondered at the time why it was. I've wondered since. You had been so close to Colom, so easy with him. It was like you were best friends. And then suddenly, you could hardly look at him."

And as she said it, she knew why.

"Do you have a picture?" she asked. "Of her?"

He nodded. Reached again into his jacket pocket. Fumbled for it. One picture, a little larger than a passport photo. Head and shoulders. She wondered if it had been taken from a case file. His hands were shaking so much that she couldn't make out the detail. She took it from him.

The face was pale, gaunt. Red under the eyes; the hint of a bruise over one cheek. The blonde hair straight, straggly. But when she looked beyond that – to the bone structure, the intelligent eyes, the shape of the nose – there was no mistaking it. She was looking at a picture of her son.

"I'd put it out of my mind," he was saying. "For years. I focused on the positive, giving Colom the life I knew he deserved. Persuading you to go along with the lie. Telling him nothing about his background; what was done to him; what he endured. Telling you nothing about his mother. I figured that if I could be a father to him it wouldn't matter whether I actually was or not. He would be healthy and happy. We would be a family. And no one would ever need to know. And then…"

"You saw her in him."

"He changed. Got taller; slimmer. His face altered, and suddenly all I could see was her. It all came back: my shame; what I'd done. I couldn't touch him. I couldn't look at him. I remember the exact moment, on that holiday. We were on the beach, he was running towards me, dragging a kite behind him

– he wanted me to help him get it airborne. The angle of the sun on his face did something to him, and all I could see was her."

He was close to tears. A broken man, sitting into his crumpled coat, his crumpled body, as if he'd aged two decades. They sat in silence.

When he moved, twisting his body towards her, she thought for an awful moment he was going to try to kiss her. Not that the idea itself repelled her, just that at this moment, in these circumstances, she could not imagine him being so insensitive. But he wasn't. He was turning, rather, to reach behind her for his backpack, resting on the floor behind the bench.

"I came to give you this," he said. He had made the decision to tell her everything shortly after his man-in-the-mirror moment, and had realized within minutes that this would involve showing her everything. He knew how wrong he had been to keep this from her. How selfish his decisions had been. It was self-preservation that had driven him, not her welfare, or Colom's, no matter how often he had told himself otherwise. He had looked for some act by which he could redeem himself. He couldn't turn the clock back, but could he somehow take the sting out of the actions he'd taken? Could he lessen the blow? The guilty verdict was delivered: was there scope now for mitigation? Full disclosure was the only action he could find that would at least make a measure of redemption possible. He would tell Fiona everything. Give her everything. Let her decide if she could forgive him.

For a moment he held the file in his own hand.

"I've lied to you, Fiona, and I've kept things from you, and I want you to know that I'm sorry. I don't deserve your forgiveness, but I'm going to ask for it. I love you, and I want you to love me again, if that's even possible. I don't want this… situation to destroy what we have; our marriage. Our family. I'm hoping there's a second chance for us, and if there is, I want you to know that I'll take it."

She said nothing. Searched desperately and urgently for the right words. Couldn't find them. Went to take the file from him; his hand still gripping it, keeping it closed.

"I don't want you to read it now," he said quietly. "I want you to open it when I'm gone. Some of it you've already seen, back then, but some you haven't. It's all here. Everything I know about Colom and about his mother. How much you tell him is up to you. Then you can decide what your next step is. I only hope it will help you, with what you're trying to do for Colom. You are his mother in every sense that matters now. I want you to see this journey you have started with him through to the end. I want you to help him."

"And if I show Miriam? Everything?"

"I'm past secrets. You must do what you need to do. For Colom. For our son."

She held the file. Let her index finger find the place where the flap folded over. Nudged it gently. Wondered what she would learn when it came open.

A question arrived unexpectedly in her mind.

"There's no chance, is there, that Colom might have been a twin?"

"No – none at all."

"You're sure?"

"We saw the birth records from the hospital. I even…" He hesitated, but pressed on. "I tracked down one of the nurses who delivered him."

"You never told me that." What she would have given to meet someone who had held Colom at the very moment of his birth.

"I know. I'm sorry."

She let it go.

"Definitely no sister?"

"No. He was her first. And only. Why do you ask?"

"Oh, it's probably nothing – just that I was thinking about his nightmares. When he describes them to me, there is often a sister in them. I wondered if she might be real."

He made no comment, shook his head. Silence enveloped them again. One of the boats lying angled in the muddy harbour had a loose line that clinked against its mast with every gust of wind. She saw gulls wheeling in the distance, but didn't hear their cries.

"Do you want to see him?"

"Can I?"

"Of course. Come on, I'll show you the house. He might even be awake by now."

He wasn't, but it didn't take long to rouse him. David took him out for the afternoon to let Fiona surrender, at last, to the sleep that was stalking her. She was grateful but, for all her tiredness, couldn't rest.

Instead she opened the file. She laid out the clippings and letters around her on the bedroom floor: the secret history of Colom's early years; a collage of accusation and regret. Inside the file she found a sealed envelope, as she had known she would. She hesitated before opening it, but forced herself to do so. Looked again at photographs she hadn't seen since the adoption: the images that had changed everything; that might just do so again. Things she had known and had forced herself to forget. Things she had kept from her son. Tears welled up until in due course she set the photographs aside. She read every article, every letter twice over; pored over those from the time before she had come onto the scene. Drank in the details David had never shared with her.

She washed her face when she heard Colom come in, David in tow. They seemed in good spirits, though she resisted the temptation to ask. David had to leave again immediately for his return ferry, and Colom took his new sketch pad and pencils off to his room, saying he had already eaten. She walked David back to his car. Thanked him for coming. Promised to let him know how things went with Colom. Said goodbye. Kissed him lightly on the cheek. For appearance's sake – not for her own.

She left Miriam to eat alone and returned to the crime scene her floor had become. Later, after she had sobbed so deeply that she almost vomited, she lay awake in the first-floor bedroom, cradled by the wildness of the wind against her window, wondering what she would do.

She had the only window on the west end of the house. If she craned her neck, by daylight, she could just catch the sea. By night she saw nothing, but heard everything. The wind hurtled across miles of ocean, hitting landfall just a stone's throw from the house. It beat against her window with unyielding ferocity. An onshore onslaught: cold, and harsh, and strangely comforting. Behind the noise of its fury was the still wilder boiling of the sea itself; ton after ton of water breaking against the rocks; relentlessly rolling onto the beaches; hammering the harbour wall. The raving and the rage of it all reached her even behind the tight security of a window that had been blocking such storms for half a century before she was even born.

She had asked David to stay, to do this with her, but had known that he wouldn't – that he shouldn't. He was right that her relationship with Colom was the best chance they had of a breakthrough – that it would be easier, not harder, with him gone. But that left her alone. She could do this thing. But not alone.

At 3:23 a.m., exhausted, she came to a decision. She was becoming too familiar with this hour to stay awake any longer. She didn't know if her call would even be answered and if it was, if she would be greeted with understanding or with anger. But she was gripped by an overwhelming need to try. Despite all that had gone on; all that had been said, and left unsaid, these past twelve years. She found her phone, scrolled to a familiar name, waited; heard a gruff and sleepy but immeasurably comforting voice.

"It's Fiona," she said quietly, hardly breaking from a whisper. "I'm in trouble. I need help."

Later, she held her breath in the stillness of the room; reached out to hear and know the turbulence beyond. She found solace in the knowledge that whatever happened to her and to Colom; whatever action she did or didn't take; whatever the outcome of their journey, nothing would change the pattern of these winds. This turbulent marriage of ocean and air would still be here tomorrow, even if she were not. Which meant that the things that were happening to her were not, after all, the end of the world. Held by this strange comfort, and cocooned in her safe room, she finally found sleep.

CHAPTER TWENTY-SEVEN

*At night I dream that you and I are two plants that
grow together, roots entwined, and that you know the
earth and the rain like my mouth, since we are made of
earth and rain.*

Pablo Neruda, *Regalo De Un Poeta / Gift Of A Poet*

A little under six hours later, Fiona stood with the small knot of people spread like a dollop of jam on the cathedral-like concourse of Nantes airport. A few held up the obligatory name cards – "M. Delponte, Orion Finance" (nicely printed, black on white), "Smith" (hastily scrawled in reusable coloured pen). Most of those waiting were casually dressed, friends or family members here for reunion.

Moments earlier there had been a brief flurry of excitement as a black-robed woman flew into a rage at one of the check-in desks. She had arrived at a run with too much luggage and a tired small child in tow, and was stressed even before they refused to check her in. She protested at higher and higher volumes, her child screaming at her feet, until the whole cavernous concourse echoed with her voice and the departures and arrivals crowds alike were treated to a live soap opera. Supervisors were called and she was taken to some private office to calm down, returning the concourse to its museum-like hush.

Fiona wondered what the poor woman's story might be. Was she simply late, and being unreasonable as the ground staff seemed to believe? Or was she the victim of a misunderstanding or, worse still, of racism? Even small regional airports, these days, were places of suspicion. She wondered how she would feel were she to meet with such hostility. David had not reported them missing or accused her of any kind of kidnapping but the haunting feeling she had carried for days – of having done something terribly wrong – was still with her. Would she find sympathy if she attempted to explain her actions, or suspicion? Was she an understandably concerned mother, or dangerously unhinged? If Colom's condition deteriorated here in France, God forbid, who would she turn to? How would she deal with such events without David by her side?

All these thoughts flowed through her mind as she waited, the emotional echo of the screaming mother fading.

The doors slid open and a crowd poured out like ketchup from a bottleneck. He had always been tall, easy to spot in a crowd. She stood on tiptoes – not so that she would see him, but to be sure that he would see her. She spotted him even though he had distinctly less hair than the last time they'd been together. She caught his attention with a wave and he came straight towards her, dropping his bag to the floor and sweeping her into a hug that took her feet off the ground.

"So good to see you, Fiona," he said. "It's been forever."

"It's good to see you too; it really is." She marvelled at her own capacity for understatement. Phoning in the early hours had been a habit in her teens, not least if she needed to be picked up from some party she had wandered into. But it wasn't something she had done recently. She had mumbled tearfully through the headlines of the past weeks; had described the crossroads she had now reached. Her inability to choose a road. His response had both terrified and mollified her. He had been quick to say that there was only one thing she could do, only one road she could take, but he had also, miraculously, agreed to come and do it with her. He had asked for the nearest airport and promised he would do the rest; had texted her over breakfast with an arrival time that same day. She knew that this is what journalists do, what he had done for more than twenty years, but it was the first time he had ever done it for her.

"So how are you?" he asked, breaking the embrace to make eye contact.

She didn't answer. Buried her head against his shoulder, clinging for just a moment longer to the bliss of surrendering to that which is both strong and familiar. Fiona was twenty years away from any meaningful contact with her father, and her brother Mark's tall lean frame; his old-fashioned taste for blue blazers; the combined residual scent of his three favourite after-shave lotions: these were substitutes enough for a girl who needed reassurance.

"Let's get moving," she said at last. "We can talk as we drive."

She pointed him towards the car park and they set off, arm in arm.

"So whose house is it you're staying in exactly?" he asked. "I still don't know."

"And you're not going to know until we get there, either. You'll meet her soon enough. In fact, she's been looking forward to seeing you again."

"Again? So we've met before?"

"Oh yes, more than once. But it was a long time ago. Don't try to guess – you never will in any case. Just be patient – we'll be there in just over an hour. Unless you want to stop for lunch on the way?"

"I'd love to – but I couldn't bear the tension. French or English?"

"French – but honestly, you won't guess. Just be patient, and tell me what you've been working on lately."

"Well that, my fair sister, is a fascinating question, which will probably take me most of this journey to answer."

Traffic was light as Fiona swept around the Nantes ring road, and they were soon speeding west on an almost empty N12. She pulled into the outside lane to pass a convoy of caravans, each towed by a white panel van. In front of them, three sports cars in turn towed small covered trailers. Making slow progress. Sticking together. The solidarity of a gypsy community, of family.

"So what's this ever-so-interesting story you've been working on?" she asked.

He answered, and their journey was absorbed in a blur of him talking; her asking questions. Closer to Quiberon, off the motorway, he asked if she was sure of what she was about to do.

"I'm not sure of anything," she said, "but I have no choice. You were right about that. I just want to get it over with."

"Today?" he asked.

"Today," she said, with more conviction than she felt.

Forty minutes later they were standing on opposite sides of the dining table. Between them was a manila envelope. They both turned to the door as they heard the latch.

Miriam's face broke into a smile.

"Mark!" she said. "How wonderful to see you."

"Miriam? My goodness, I really wouldn't have guessed. Good to see you too." He opened his arms in time to receive and return her embrace. "This is your home?"

"Not exactly. I live in England, near Brighton. This was my childhood home, and my mother's until she died."

She noticed that Fiona was silent; could see that she was fighting tears. She returned her stare, a silent "What is it?"

"Colom is sleeping upstairs," Fiona said quietly, "and he's unlikely to surface in the next hour or so. There's something we need to show you. We need to do it now."

Her voice was quiet, strained, as if she was speaking through a blanket. Her hands were shaking. Miriam thought that perhaps she was about to faint. She stepped forward to catch her if she fell. Fiona regained her self-control and turned back towards the table and its mysterious contents.

"These photographs were taken two days after Colom came into our home," she said somberly. A dull, detached monotone. "Colom slept through the whole experience. I hadn't seen these images for twelve years, until yesterday. It was Mark who insisted we take them back then, so that there was an independent record." She nodded towards her brother acknowledging, ever so slightly, that he had been right to force her hand, now as then. "It was Mark who finally persuaded me to show them to you now. I didn't even want to see them again, let alone show them to anyone. Even to you, Miriam. I'm sorry."

"They're not pleasant, Miriam," Mark said, "so please be prepared. Do you want to do this, Fiona?"

"No, you do it."

She sat down heavily at the table, her head resting in her hands; her fingers buried deep into her hair, pressed into her scalp. Miriam took up a position behind her, her hands on the chair back. Mark remained standing, and reached for the envelope. No one spoke as he removed a pile of colour photographs, and began to lay them out, like a dealer setting up a game of patience.

By the time the third image had found its place, Fiona's quiet sobbing had become a torrent of tears. Miriam laid a hand gently on her shoulder. The other went to her mouth in shock at the horrors unfolding like a murder scene before her. All the pictures were of Colom. He was younger than in other images Miriam had seen, but there was no question this was him. He was wearing *Toy Story* pyjamas and appeared to be asleep. In most of the images an adult hand appeared – Fiona's? – to hold up the pyjamas. There was a sequence to the images. The first two simply showed Colom asleep, then a third showed his stomach, red and bruised. Each of these signs of injury would be afforded an image of its own: the close-ups amplifying the horror. The same pattern was pursued on Colom's back, then his legs, then – in a final set of images that Miriam could hardly bear to look at – his thighs and buttocks.

Miriam marvelled that Fiona had been able to keep her son asleep throughout this process of cataloguing the abuses he had suffered. She wondered what might go through a new mother's mind at such a time. There were bruises and cuts at various stages of healing, and two injuries that shook Miriam more deeply still. Her guess was that they were cigarette burns.

Miriam pulled out a chair and sat down heavily, across the table from Fiona. "Tell me," she said, to no one in particular.

"We counted thirteen separate injuries," Mark said. "There may have been more: some of the bruises were on top of earlier trauma. All the injuries were carefully placed to avoid detection – nothing to the face or lower arms, the worst in places that would be covered most of the time."

Miriam was already beginning to calculate the impact of this new information on her conversations with Colom. Buried deep in the shock and horror she felt, there was an acute sense of relief. Naming at last the ghosts that had been haunting Colom was a strange kind of progress. It wasn't the end of the journey, and nor did it guarantee recovery, but it was a huge step. Identifying the poison was a crucial move towards finding the antidote. But it did nothing to relieve the sick sensation she now carried in the pit of her stomach.

"Who did this?" she asked, her tone suggesting, had such a person been here in the room, that she would happily have killed them with her own bare hands.

"The foster carer," Fiona said flatly. "Colom was already two by the time he came to us. He had been in foster care since he was a few days old." She couldn't say any more.

Mark took up the explanation, the facts engraved as deeply in his memory as in that of his sister. "His name was McAllister," he said. "He was as deeply disturbed as a man in such a role could be. His wife was no better – she was as involved as him, sadly. They were jointly prosecuted. They had been responsible for the care of twenty-three children over seventeen years. They sometimes had as many as eight at a time. They both received long sentences, though I suspect they are free now. I doubt that they will have stayed in Newfoundland, though – their names were all over the papers at the time, and memories are long on a small island."

CHAPTER TWENTY-SEVEN

The three maintained a reverent silence as the import of this information took its place at the centre of the room.

"Let's hope they can be shorter for the victims," Miriam said at last, though she did not believe for one instant that they could be.

CHAPTER TWENTY-EIGHT

Rain drops are not the ones who bring the clouds.
Sorin Cerin, *Wisdom Collection: The Book of Wisdom*

"Are you very angry with me? For not telling you sooner?" Fiona asked Miriam. After the pictures, they'd shown her the letters and clippings; explained about the social services investigation; the adoption process; the decision to tell Colom none of it. Mark had taken the opportunity to register for the hundredth time his anger at the choice they'd made: Fiona wilting, shrinking into herself with the weight of it all.

When they heard Colom stirring, the papers and pictures were returned to the file. Reunited with his favourite nephew, Mark persuaded him to act as tour guide on a walk around the village, and a visit to its ancient café. Miriam and Fiona sat in the non-matching armchairs: the room unchanged; the scene familiar, yet everything different. An unknown galaxy.

"I'm too shocked to be angry, Fiona," Miriam sighed. "I knew that there must be something you hadn't told me, but this is horrible. Horrible. The poor child."

"We thought we were doing the right thing. By not telling him. By lying to him."

"Maybe you were. Maybe you did the best you could in impossible circumstances. Who knows how any of us would react to such a situation? It's not you that hurt him, Fiona. It's not you that held him down with one hand while with the other…"

She stopped. Tears pressing at the back of her eyes like teen fans trying to force their way into a concert. The doors bulging, threatening to give way. Her face was set hard in a way Fiona hadn't seen before.

Fiona was twisting and rotating her wedding and engagement rings, turning the stone, a small diamond, now inward into her hand, now outward again, into the light.

"By the time David adopted Colom," she said distractedly, "he had lived through more suffering than most of us meet in a lifetime. We just wanted to give him the alternative – to give him the childhood he should have had in the first place. We wanted to erase every bruise until there wasn't a trace of the torture he had endured."

"I know you did, Fiona, and I think I know why." She reached across, her hand on Fiona's arm, made eye contact. Held it. "But these things can't be erased in that way. Lies, denial, fabricated histories – these only bury the bruises, sometimes in a place where they can even grow and spread, because no one's watching them. Did you never consider even telling him he's adopted?"

"No. Not once. It was like we'd banned the word from our vocabulary. We wanted to treat him as if he'd been ours by birth, so we created that myth and held to it. We worked so hard to convince him that we convinced ourselves. This reality, this nightmare, belonged to another world. We didn't want or need to bring it into ours. It feels terrible to say it now, but it was a kind of experiment. We wanted, David wanted, to see how far a positive outlook could go in redressing negative experience."

"You didn't agree?"

"I went along with it, because I had no better ideas, and it did seem to be working. Colom was a wonderful child. We bonded – at least it felt as if we had. And then it just seemed wrong to tell him. At first it was too early to tell him – he was too young to understand – then it was too late. We couldn't admit that we'd lied to him."

Miriam leaned in, elbows on her knees. "And he had no memories from the foster home? Nothing from his first two years?"

"I think he did; he must have done." Dredging up the memories. Addressing her answers to the carpet. "But we replaced them with our own. We told him stories, showed him pictures, and the other life gradually disappeared. By the time he was five or six, it was as if those other years had never existed. We even added three years every time we celebrated our wedding anniversary, in case Colom did the maths and became suspicious."

"You must have known that it would come out in the end?"

"Must we? I suppose so, but we put it out of our minds. Maybe we thought that we would tell him one day, as an adult. I don't know. We poured the positives into him like medicine, because we felt that was what he needed. We weren't going to bring him into our home and remind him every day of what had happened to him. But then when the positive memories became part of him, of his story, we felt we couldn't take them from him, that it would be a renewed cruelty to do so."

"Hence the other pictures? He said you had a whole series, from his earliest years?"

She nodded.

"So what changed?"

"What do you mean?"

"You said you thought it was working. He was adjusting well. Bonding. But you came to me last month because Colom was in crisis. Your fears for him were at fever pitch. What triggered the change?"

"We assumed at first it was his age. Puberty; hormonal changes. But there was something else. I saw it but didn't understand, until yesterday. It was David. David changed. A complete U-turn. They had been so close; like best friends in a way. But it was as if David decided, after, what, ten years, to reject him entirely. I didn't know why. I couldn't make sense of it. But I know now."

"Because he looked like his mother?"

Fiona's eyes widened. "How did you know?" The ring was turning again, the dry skin reddened underneath its imprint.

"Her picture, in the file. The likeness is striking. I remembered you mentioning that David had known Colom's mother, as a client. It struck me then as odd and has been working away at me ever since. Too much of a coincidence, I suppose. Forgive me for asking, Fiona, but was there perhaps more to their relationship?"

"Yes. I didn't know. Until yesterday."

"Is it possible that David might actually be Colom's father?" The knots were unravelling now. So much beginning to make sense.

"No. He's not. He did a paternity test, last month."

"But until last month he thought he might be Colom's father?"

Fiona nodded. Mute.

"So everything he did: adopting him, giving him the best life he could imagine, even making it up where he needed to – all that was because he might, indeed, have been his son?"

"Yes. I honestly don't know if it was from guilt, or from love."

"Does it have to be one or the other? Don't all our actions show a little bit of both?" She'd put down her pen and notebook. Her repository of facts and observations. Was running, now, on instinct.

"You're being very kind to him." The ring again; turning.

"Perhaps so. But think of those pictures. Isn't kindness exactly what is needed here – for all three of you?"

"But will it… can it… can we unravel this, Miriam? Is it too late to put right what we've done?"

"My honest answer is that I don't know. I have hope, but I won't make empty promises. But there is something I need to say to you, Fiona." She shifted in her seat; moved even further forward. Hardly ten centimetres between them. Her voice clear. Deliberate. The conclusion she had been working towards. Hardly knowing, herself, that it was where they were headed. "I don't know if you are in a position to hear it right now, but I do believe it needs to be said."

CHAPTER TWENTY-EIGHT

Fiona looked up. Wide-eyed again. Was this where the axe at last would fall?

"When I saw those photographs this afternoon, it broke my heart. I wept inside for the child who had to endure such cruelty. But I also thought of Colom – this young man I have been getting to know these past days. I thought of this Colom who pretends to have nothing to say to me, knowing that moments later he will spin a world of words. This Colom who speaks articulately and intelligently of his own feelings; who is sensitive to the feelings of others."

Fiona was surprised by the turn the conversation was taking; thrilled that someone else had seen what she had always known to be true: that her son was a strong and an honourable young man.

"Looking at those pictures, those injuries," Miriam continued, "I would expect to find a child in acute trauma. I would expect some of the symptoms Colom has exhibited, but I would expect more. Much more. Unless something else – a more positive influence, a secure relationship, a genuine love had come into the picture. Something has made that difference. Something good and pure and strong has already helped Colom not to be subsumed by pain and anger."

"And what do you think that something is?"

"You don't know?"

"No."

"It's you, Fiona. Your love. Whatever else you've done, you've loved your son, and I think I know enough to say that your love has made a difference."

Of all the emotions Fiona had expected to endure through the length of this day, peace was not one of them. But she felt it now. It was spreading through her body, from her feet upwards. It was filling her chest, climbing her neck, taking hold of her head. She had beaten herself senseless over the things she had done wrong. It was a joy; a relief; a precious gift, to be told by someone whose opinion meant the world to her, that she had at least got something right. The tears that now poured from her were, at least in part, tears of relief.

CHAPTER TWENTY-NINE

*... with you, I find peace from pain – You are gentle
and healing like the landscape – like rain...*

John Geddes, A Familiar Rain

In the evening they attempted to build a fire. Though spring
was evidently on its way, the nights could still be cold. The logs
were smouldering, not quite taking. Their smell filled the room,
the flames fighting for a hold. Miriam had now read everything in
the file; had pieced the story together with the added details Fiona
had shared with her. She'd spent the later part of the afternoon
with her notebook; looking back over her conversations with
Colom; setting them against this new information. She wanted to
talk now with Fiona, about what her next steps might be.

Mark and Colom had gone their separate ways – the nephew
to his attic, the uncle to deepen his acquaintance with Pierre's
various beers. Their afternoon tour had stretched beyond the
village itself to take in the clifftop walk out to the stone table.

"He's boxing an opponent he can't even see," Miriam said. "He
needs for his own sake to forgive those who have hurt him. But he
can't do this without knowing who they were and what they did.
He's hurt and angry, and not knowing why makes it worse for him.
By telling him everything, we give him the information he needs to
be able to manage his emotions. We don't do it all at once, and we
think carefully about how it's done, but ultimately you must trust
Colom to be able to deal with reality just as you have had to."

She could see that Fiona was struggling with this: unable to
make the decision with any degree of finality.

"Do you read French?" she asked.

"Very little," Fiona said. "Signs, menus, that kind of thing. I can sometimes manage a magazine."

Miriam crossed the room to the bookshelves; quickly found what she was looking for; passed it to Fiona. It was a French paperback. The title *Les Enfants de Jaïrus* – The Jairus Children. The author was Miriam Casselles. Fiona raised her eyebrows.

"It was my doctoral thesis, adapted for publication. It's a small academic publishing house, there are only a few hundred copies in circulation. It was the cover I wanted to show you."

The image was of the raising of Jairus's daughter. The fly-leaf credit confirmed Fiona's hunch that the artist was William Blake.

"You recognize the picture?" Miriam asked.

"I hadn't seen Blake's version before, but I know the story, yes."

"She's twelve or thirteen years old; in some kind of early teenage crisis. Her father doesn't know what to do; the adults around her have already given her up for dead. And this rabbi comes in. They tell him not to bother; that he will be too late, but he comes anyway. And what does he do when he gets there?"

"He prays for her; heals her. Brings her back to life."

"Yes, but before that. What does he do when he first walks into the room?"

"He asks them to leave?"

Miriam nodded. "Throws them out, every one of them. The weeping relatives, the bereaved adults. He asks them to take their wailing death song elsewhere. He clears the room, and he speaks life into the girl. So why do you think he would do that?"

"To get rid of the noise, so he could speak to her in peace?"

"To *focus* on her. They are mourning her death, but he says she is only sleeping. They haven't understood her; haven't spoken to her. She is the object of *their* sufferings. He makes her the subject of her own. He is the only adult who addresses her directly; the only one who places her at the heart of her own story. It's the whole shape of the room; the dynamics. In their story she is dead already. In her own she is alive still. He restores her to the centre."

Fiona could see in Blake's composition the point that Miriam was making. A circle of light, central to the picture, illuminating only two faces: Jesus and the girl. All others present pressed back into the shadows. Peripheral to the miracle unfolding.

"An adolescent in crisis is always a family in crisis," Miriam continued, "but adolescence is about identity; about becoming an individual. My thesis suggested that healing can't begin until we acknowledge the child as the subject of their own story: the actor in their own journey. The adults who have held the child as the object in their story must let go. It's the whisper of identity they're waiting for. Life, spoken into them again."

"And telling them terrible things about themselves; recounting horrors they have suffered – this helps?" Fiona asked. She needed this to be about Colom; needed answers she could take to the bank.

A gust of wind found its way down the chimney. Flattened the infantile flames, but couldn't fully defeat them. Miriam took a set of bellows from their hanging place on the wall beside the fire. Red wooden handles; leather concertina; a brass nozzle. She aimed this at the centre of the fire, leaning forward in her chair; worked the bellows; saw the flames rise. Sat back.

"Not always, no, because that is not always the issue. But telling them the truth about themselves, whatever it might be, yes. Adolescents are designed to be warriors – they sense a strength growing in their bodies preparing them to fight. By telling them the truth, we give them weapons to fight with. Like all weapons, the truth can harm as well as heal – a sword can cut your own arm as quickly as it can pierce the heart of your enemy – but if we are careful, if we not only give them the truth but train them to live with it and use it well, then they will take up the fight for themselves. If we lie to them, we are keeping them as children. Forgiveness is a weapon Colom can wield for himself, but we have to help him by letting him know who to forgive. We aim. He fires."

She could see a hesitancy still furrowing Fiona's brow. She had so long protected Colom from this truth: how could revealing it now be to his benefit?

"You can't save Colom, Fiona," Miriam said, the words quiet, soft, but spoken with intention and authority. "It's too late for that. But he can save himself. This has to be his battle now, not yours. We have to give him what he needs to fight for his own life."

Fiona's eyes were closed now, concentration written across them. Miriam couldn't begin to imagine the images and words, the arguments and counter-arguments, that were scrolling across the screens of those closed lids even now.

"But surely telling him now that he's adopted, telling him what happened to him, will send him into an even deeper crisis? That's a trigger if ever there was one." It was her best shot. Her last bullet.

"I know. It seems illogical, but I'm convinced that what's really needling Colom is that he has deep feelings – of loss, even of pain – but he doesn't know why. Nothing in his environment explains what he is feeling. We have to help him to account for his feelings, and therefore deal with them. We have to take off the bandages you so carefully wrapped him in to see the true condition of his wound. We have to let the air get to it. And we have to trigger his own healing response."

Silence swept in to fill the seconds stretched between the two women. There was no more to be said. It was enough, or it was not enough: more words would only weigh Fiona down. The room was warming now; the flames sending flickering shadows across its white walls. In Blake's imaginative work the eyes of Jesus were fixed on those of the troubled girl. To the exclusion of all others. A world of meaning and compassion in his gaze.

CHAPTER THIRTY

The most successful attempts at influencing weather
involve cloud seeding, which includes techniques used
to increase winter precipitation over mountains and
suppress hail.

"Rain", Wikipedia

"I don't think I can do it," Fiona said, still fighting the tears that had interrupted her breakfast conversation several times already. "How can I tell him he's not my son?"

"Well, you don't tell him that, for a start," Mark said firmly. They had slipped out early, leaving Miriam to her breakfast reading and Colom to his pillow. They had driven down into Quiberon itself; parked near the harbour and fishing port. There was a café there offering a *"Petit-Déjeuner Complète"*, which Mark naively hoped might be a full breakfast in the sense that he was used to in Camden. He was disappointed to discover that it consisted of coffee, bread and jam. He made up for the let-down by ordering refills of coffee, and making sure that neither a crumb of bread nor a gram of butter went back to the kitchen. The bread, at least, was heavenly.

"You can't use blunt, limiting statements like that," he said. "You're not my son; I didn't give birth to you. Not because they're not true, but because they are not the whole truth. Adoption doesn't define Colom – he is the person he is no matter what his history. And he is your son in many senses of the word. Don't close any more doors than you absolutely have to."

"You're very good at this," she said. "How do you know all this?"

"I read," he said. "I ask questions. I have friends. You'd be amazed at how many people think a single man is the ideal confidant when their family is in trouble."

"I just don't know where to start," she said at last. Despondent. Lost.

"But you do know you have to. You can't leave this any longer: it's only as hard as it is now because you've left it this long – every day that passes has the potential to make the telling more painful still. You have to do this, Fiona, and you have to do it today. Look at it this way: for better or worse, by this evening, it will be over. You will have done what you should have done years ago."

A refilled coffee pot arrived on the table; Mark quick to pour from it; Fiona saying no. She wondered how his constitution could stand to ingest such quantities; wondered if, like for many journalists, it was his primary fuel. The one remaining piece of baguette, appropriately spread with butter and jam in generous proportions, accompanied Mark's coffee. She feared for the last remaining crumbs. Their days were numbered. They would be mercilessly hunted down and captured.

"Thank you for not saying I told you so."

"I won't. But I did. David all but banned me from seeing you because of it."

"I know, and I'm sorry."

"For me? Don't be. But for Colom, let's both be sorry enough that we won't rest until this thing is done."

She put her hand on his. Took a deep breath.

"Will you come with me? Be there when I talk to him?"

He put down his coffee cup. Wiped his mouth with the crisp linen napkin. "You know I will help you in whatever way I can. I'm here for you. One hundred per cent. But no, I won't."

Her brow furrowed. Tears threatened again. He had never seen her look so alone; so lost.

"I was asked to do a piece on adopted teens a while back," he said, his voice more gentle now. "I was thinking of you every moment, believe me. It took every ounce of discipline I possess not to phone you and start the argument all over again. I researched parents who had told their children, late on, that they were adopted. The one that still stands out to me was a woman who said, 'It's not just what you tell them, it's how.' She talked about this cloak of shame and embarrassment that surrounds adoption – at this moment in particular. You feel ashamed. You feel guilty. You've let your son down by not telling him earlier. He's not the person he thought he was. The whole thing should never have happened. Secrecy is so closely linked to shame. The danger she talked about is that all that shame, that brooding storm cloud of emotion, will be taken on by your child as his shame. He'll think you've kept this secret because adoption itself is shameful. That you're ashamed of him. You have to convince Colom that there is no shame in being adopted. He hasn't failed, or fallen, or sinned, or done wrong in any way. He has nothing to be ashamed of. But if he sees it in your eyes – just the shadow of it – he'll fall into it."

It was a long speech, and she understood what he was saying. What she didn't see was the connection. She looked at him, confused.

"If I'm with you, he'll know you're scared. He doesn't need to see that. He needs to see you strong, and certain, and offering him confidence."

"But I'm not."

"No, you're not. But you need to be by the time you tell him. If you don't believe you can get through this together, then he never will. Even if he bursts into tears, or runs away, or beats his fists against your chest, he needs to have heard you say that you love him and you know it's going to be OK."

She rubbed her eyes, pressed her face into her hands. "I just don't know where to start."

"It's not easy, I know. You have to put yourself in a position in which you have no choice. We do it when we have to interview a tricky customer – a politician who's fiddling his expenses; a business exec hiding the company's losses. We never start in with the real questions. We know the information we want, and we know the question we'd like to ask, but we don't ask it. Instead, we move sideways and ask some related but very different questions. I don't mean about the weather – we will talk about the business, about the politician's record – but before we get to the question he doesn't want to answer, we ask several that we know he won't mind answering."

"To lull him into a false sense of security?"

"Not exactly, no. More to create a flow; to get a conversation moving. That way we can edge towards our real goal gently, not trumpeting our intentions."

"And you think Colom is a tricky customer?"

He looked at her over his glasses, the way her chemistry teacher had done when she confused sulphuric and hydrochloric acids. "The tricky customer isn't Colom, Fiona; it's you. There are some things you are afraid to say to your son, and you'll duck and dive like the best of them to avoid saying them. So you have to trick yourself. Before you tell Colom the thing you're scared to tell him, tell him some things you're not so scared of. Tell him something that points in the direction of the truth, but isn't so blunt and devastating that it's impossible to say. Get up the mountain your fears have made by starting in the foothills."

She thought about this for a moment; felt a glimmer of hope. "Thanks, Mark. For being here. For this. I want you to know that you really have made a difference. I couldn't have faced this alone."

He smiled. Didn't speak. Was wondering if the tears might be infectious.

CHAPTER THIRTY-ONE

If I were rain, that joins sky and earth that otherwise
never touch, could I join two hearts as well?

Tite Kubo, "The Death and The Strawberry", *Bleach*, Vol. 1

As soon as Fiona opened her car door she realized the wind was too strong to even contemplate a clifftop conversation. She hadn't noticed it on the bay side earlier in the day, but here on the Côte Sauvage it roared.

She had not wanted to talk to Colom at the house; had sensed that he might feel in some way trapped. She'd seen how relaxed he was out in the open, with a view of the sea; wondered if a walk might offer the ideal combination of privacy and space. The plan was to park in the Le Vivier car park, walk out along the cliffs, then double-back to the café. But any talking they did here would be shouting – the one thing she was hoping to avoid. She had no choice but to try the café.

She took the few moments on the way from the car to show Colom the vivier itself, remembering Miriam's explanation of the Portivy installation. This was an older, wilder arrangement, unused for many years. It was a stone-walled pool, built into a natural inlet in the rocks. A primitive system of drainage using metal sluice gates had long since surrendered to redundancy and rust, as had the ladder leading down into the pool. But the system's main functioning remained intact, provided not by metal or mechanics but by the moon's magnetic field. With every tide a refilling and refreshing of the vivier's water. Any fish left here at low tide these days would be accidental tourists, occasional visitors too slow to quit with the receding waters. Long gone were the more crowded populations placed here to be kept alive until paying customers demanded their execution.

Today's "Le Vivier" was a popular seafood restaurant, benefiting from proximity to the fresh and living fish, even though their stocks were now delivered from Port Maria and further afield. Generally crowded in the summer, and often so on winter weekends, it was quieter today: one table finishing off a late lunch; another taking an afternoon break from their clifftop walk; just one local at the bar. Fiona found them a table in the corner, far enough away from other occupants to free their conversation. They were closer, though, to the bar's non-human population: a tank of lobsters, floating, crawling, flicking their antenna lazily through bubbling waters. Beyond them the view to the open sea, where their brothers and cousins still roamed, unaware that they might soon be residents of this same tank.

So here they were. She panicked. Was this the right environment? The right moment? She had not planned to speak to him in such a public place. She knew what Mark would say to her, were he here. There will never be a right place. There is no perfect moment. You just have to do it. She knew he would be right. She felt wretched.

After talking to Mark over breakfast, she had looked for something to tell Colom that was big enough to get the conversation moving, but not so big that she would let show the fear and dread she was feeling. Something to move them to the place where telling him seemed natural. She had quickly come to what that something would be.

Testing the volume of their likely conversation, she said, "There are some things we need to talk about, Colom."

No one looked around. No one was listening. Perhaps this was, after all, a safe place. Colom obviously thought so, too.

"We're not going to do the sex talk, are we? You know I've done it at school. I know everything I need to know. It's all good."

She smiled, despite everything. "No, it's not that. More about our family and what we've been going through."

"You're going to get a divorce?"

"No, not that either. We're not getting a divorce." She said it emphatically, but wondered if she should have crossed her fingers when she said it.

A pause. He waited. She breathed; readied herself; dived.

"I know about the letter."

"What letter?" Genuine. Could he even have forgotten?

"The letter you wrote with Daniel, for that website." Recognition coming to his face. Shock. Fear.

"I wasn't spying on you, love." How to explain? She didn't want to mention the police, for fear of spooking him. "After Daniel died, his parents found the letter he had signed. They told us because they knew you two were close, and wondered if you might have signed one too. That's why we looked. That's when we found it."

"OK." Hesitant. Guilty. Afraid of what would follow.

"I'm not mad with you. Colom, believe me. It's not that at all. I know how hard things have been for you lately; how you've been struggling. The thing is… I think I know why."

She left a space. Heard him begin to form words. Had to listen hard to catch them, half-whispered, half-mumbled, directed not at her but at the table.

"I don't."

"No, I know you don't. That's just it. There are some things that I know, that you don't, and I think they might help you to understand what you've been feeling."

He looked up, his eyes clouded. "What things?"

And there it was. The open goal she had tricked herself into creating. She breathed her silent thanks to Mark.

"Colom, there are some things your father and I have never told you, about your history. We should have told you, and I'm so sorry we didn't. I love you, we both love you, and we should have told you the truth."

231

She could see, on his face, fear descending like a cloud. His eyes were on hers, but spoke of terror, not embrace.

"About your birth. About how you came to us."

The fear now contorting him, darkening his eyes. Self-doubt; horror. She could almost believe that he knew already, understood what was coming.

"You were born in Canada, that much is true. But not to me. Your real mother's name was Chevonne. Chevonne Richards. She was from Newfoundland. She died not long after you were born."

She wondered if she should stop; let him react. But she could see he wasn't going to; was working hard to take this in, his mind spinning even as she spoke.

"Your father and I adopted you when you were two years old. We chose you because we loved you. I've always told you that seeing you for the first time was the happiest moment of my life. And it was. It really was."

He had closed his eyes now, was swallowing his tears; his body shaking slightly.

"I'm so sorry we didn't tell you sooner, Colom. Truly I am. It was the biggest mistake of my life, and I would give anything to go back and change it. But I can't. That's why I want you to know the truth now. We love you. You are our son, nothing changes that. But you need to know that you had another mother – a birth mother."

She slid the photograph across to him; let him see what it was. He took it gruffly; refused to look at it; replaced it on the table between them. She waited for some response. Got the merest hint of a shrug, his face twitching now. Should she stop? How could she? Full disclosure – that was what she had committed to. She hated the cruelty of this, but knew it was more cruel still to push the secrets back into their hiding place.

"But that's not all," she said, as gently as she knew how. "There's something else I need to tell you."

He looked at her now, pleading with his eyes for her to stop. She knew she couldn't.

"Before you came to us, you lived for a while in a foster home. With a family called the McAllisters. There were several children there. But they were very cruel people. You should never have been placed there. They did some terrible things – they hurt you. Badly. That's why we never told you, because it was too painful to talk about."

And he knew. That it was true. It arrived in the very centre of his puzzled, whirring mind, and as soon as it landed, he knew it belonged. Knew he couldn't scream that she was lying. Knew that he would never again reach the calm, dry shoreline of the life he had lived until now.

She put her hand on his. "Colom," she said.

Tears were rising in him now, ready to overwhelm. Suddenly he stood up from the table, the violence of the act rattling his cup and drawing stares from their fellow customers.

"I don't want to talk about this," he half-shouted, half-cried. He turned quickly and headed for the door.

"Colom, come back!" Fiona said, her voice hovering somewhere between an angry mother and a jilted friend. She got up quickly to follow him; grabbed the photograph of Chevonne; threw down twenty euros in its place so as not to be pursued for non-payment. He was out of the door and gone by the time she reached it. She ran instinctively towards the clifftop; grey rocks in menacing formation, white spray breaking over them. She couldn't see him.

She breathed a sigh of relief when she saw that he had not headed that way, but in the opposite direction, towards the car. She ran after him, fumbling for her keys as she did so; clicking the remote. As soon as he heard the locks disengage, he climbed in, pulled his seat-belt on, turned to lock his door. She had to click again to open hers. She got in beside him; saw his angry silence; tried to speak. "Colom…"

But he turned from her and she knew in her heart that, for all she wanted to say right now, it was better to stay silent. She started the car; turned towards Portivy; drove home; watched him open his door before she'd even switched off the engine; saw him run into the house; knew by the time she got there that he would be on his way up the stairs.

Not a word had passed between them on the journey home. He pretended not to notice when she slipped the picture into his coat pocket.

She came into the house to see the back of his heel disappearing up the stairs; Miriam standing in the kitchen; now moving towards her. She fell into her arms; let the tears that had been pressing against her all afternoon flow now, and express themselves. Sobbed like a wounded child on the welcome shoulder of her friend.

CHAPTER THIRTY-TWO

Whenever it rains you will think of her.
Neil Gaiman, *Strange Days, Short Story*

Fiona explained to Miriam, as best she could, all that had transpired with Colom. She felt wretched still, believed she had mishandled everything, but Miriam was more optimistic; felt that progress had been made. Fiona wondered on what evidence she based this. Was it a reasoned hope, or was she simply trying to be positive?

They cooked, but Colom didn't show for supper. Fiona knocked on his door; asked without opening it if he was coming; heard a muffled "No"; heard even in that one syllable that he was crying still. Her heart ached for him, but something told her not to force his hand.

Much later, she went upstairs to check on him again. She was determined not to communicate to him her fear – but equally determined to make sure he was OK. She couldn't go to bed herself without knowing how he was doing. She knocked, and as she came into the room saw something hurriedly slipped under his pillow.

She went to his bedside; smiled gently.

"Do you want to talk about her?"

A half-shrug; a puzzled look.

"I don't mind, really I don't. I don't know much, but what I do know I can share with you."

He said nothing for a moment, questions gathering in his mind like a traffic jam on the M25. He wasn't looking at her; was staring, rather, at a point on the wall beyond the end of his bed. There was nothing there to look at.

"Did you ever meet her?"

"No, never. Your father did, before you were born. She was involved in one of his projects." She hated that this, even now, was only part of the truth, but knew that this was not the moment to pursue it.

"Why?"

"Because of her addiction. She was heavily addicted to drugs. That's really what was destroying her life. It was very hard for her."

"Did she even try to quit?" Anger hovering under his words.

"She tried really hard, Colom. But it was too strong for her. You have to understand, she was ill. Addiction is a disease, not a choice. You can't blame her for not quitting. But you can know that she did try. For you, I think. I think she really wanted to be able to look after you. She wanted to be a good mother. But in the end, the disease was too strong for her."

He was quiet again. Examining, still, the same vacant wall.

"Did she ever hold me?"

The question landed like a dart in Fiona's heart. She fought tears, held herself in check for his sake.

"Yes. She did. She had you for just over twenty-four hours, in the hospital." Her eyes closed now, imagining what it must have been like; this scene that she herself had so often wished, so deeply longed to have been a part of. "They gave you to her and she held you, right there in her bed. She looked at you, into your eyes, and loved you. She loved you as much in that moment as any mother has ever loved a child. Enough, maybe, to last a lifetime."

His tears were coming now. She knew the conversation would not go on much longer.

"And she named you."

He said nothing. But for a moment his crying slowed. This information was arriving in his mind like a wave onto the shoreline. Climbing the sands. Making sense.

"She did? Not you and Dad?"

"No, not us. She named you right then, in that moment." Understanding, even as she said this, the great elephantine truth she had been blind to these past twelve years. "Every time you hear your name, it's a memorial to that moment. She loved you, and she named you, and I'm so sorry it's taken me so long to tell you."

She meant it, now, not just for him, but for herself. How could she have feared this moment; have run from this beauty? She meant it because she wanted to remember too. She wanted to honour this woman who for one brief moment in a life of chaos and confusion was able to love clearly, unconditionally. To receive her son; to welcome him; to name him with a name that had been formed and spoken in the very depths of her heart. She spoke a silent apology to Chevonne, for having resisted her memory; for having tried to erase her; for not having shared with her son before this night the sacred duty of remembering. How could she not have known that the love, the clarity, the holy beauty of those twenty-four hours were a treasure for her son to hold on to?

"I think I'll go to sleep now."

"You should. But it's also OK to think about her for a while. It's OK to miss her. OK?"

"OK."

She got up from her knees. She sensed as she moved away from him that they had a new connection. It was fragile; partial; a makeshift bridge. But it was there. The beginning of a new kind of friendship, a partnership not derived from excluding Chevonne but from loving her. Sharing the task of keeping her memory alive. She left the room with a new commission; a new purpose. The first, she now realized, that she had ever so completely co-owned with her son.

The peace lasted well into the night, until her sleep was once again disturbed by his cries. The same dream. The same fierce terror. She soothed him once again, their conversations of the day forgotten, it seemed, in the urgency of the night-time crisis. She wondered if it was of Chevonne that he dreamed. Was it possible that it was his mother beside him in the water? Or was there someone else still; someone for whom they didn't even have a name?

CHAPTER THIRTY-THREE

Rain starts off as ice or snow crystals at cloud level.
A droplet of water will stay in Earth's atmosphere for
around ten days.

"Rain", Wikipedia

Nobody knew what the morning would bring, but the weather, at least, was on message. A calmer, warmer day broke over Portivy harbour; the sea still but for a tiny, rippling breeze; the sky a hazy, white-glazed blue. The tide was as low as Fiona had seen it so far; the little tribe of boats all leaning on their sides in the mud like sleeping sunbathers. Where the long stone launch ramp usually met the water, it was now dry and exposed, the drainage pipe buried under it showing now where it came out onto the sea bed. She watched a group from the diving school make their way to their dinghy, walking further than on most days they would need to; black-suited; struggling to carry their flippers, their oxygen tanks; pleased, in due course, to heave these burdens into the waiting boat.

She had come down to the harbour to get some fresh air, knowing Colom could be up at any moment, or equally could sleep until lunch-time. For her own part, she had again slept little; drifting in and out of shallow slumber, the waking spaces in between spiked with regrets, fears, self-reproach. She had not yet spoken to Miriam this morning, nor Mark. But she knew that they had no greater clue than she had of what the day would hold. Only one thing would tell them. In due course Colom would wake. She would try to speak with him again. And they would know.

She was surprised to see Mark heading down the hill towards her. Wondered what it was that he was carrying.

"Thought I might find you here," he said. "You OK?"

"Yes. No. I don't know."

"I bought something for Colom. Wanted to know if you're happy with me giving it to him this morning?"

"What is it?" It was wrapped around with a carrier bag. He brought it out to show her. She saw colours: a rainbow display on what might have been a chocolate box.

"They're pastels," he said, "oil-based. You use them like a kind of coloured charcoal in some ways, but they can also be like oil paints; you can blend and mix them, rub them together. They're a great way to discover how colour works."

"You think he'll like that?"

"I think he's ready for it. He loves Thierry's work, but I don't think he's going to take up a palette knife any day soon. This is a step in that direction."

"You think he should paint?" They had instinctively turned towards the Café du Port and were walking now in that direction, Thierry's excellent early-morning coffee beckoning them.

"I don't know. But he's concentrated on drawing so far, and he's really very good. It would be good to find out if there's a painter in there, trying to get out."

"He reminds me a lot of you at his age."

"Me too. Odd, isn't it. There are times when I could swear I can see a family likeness. Physically, I mean… Anyway, you don't mind?"

"Not at all. It's very kind of you."

"It's not just about the painting. I really felt it might do him good to have something to focus on right now. Take his mind off things a bit." He held the café door open for her.

"I hope you're right."

And he was. Brilliantly so. Colom couldn't wait to try the pastels, and immediately assumed this would mean working outside. The rain had decided to be elsewhere for a while; the light was good; the colours of the sea were as iridescent as they ever could be. The pastels got him out of his room; out of the house; into fresh air and the ocean's benevolent presence. After his first experiments, which were mostly attempts to understand how the colours worked, Thierry lent him a big board. He could hold this on his knee, paper held to it with masking tape, and have both hands free to manipulate the colours. He was still tense around Fiona; still reluctant to talk further. But he was at peace, more than he had ever been, with the sea, the sky, his board and the pastels for company.

They found a new rhythm; a new routine. Spring was making evident progress in Brittany, and early sunlight brought an earlier breakfast all round. Colom didn't tend to make the first sitting, but he wasn't far behind and once Miriam had reiterated her willingness to talk, he responded well, giving her an hour each day, sometimes two. He'd try to get out drawing before lunch; would return to it in the afternoon. In the evenings, when the light was gone, he would continue working in his room; touching up the experiments of the day, bringing each piece to the point where he was prepared to title and sign it. He wasn't quick to share the results, but both Mark and Thierry were treated to the occasional glimpse. Both responded with encouragement; reported to Fiona the unexpected maturity and accomplishment of his work.

Fiona longed to talk more but resisted the urge to force it on him. She loved that he talked more over meals; had energy. Loved, too, that he would allow her to come and see him late each evening, to talk for just a little while. These were precious moments for her. She urged him to ask whatever he needed to know; tried to give him every detail possible.

It was Miriam, not Fiona, who showed him the photographs. She talked him through the pictures, making sure he only saw each one briefly. Enough to know that he had seen them, not so much as to rub his face in what had happened. She knew after the first few images that they had made the right choice. He was separated now from these tragedies by twelve years or more: a safe distance from which to know and understand what had happened. She hoped that he would even come to see the adoption as his rescue. Fiona and David had not been wise in keeping the trauma from him. But they had been more than wise, more than loving, in taking him away from the trauma.

They talked for a while: about pain and how we deal with it; about the things people can feel, even years later, when such things have happened. Colom didn't say much, but his occasional nods and his evident attention convinced her that he was familiar with many of the feelings she described. He had an explanation, at last, for the strange sadness he had felt, the random anger that from time to time had gripped him. To say "I miss my real mother" and "somebody hurt me" was too simple; words too shallow to explain his whole life: but the words represented, all the same, a truth he could recognize; could stand on. A truth easier to live with than wanting to die but not knowing why. At last she broached the subject she had been steering towards.

"Do you think you might be able to forgive these people, for the hurt they caused you?" she asked, intentionally tentative.

"I don't know. What would I need to do? Do I need to talk to them?"

"No, nothing like that. I just mean for you, for your own sake, might you be able to speak out that they are forgiven? And your mum and dad, for all that's happened?"

"I think so. I'm not sure."

"Well, we don't have to do it right now. It's something I'd like to get to if we can – if you feel able." She explained a little about the power of forgiveness, how it takes the sting out of the things that have happened to us; frees us to move on. How it can touch areas that are so hidden even we hardly know they're there.

"I'll try."

242

* * *

"I think he's doing well, to be honest," she said later in response to Fiona's questions about progress. She had agreed not to ask for details, though she would have liked to. But she needed to know, as time passed, whether they were moving in the right direction.

"Maybe he'd be ready to talk to you again now? It's worth a try."

She asked him to walk with her again; not this time on the cliffs but here, in Portivy; to the harbour and along the beach track. The sun was setting in breathtaking colour, across a sky as wide as forever. She saw it through his eyes, imagined him taking the stripes of such a sky, converting them to pastel, pouring them out onto a blank white page, secured with masking tape to a board held on his knees.

"So how have you been feeling?" she asked clumsily.

He shrugged, but not dismissively. "OK."

"I can't tell you how sorry I am. For all this. For not telling you. For what you've had to go through."

"I know."

She stopped walking. Turned to face him. "I love you, Colom," she said. "I always have, but here, now, after all you've been through, I love you more than I could have imagined. I'll do everything I can to help you through this."

"I know."

"Is there more you want me to tell you? Do you have questions? I really don't mind answering them."

He turned to walk again. She fell into step beside him. Watched him thinking.

"Was it my fault?" he said quietly.

"You mean with your mother?"

"Yes. Was it my fault that she couldn't cope? Did I do something wrong?"

243

Again her heart lurching. Pain like an arrow.

"No, Colom, absolutely not. You did nothing wrong, nothing at all. You were the one who came closest to saving her. How could you believe it was your fault?"

"But why would she have given me away if there wasn't something wrong with me? Nobody gives a good baby away. I must have been too difficult for her, cried too much, something."

Mark had told her of an adopted teen he'd researched who was convinced the whole event had been his fault. Nothing could shift his belief until a therapist backed him into a corner, placed an infant in his arms and asked how such a child, such a helpless baby, surrounded by adults, could possibly be the one responsible for such harm. The boy was shocked; a little scared. But he understood at last.

She stopped again. Turned again to face her son.

"No, I promise you. You did nothing wrong. You were a tiny baby. How could you? You mustn't blame yourself. Or her. If you want to get mad, get mad at her addiction. Get mad at the drugs that can come in like a forest fire to destroy a useful life. It wasn't you, love. It wasn't her. It was something dark and evil that just at that time was stronger than both of you."

"Will I get sick too? Will I get addicted?"

"No, I don't think you will. You're stronger now. You have us to support you. You have me. We can get through this. Together."

He paused. "I know," he said, and turned to walk on.

And so it continued. With each conversation a new question. Colom exploring in his own mind all the scenarios this new information, this new identity, had rendered possible. Fiona doing her best to respond to each one; not being naive or falsely positive, but not being pessimistic either; trying to give him a realistic, feet-on-the-ground chance of getting through. Where she didn't know, she said so. Who was his father? She didn't know for sure – no one did. It was sad, but in all probability they never would. Were there relatives? Brothers? Sisters? She didn't know of any. A grandmother? Cousins? Maybe they could try to find out. She could help him search, if he wanted to.

And each time, she saw a tiny window of progress. A small step forward. His demeanour changing by the day. Her gratitude to Miriam and Mark was unmeasured. Mark had stayed on; arranged a two-week leave; was fast becoming firm friends with Thierry, asking if he might write about his work. Miriam was holding true to her word, to see this thing through with Colom to the end; until he could truly stand on his own feet emotionally; until he was ready to take on the world alone.

Only two clouds hovered in this otherwise promising sky; two fears that pulled at her optimism, demanded her attention. The first was, in the wider scheme of things, a small thing. But it nagged her like a toothache. She hadn't told Colom the whole truth about his father and Chevonne. She didn't know if she should. She didn't want to. But neither did she want to face him if it came out some other way, and he asked her, yet again, "Why didn't you tell me?" She wanted to promise him that she would never again withhold from him a secret that might matter in his life, and she needed to be able to mean it. She wondered if he would see his father's involvement with Chevonne as such a secret. Did he have a right to know? Did she and David have a right not to tell him? They were doing so well. Could she risk destroying that good work for the sake of this one fact?

And if he knew, could he forgive his father?

The second was a darker cloud altogether; a cloud heavy with rain, promising to burst at any moment. Colom's dream – of the water; the girl; the sensation of drowning – continued to disturb his nights. It had come more frequently since coming to Portivy. He didn't always wake up screaming. She didn't always have to go to him. But she could tell each morning which nights had been disturbed. It was a cloud that could be seen on his face when it passed over: there was a heaviness, a deep sadness, associated with this dream. And nothing was stopping it. Nothing they were doing, or saying, or achieving, or changing was having an impact on that cloud. If anything, the broken nights were getting worse.

She had begun to make some connections; had understood that the strong man forcing him under the water must be McAllister. She was certain that the sensation of drowning must be an echo; a residue of the trauma from that time. But who was the girl? It was her fate, not his own, that Colom spoke of, cried for, when he woke. Whoever she was, whatever the dream meant, all Fiona's joy at seeing her son improve evaporated like a morning mist with just one look at the terror in his eyes each time he woke from his dream.

* * *

It was after I lost myself that I stopped eating. I had this feeling that I took up too much space in the world. I stopped wanting to be whatever it is people want to be by eating; by living for another day; by playing ball and getting married and going on holidays and riding on camels and taking pictures of the camels to look at when they get home. I stopped wanting anything. It was another question that was only a question because it was a question. Why won't you eat? Because I don't want to eat, and to want to eat I would need to eat, and because I don't want to eat I can't eat. You might say "I lost my appetite," but that doesn't really capture it. It's like asking someone who does eat, who hasn't lost their appetite, "Why don't you chew rocks?" "Why don't you put marbles in your mouth?" They wouldn't answer, "Because I've lost my appetite." They would say, "Because I don't eat rocks or marbles." And that's how it is with me, with food. I don't eat food, and once I got to the place of not eating food I could no more imagine eating, and liking it, than you could imagine chewing bricks for entertainment.

People tell me I am thin, and I know that I am weak, but whatever part of you is supposed to care about such a thing clearly doesn't for me. I hear my parents arguing about me, or I

*listen to the doctors telling me that if I don't eat I could get very
sick and even die, but none of it gets through to whatever part of
my brain that is supposed to want to keep me alive at all costs.
All I know is that whatever they are saying to me or about me will
come back in due course to eating, and since I don't eat there is
little point in discussing it all. They find a million ways to start
the conversation, but only one way to end it, which seems totally
uncreative to me. All that education; all those machines and pills
and operations and white coats and brilliant minds, but they
can't generate a single genuine alternative. They tell me I might
die, but they don't have a single good idea about how not to.*

CHAPTER THIRTY-FOUR

The cause, torrential rain, was natural enough.
The timing of the rain, however, may have been
supernatural....

Linford D. Fisher, *The Indian Great Awakening: Religion*
and the Shaping of Native Cultures in Early America

In the garden of the tiny chapel Fiona had found a cross – old stone, moss-marked, weathered by the winds of a hundred generations. It had become one of her places of prayer. She had taken to praying again since the conversation at Le Vivier. While Miriam was talking to Colom, or when he had gone out to draw the sea, she brought here all the longing of her heart for her son's health: poured it out like an offering. Even when it rained, as it had decided to today, she would come, turning up her collar against the elements and pressing on with her pilgrimage of prayer.

A tiny plaque, barely decipherable, declared the cross a twelfth-century relic – old already when the monks of the thirteenth century took up tools to build their priory here. The figure of Jesus had been eroded; smoothed over until he was little more than a blurred shape on the surface of the cross itself, as if the two had merged over time; the crucified becoming one with his crucifix. The tiny, indistinct figure looked to Fiona like a prenatal scan. You could only just see that there was a body there; only guess that it was human.

She considered this symbol that had outlived her twenty times over. Generations before her had stood or knelt here. Wandering monks; impoverished fishermen; wives and mothers desperate for news. She thought of infertile women praying here for sons and daughters; of those burdened with guilt trying to offload it. Those blessed with innocence trying to hold on to it. She thought of Marie-Françoise Sonic, reciting remembered prayers until she was interrupted by the Mother of God herself, speaking in her local dialect and urging her to stir the indolent parish to action.

She knew at once that this was not the bright, plastic Jesus of the modern era; strong and shining and resisting all decay. The neon Jesus of churches looking to rival Las Vegas. This was a humbler Jesus, stuck forever on the strange frame of his cross, open to the elements: the rains of centuries thrown in his face. This was Jesus accepting his imprisonment. Letting them abuse and curse him, ignore him, even. But here, still. A thousand years on, outlasting them all. This was a Jesus older than the revolution; deeper than Hiroshima; more certain than the claims of Nike and Apple. This was the Jesus she would like, if such a thing were possible, to get to know.

She turned back into the wind, rain meeting her like a bucket thrown. She pulled her coat around her; bowed her head; walked into it. Took the path that ran behind the church and down a tree-lined incline, to the second place she had begun to see as sacred – the site of the ancient village well: the field of miracles.

The waters here had been declared miraculous in every generation – by the pagan hunters; by the praying monks; by the Catholics who built the church and made this place their home. Local legend had it that babies washed in this water would walk at three months; that life and health, prosperity and peace would be theirs in perpetuity, all from the splash of a well whose waters had run for centuries and were running still.

She didn't believe it. Wasn't here for such a miracle. But there was a peace here she could not deny, a sacred, trembling presence. She had chosen to name this a thin place, and to let her deepest dreams be spoken here.

She waited by the well. Distant sounds of village life rumbled faintly – a car passing, a hammer on wood – but she was alone here and thick silence enveloped her. It was not so much the absence of noise as the presence of something altogether deeper. The well was stone-built; a low rectangle of wall, at its centre a round, covered well-head. Rich green grass gave testimony to the presence of water close to the surface. A low, sweeping willow tree, its own green a shade lighter, formed a kind of roof over the glade; protecting it; nurturing its silence; centring attention on the well. It was easy to see how this place could be thought of as miraculous; a place to bring impossible questions to be answered. Hers arising from the mystery of a child's repeated dream.

She silently recited a short prayer – of readiness; of listening. She wasn't here to mumble words, to work through her roll-call of petitions. Her years of faith had been an endless stream of words. Only now did she see that, and see it for what it was: a fear of silence; a deliberate immersion in distraction. An infinite cavalcade of high-sounding words that seemed now to lack substance, as if she had mistaken the smoke for the fire, the echo for the voice. She tried hard, now, to still the words; to create a space to make true listening possible. She heard nothing. The car. The hammer. Her own thoughts darting here and there like sparrows. But nothing of use. Nothing new. She wondered was it her inability to listen, or was there indeed only silence to be tasted here? Were those who had come here to find hope as deluded as the cynics would suggest? The pagans hearing the echo of their own fears; Marie-Françoise Sonic dressing her own thoughts in the robes of Mary; monks and mothers, petitioners and penitents, all throwing their own desires against the quiet, and hearing what they wanted to hear?

Was it foolish, now, to believe that her God might speak to her?

She abandoned her ill-fated efforts at stillness and let herself mumble. Pleas, entreaties, the desperate whisper of a mother seeking hope for a suffering child.

"What I'm asking for, I don't deserve," she found herself muttering. "I've done nothing right for Colom and everything wrong. But it's not for me. It's for him. For his future. For his freedom. For his inheritance."

And on she went. Mumbling. Muttering. Circling the well. Speaking to the silence. Pleading with her God. Letting sense emerge if it could from the overflow of her troubled heart. She was being honest – this at least she knew. If prayer was built not on eloquence but on the raw expression of true feelings, then she was at last praying. Regret poured from her like wine from a slashed gourd. She spoke the truth about herself; about her marriage; about the construction of convenience that religion had so often been for her. She saw the danger her decisions had placed her son in. And she confessed her love for him. Her desire, unconditional and unconstructed, to see him thriving in the gifted beauty of his humanity. Her willingness, even, to see her own needs unmet and unmeasured if only it might mean that he would find peace. She understood, as never before, what it is for a mother to count as nothing her own life that the life of her child might be saved.

"I just need to know what to do for him," she said. "I want what's best for him. Even if I have to give him up. I want him to be free."

And all at once the words were done with. She had used all the sentences her soul had been saving. Had reached the runway's end. Now there remained only flight, or the humiliating crash into the wasteland beyond the tarmac's end. She turned to leave, knowing now that if there was no answer it would not be because she had failed to ask. She had looked into the shadows of her soul; had spoken everything she found there. If heaven remained silent, the door unopened, it would not be for want of her knocking.

Her back was to the well now. She climbed the gentle slope towards the road.

And like birds at last settling because they felt it safe to do so, they arrived. Three words; unadorned; uncomplicated. Not voiced or heard as such, but present nonetheless. Three words so unimpressive that at first she didn't know they mattered. But all at once she did know. That for all her outpoured longings these three words were enough. The next step. The key to unlocking the puzzle she was caught up in. The end of the sticky tape – still to be picked at and peeled clear, but definitely there, and firm enough to begin the unravelling. She knew what she had to do.

CHAPTER THIRTY-FIVE

*The sun did not shine. It was too wet to play. So we sat
in the house. All that cold, cold, wet day.*

Dr Seuss, *The Cat in the Hat*

Every crime has its incident room, and the dressing table in Fiona's bedroom was now spread with the contents of David's file; her make-up and toiletries relegated to floor space beside her bed. She wanted the information in front of her. Keeping the photographs there, no longer hiding them, was robbing them of their horror, like colour slowly bleaching from old prints. Nothing would ever make the images of Colom's injuries any less cruel, but exposure was making them less shocking. Fiona was finding day by day that she was less afraid to look at them.

She had explained to Miriam her experience at the well.

"Just those three words?" her friend had asked.

"Just those words: 'Find the girl'."

They had agreed it made sense; that it was the right next step; that Colom would not be fully at peace until he knew who it was he was dreaming of. Fiona knew that he himself had no clue. The emotional strength of the dream was self-evident – it touched something deep in the boy's memory – but what, or who, it was about he simply didn't know. She also knew, though, that she had a serious weapon at her disposal: a professional journalist who, before specializing as an art critic, had learned his trade in the newsroom.

Mark was glad to help, relishing a brief return to the investigative role he still at times missed. David's file was their starting point. This was the time in Colom's life Fiona knew the least about: the most likely time for him to have been connected in some way to a girl none of them knew. Mark had mobile internet access on both his laptop and his iPad and was able to verify the clippings, but the events around Colom's adoption were too early to have registered much on the web. Pre-Twitter; pre-Facebook; a golden age when not everything was talked about on blogs. And Newfoundland, it seemed, was not the world's most tech-savvy province. It was the local papers, he was convinced, that would most help them. This was his world – surely he could turn up something? He soon discovered that David already had everything that mattered. Archive searches turned up repetitions, but no new information. They were wading through treacle, moving at a snail's pace, if they were moving at all.

The papers had been scrupulous in not publishing the names of the children fostered by McAllister. Throughout the investigation, references were made to "baby A" or "child P". Mark found himself admiring the ethics of the journalists concerned even as he searched for a loophole in their excellence.

Official avenues were closed to them. The most they could expect to be allowed to see would be records relevant directly to Colom, and even then it would be David, not Fiona, who would be given access.

"Maybe there isn't a girl to be found at all," Fiona said despondently after another fruitless hour of searching, moving between the clippings and the web, Mark doing the same on his iPad across the table from her.

"Don't give up," he said simply. "There's a story here; we just need to find the right thread and follow it."

She marvelled at his perseverance. Knew that it was part professional, part personal. He was good at his job, was enjoying reviving old skills. But he was also driven by love. For all his bachelor posturing, Mark's love for Colom was as evident as it was uncomplicated. This was not a reporter reviewing his material for the hundredth time. This was an uncle.

CHAPTER THIRTY-FIVE

While they continued to pore over the articles and clippings, Miriam was in the tiny courtyard at the rear of the house with Colom, undertaking a different task altogether; one she had told Fiona must also be addressed. She had taken a walk with Colom to discuss what must be done. He had agreed to it; had the letter now in his jacket pocket. Miriam had commandeered her old barbecue for the purpose; had raided the shed for a bottle of white spirit.

The familiar words were invested with an unexpected depth. She heard in her own voice that Colom had become more than a friend to her. She thought of her own lost son. Might she be allowed to give this other boy, blown into her life on the winds of a long-delayed spring, just a small part of the love she had stockpiled? She looked at him. A tiny tremble in his lip: the cold? The wind? The moment?

"You ready?" she asked.

He nodded. Took the letter from his pocket; opened it out; laid it, face-up, readable, in the bed of the barbecue. Miriam poured spirit over it; reached for the matches. Stopped. Looked to him.

A slight movement of his hand and she knew he would do it. She handed him the box. He struck one match without success; another, the wind stealing the fire before it could be used. She showed him how to cup his hands, then stepped back to let him try again.

He did, and the match went gingerly to the edge of the paper. It caught. They watched together; the paper curling at the edges; the ink taking on a different hue just before it disappeared. The thumbprint throwing up a tiny plume of differently coloured smoke.

* * *

"Cup of coffee?" Fiona offered as she got up from the table, her legs stiff from sitting for too long.

257

"Please," Mark mumbled. Still concentrating. Still engaged.

She went down to the kitchen; filled the coffee machine; took a filter from the drawer; spooned in the right amount of ground coffee. Added more for good measure. If ever they had needed caffeine it was now. Then she heard Mark's shout. Left her task unfinished as she ran back up the stairs.

He had found it on his hundredth read-through of the report summarizing the investigation. There was a picture of the convicted couple's lawyer, taken outside the courthouse; some of the victim's families in the background. He had pored over it, time and time again, in the hope that their presence would trigger something. It hadn't occurred to him that the small print would matter. The by-line for the photograph; barely legible on its ageing newsprint. Dermott Mitchell's name.

* * *

"Can he help us?" Miriam asked over lunch, when Mark reported to her the information he had already shared with Fiona. He had met Mitchell at an awards dinner. He knew he was now the picture editor on *The Telegram* in St John's but hadn't realized how long he'd been there. Had found out now that the McAllister case had been his first really big story; that he was credited on at least half the articles and pictures.

"He may well be able to," Mark said. "With stories like this, there are always things that reporters know that they are not allowed to print. If his memory is as good as his reporting, he might just have information we can use to find the girl."

"What's the next step? To phone him?"

"Already done. The last thing he said to me in Prague was, 'If you're ever back in Newfoundland...' Newfie hospitality is legendary. I phoned him this morning. If I fly tonight, I can talk to him over the weekend. He'd be more than happy to host a visit; show me around; talk about old times and new..."

"You're going? To Canada?"

"Already booked a flight. I've been meaning to visit again for years, just never had reason enough to book. I've reason enough now. I'm packed and ready."

He had found a morning flight to Paris from Nantes, then Air Canada via Toronto to St John's. If he could handle the jet lag he could get talking to Mitchell that same evening. He hoped to persuade him to break out any notes he had kept. More than anything he wanted to plunder his memory. He knew from their beer-soaked conversations in Prague that Mitchell liked to talk. At the time he'd found it entertaining but unimportant. Now he was grateful to know of the man's propensity to tell and re-tell the stories of his triumphs.

Miriam saw the smile on Fiona's face. Her pride in her brother. Fiona had offered to pay for the flight, but he would have none of it, muttering something about accumulated air miles. Here was an opportunity for the things he was good at to mean something to his nephew. He was glad to do it. Would chide her if she tried to stop him.

"I'll leave my iPad here with you so I can email you," he said to her. "I've got the laptop. Anything I find, you'll have immediately. We wondered, Miriam, if you would take me to the airport, first thing? Fiona needs to spend some time with Colom, I think."

CHAPTER THIRTY-SIX

*All partake of one common essence, and necessarily
coincide with each other: and like the drops of rain which
fall separately into the river, mix themselves at once with
the stream, and strengthen the general current.*

**Basil Montagu, *The Private Tutor, Or, Thoughts Upon the
Love of Excelling and the Love of Excellence***

It was drier than the day she'd come with Thierry. A strong
morning sun sharpened the profile of the fort as they moved
towards it. The silence they kept as they walked was not the silence
of tension. More of contentment. A "companionable silence" Jane
Austen might have said. She led Colom to the steps, climbed
down, found the tunnel entrance and repeated the ritual of eye-
closing. She explained, just as Thierry had to her, the origin of the
monument – the fifty-nine prisoners shot just weeks before the
end of the war; the deep sense of responsibility felt by the villagers.

They came back out into the light and Fiona led Colom to the
displays, showed him the letter, translated the gist of it for him.
She was standing behind him, a hand at his back, reading over
his shoulder.

"Wow," he said.

"I wanted to talk to you about your father," she said. Hesitant
but committed. She had decided to brave the conversation and
would see it through.

He nodded.

"Colom, your father has done some fairly stupid things in his
life, and I've known about most of them. But this I didn't know –

not until he came here last week. I could have chosen not to tell you, and until recently that's the choice I would have made. But I think you have a right to know. I think you are old enough to deal with knowing. Is that OK with you?"

He shrugged, uncertainly.

She pressed on.

"Your father had… David had a relationship with your mother – your birth mother, I mean. It was before we met – I wasn't even in Canada at the time. It shouldn't have happened – it was against all the rules of the project he was running – but it did happen."

"Are you sure?" He was screwing his eyes tight. She saw it in his reflection in the plate glass display. He might have been holding his breath.

She turned him towards her. Brought their faces level. Held his shoulders.

"Do you want me to tell you more? I don't want to keep anything from you, not any more. But I won't tell you if you don't want to know. Should I carry on?"

He said nothing, but nodded. His eyes still shut.

"Yes, I'm sure. It didn't last long; it was over very quickly, and she left the project – no one knew where she was, and he didn't see her for a year. But when she came back she said that she had had a child and that he had been given up for adoption. She said he could be the father, and asked for money not to tell anyone. He didn't know if she was telling the truth or tricking him – he knew she wanted the money for drugs: he could tell she was back on them in a big way."

"Was it true? Is he my father?"

"No, he isn't. It wasn't true – we're sure about that now. But he did give her some money; the first time and then twice more. But she didn't come back after that, and not long after he heard that she had died."

He was fighting tears. "But he didn't come and find me."

"It's complicated, Colom, but no, he didn't, not at first. He was scared, to be honest. If it came out that he had had a relationship with one of his clients, he would have lost his job and the project might have had to close. He was told that you were being well looked after, waiting for an adoptive family, and he thought that would be best for you. He didn't know anything about what was happening to you – none of us did. Then when it all blew up, two years later, he did the best thing he could to help you, which was to apply to adopt you. He had a better chance at the time of helping you by adopting than by finding out if he was your real father – that would have involved losing everything, and he still didn't know if it was even true. He wanted to be able to provide for you; to give you some kind of life. Adoption seemed the best option at the time."

He said nothing. Pushed his fists against the bridge of his nose. Into his eye sockets.

"I'm telling you this because I think you have a right to know. I don't want you to be hurt any more than you have already. He loves you, you know."

Still nothing. Was this too much for him? Did he even understand what she had told him? She waited. Gave him space.

"How did she die?"

The question took her by surprise. Hadn't she already told him? Had she missed out these all-important details; assumed that he would guess, knowing that she had been an addict?

"She took an overdose – not on purpose, but by accident. Heroin. She was with her boyfriend, who was also an addict. They'd got hold of a lot of drugs, and by all accounts had just taken too much too quickly. I think it's possible that he may have been your father, but we just don't know. They both died, Colom. I'm so sorry."

"I wish I could have known her. I wish she'd lived."

"So do I, Colom, with all my heart. And I wish your father and I had been more honest with you, from the very start, about what happened. I wish we'd understood that you needed to know, instead of thinking you'd be better off if you didn't."

She saw that he could no longer fight the tears. She took the risk of pulling him to herself; holding him against her. He didn't reciprocate, but neither did he try to break away. As his face burrowed into her shoulder, the tears came in earnest. He sobbed and sobbed. She stroked his hair, held him more firmly still. Heard him mumbling words, but couldn't make them out. Pulled back from him just in time to catch them as he repeated them.

"I'm sorry, Mum."

"Sorry? For what?" she asked in genuine amazement.

"For the letter. For saying I wanted to die."

"Oh Colom," she said. "You have nothing to be sorry for. I'm the one who should be sorry. Me and your father. It's our fault, not yours."

He looked for a moment as if she hadn't heard him; hadn't caught what he was trying to say. His eyes were open now; his tears drying.

"But I am sorry," he said firmly. "About the letter. I'm sorry I hurt you. I love you, Mum."

And in that moment she knew that the danger truly had passed. The letter had been burned and there wouldn't be another. For all the shocking information her son had taken in during these past few days, enough to make a superhero suicidal, he had decided that he wanted to live. She pulled him to herself again; held him; prayed that this moment could go on forever.

"And I love you, Colom Dryden," she said. "More than you will ever know."

It wasn't the last time she would need to hold him that day, though. Tired from their walk, he went to bed unusually early. Still more unusually, he was soon asleep. But shortly after midnight Fiona was back at his side, drawn from her own room once again by his screaming. Talking him down from the same dream. Changing the wet sheets. Settling him again as best she could.

Whatever stage his journey had reached, it wasn't over.

CHAPTER THIRTY-SEVEN

*When air turbulence occurs, water droplets collide,
producing larger droplets. As these larger water
droplets descend, coalescence continues, so that drops
become heavy enough to overcome air resistance and
fall as rain.*

"Rain", Wikipedia

It was early evening the following day by the time Mark called. He was only just breaking for lunch.

"How's it going?" Fiona asked impatiently. "Have you had a chance to talk to him yet?"

"Yes, I have. And I've had plenty of time to listen! This man is a talker, I can tell you."

"And what about the girl? Have you been able to identify her?"

"I may have – that's why I'm calling. There's a photo – it's in the scanner right now and I'll email it to you as soon as it's done. I need you to take a look and tell me what you think."

"But I don't know the girl – I don't know anything about her. How can looking at a photo help?"

"You'll see, I think. Let me tell you who she is, and then take a look at the picture, OK?"

"OK. If you say so."

"So, her name is Amy; she's about two years older than Colom. She was already with the McAllisters for about a year before Colom got there. The picture I'm sending over was taken before she would have met Colom, if she did. OK, it's done. I'll email it – pick it up and call me back in five minutes."

He had hung up before Fiona could speak again. She quickly opened up the laptop to log on to her email. His had arrived by the time she opened the programme and there, in the preview pane, was the image he had sent.

She thought that the picture might well be of a birthday party, judging by the dress the girl was wearing. It was pink, in a silky material. It wasn't completely clean, and there were creases that suggested it had not been well ironed. But it was a party dress for all that. Her dark hair was gathered into two slightly uneven bunches, each held by a red bow. She was seated at a low table with an ancient lace tablecloth, set with miniature teacups and a plate of cupcakes. The two other places set were not for her friends but for her dolls. She was not much out of toddler years but already had the face of a child. A look of intense concentration as she poured imaginary tea. She was olive-skinned, neither smiling nor grimacing, her face a study in responsible hosting. And there was something in her wide eyes as she focused on her task. Defiance? Strength, certainly.

Fiona wondered what she was supposed to be seeing. She didn't know the girl. Didn't know what she was looking for. Then she saw him: the fourth guest she had not at first noticed. Beside the girl's plate was a napkin, and beside that, an old and worn soft toy, positioned to share with her the pleasure of the party. Fiona's eye was drawn to the toy. She swept her fingers across the screen to enlarge the picture, centred it in. Looked more closely. Stopped breathing.

Even with the picture beginning to pixelate, and blurred to start with, she knew that there was no mistake. She grabbed her mobile and punched the number Mark had given her. He picked up straight away. Spoke immediately.

"What do you think?"

"It must be her," Fiona said breathlessly, barely breaking a whisper. She could hardly believe it. "Why would she have the toy beside her if it wasn't her favourite? And why would she subsequently give it to Colom unless they were close? Very close?"

Was that why Colom had held on to the toy like an old friend all his life? Clung to it, reluctant to release it even to the washing machine and drier for twenty-four hours? She had always assumed that it had come to him from his birth mother – that it was his last link with her. But it was another relationship altogether, it seemed, that had been sealed with the gift of Oscar: another friendship of which the toy was a lifelong memento.

"I think it's enough to be going on with," Mark said. "I've filed stories on weaker evidence more than once. Dermott has said that if we're sure this is the girl, he thinks he can find out where she is now. The files are not public, but he can get access. If you know you have the child's number right, you can make the connections and trace them through. He says it may take a day or so, but he thinks he can do it, and he's willing to try."

"Will you thank him for me?"

"Of course I will. He seems happy to help – between you and me I think he's enjoying it. He's glad to do anything for the kids – broke his heart, he says, hearing more and more of the evidence come out every day. There are two pictures he's carried in his wallet ever since – no one we know but two of the victims. Regrets every day, he says, that he couldn't do more to help them."

"So what do we do now?"

"Give me twenty-four hours or so. Everything I get I'll update you by email. As soon as I can get a confirmed location, I'll let you know."

They said their goodbyes and Fiona breathed a deep sigh – not of frustration but of relief. After all they had been through, it seemed at last that they were moving forward.

* * *

The confidence this gave her was sorely tested just a few hours later. She took the stairs two at a time to get to Colom's room; was at his bedside by the time the echo of his screams had faded.

He was sitting up, sweating. She wasn't at first sure if he had woken or was still dreaming. She noticed, on the floor around his bed, pages torn from his sketchbook, several with a single charcoal image of a girl.

"Nightmare?" she said.

He nodded; seemed unable to speak.

"I couldn't save her," he said at last. "She was in the water with me, but I couldn't save her. Then there was a hand, a man's hand, forcing me under. I couldn't breathe, but all the time he pushed harder. I couldn't get away from his grip, and I couldn't reach her. I knew she was there, not far from me, but I couldn't reach her."

The panic in his voice tore at her heart.

"It's all right, my love," she said as soothingly as she knew how. "It's just a dream. It's over now."

He was calming, slowly. Coming to terms with where he was. Awake. In his room. The dream fast fading. He lay back down on his pillow. She stroked his hair. And she realized he had fallen back into a sleep. He seemed, at least, to be at peace. She tucked his duvet around him; rearranged Oscar beside him. Went quietly back down to her own room. Prayed, in the few moments before she too fell back into sleep, that they could find this mystery girl.

She couldn't tell if her dark mood over breakfast was from interrupted sleep, or the tension of waiting for word from Mark. She knew she could trust him to stick to his word and call as soon as he had news, but for much of the day, there was nothing. She checked her email repeatedly, to the point of beginning to worry that the system wasn't working. She couldn't concentrate on anything, so spent most of the day in mindless routines of cleaning anything she could get her hands on. Miriam was a less obsessive clean-freak than she was, so there was plenty to work on. She took particular pleasure in investing ninety minutes returning a supposedly stainless-steel sink to some semblance of stainlessness. She wondered momentarily if, like Lady Macbeth, she was trying to clean some inner spot that simply wouldn't budge, but the effort of reflection was too much for her. She channelled her energy, instead, into the scrubbing.

It was gone five by the time Mark's email arrived. Courting melodrama, the subject line read: Amy's location. The message itself was just one word.

She dialled his number straight away, and once again he picked up on the first ring.

"Amsterdam?" she said. "What's she doing in Amsterdam?"

"Living with her adoptive family, we assume."

"But why Amsterdam?"

She wondered at first why his tone of voice was so deadpan, until she realized he was now reading from his own notes.

"The father's English; graduate of LSE; was interning at Memorial then stayed over here for several years. The mother's a Newfoundlander, born and bred. They married here; adopted Amy soon after. Moved to Europe six years ago; four years in Brussels and now two in Amsterdam. He's with ING; big Dutch bank, now global. He's something big in insurance; to do with the algorithms they use for risk assessment. Apparently he's writing some hot-stuff programme that could save the industry millions. Not short of cash, by all accounts. No other children as far as we can tell, so it's just Mum, Dad and Amy."

"How did you find all this?"

"The early stuff came from Dermott, but once we had a name for the father, the rest is Google and a bit of digging. We have an address: Amsteldijk. It's a riverside location just off the city centre. Not a deprived neighbourhood. And we have an email address. And a mobile phone number that we think may be the father's. That's it for now."

"You've not made contact?"

"No – I'm leaving that to you. Should we go, do you think – to Amsterdam?"

"I don't know. I think so. Should we contact them first?"

"I would say yes – but contact them to let them know you're coming. Don't say that you might come if they'll invite you. Tell them you're planning to be in the city anyway. There is one other thing."

"What's that?" She didn't like the nervous edge to his tone, or the fact that he'd had cause to hold back this last discovery.

"The reason Doug, Amy's father, took the internship at Memorial is that he had an uncle in St John's. Not at the university – but he was well connected. Served on the city council for several terms. He died quite recently. His name was James O'Brien, and a few years back…"

She finished his sentence for him. "He worked with David."

Even as she said it she wondered if this was good news, or bad. What she didn't tell Mark was that David had comprehensively fallen out with James O'Brien in the closing months of his time in Canada – some dispute over a planning application for a project. She wasn't aware that they had ever made up. David's last description of his friend, to her recollection, had been "stubborn mule". It was difficult to imagine the feeling not being reciprocated, possibly in the very same words.

* * *

So, this week I found out something really weird. I thought I was doing great – I lost about ten kilos in three weeks, but I kept getting this terrible thirst AND I kept needing to pee all the time. We went to the doctor's but he said it could just be an infection, and gave me antibiotics. They didn't make any difference and yesterday I had an accident at school, and Mom found out. And then there's this really strange smell. It's not sweat; it's a kind of sweet chemical odour. At first I thought it was in certain rooms, then I noticed it in the car and at school, and I realized. It was me. So we went back to the doctor's, and they did some tests – and it turns out I have this disease called DIABETES. Type 1 they call it – there's another kind, that I haven't got. I had no idea. Turns out that's why I've been losing weight. And why I've been so darned tired all the time. And the weird mood swings. That's all part of it too, apparently. So I'm going on this programme to learn how to use insulin – and I have to inject myself, usually twice a day.

They told me everything I have to do, and think about, and remember. I wrote it down –

"If I want to live, I will:

Test when I should.

Never cheat.

Shoot the way I've been told to.

Take responsibility for my condition."

I feel really weird about this. No one else at home has this disease. It's not like they're used to it or anything. Sometimes I feel I want their sympathy – I want them to understand. But other times I just want them to leave me alone. I don't want to be treated differently all the time. Mom's started talking about how hard college will be, and whether maybe no one will want to marry me now; and how I might never be able to work... I KNOW she's scared at the thought of having to look after me FOREVER. As if it was her disease or something. We used to argue a lot anyway, especially about FOOD, but this is making it way worse.

So that's me. The anorexic diabetic. They say it's inherited, but who knows? No one knows what I might have inherited. How could they? Welcome to my world.

III

AMSTERDAM

CHAPTER THIRTY-EIGHT

*Sometimes it rains and still fails to moisten the desert
– the falling water evaporates halfway down between
cloud and earth. Then you see curtains of blue rain
dangling out of reach in the sky while the living things
wither below for want of water. Torture by tantalizing,
hope without fulfillment.*

**Edward Abbey, "Desert Reflections Part 2: Phantom
Rain and Ways of Being"**

Mark brought the white Volvo to a gentle stop in a narrow street that ran perpendicular to the waterside, connecting two canals. Finding the street, let alone the house, had been a challenge worthy of Commissaris Van der Valk. It was approached from the Singel – the most central of Amsterdam's city canals – and even locating that was a puzzle, solved by first finding the city centre and then negotiating a complex sequence of one-way streets and bridges. Calling the canals of Amsterdam a maze would be like calling the Amazon rainforest a wooded copse. They had no satnav and were dependent on a street map read by the inadequate glove-box light. Fiona had volunteered for this responsibility while Mark drove, trying and failing to get his memories of the city to offer up information that might be useful to them. It didn't help that the street names were unpronounceable to a car-load of anglophones and francophones. By the time you'd worked out where you were, you weren't there any more. Half a dozen false turns later Fiona was surprised and relieved to find that the road they were looking for did exist.

Like all the houses that line and link the canals of central Amsterdam, 6 Romeinsarmsteeg was tall and narrow, brick-built, terraced. It ran to four storeys, the main rooms having large, curtain-free windows. Theirs were dark, but in houses alongside and around them lamps and candles burned, showing off an eclectic range of interiors with paintings, ornaments, shelves of ancient books. Cars were not banned from the narrow streets, but they were not greatly encouraged either. The strong possibility of being held up for two hours while a truck with nowhere to go unloaded a piano through a third-floor window meant that those who knew these roads were sensible enough to leave their cars at home, or park outside the city and tram in. Only bikes could roam freely here and did, in their thousands. Cyclists still filled the streets as Mark edged the Volvo towards its destination, though it was close to midnight. The city that never stops pedalling.

For a small nation, perched on the inhospitable shores of the North Sea, the worldwide reach of Dutch commercial interests was breathtaking. Slavery had had its part to play, and diamonds, but more mundane commodities – tea and coffee; cotton; spices; rice – had also found their way here, stored in warehouses labelled with the days of the week. There was money to be made from such movement, and much of it went into the homes and houses, the churches and monuments of these canal-side neighbourhoods. Trade and shipping still paid a share of mortgages here, but other industries now nestled alongside them: banking and finance; computers and software; media interests. A new generation had shaken off the puritan strictures of the Protestants and the ancient rituals of the Catholics to create a postmodern, art-and-party culture, for which the one-time merchant houses offered the best possible home.

The panelled garage door they had stopped beside took up most of the building's ground floor, with just enough room for a narrow front door beside it. The garage, like those both adjacent to and opposite it, carried a large sign advertising its need for twenty-four-hour access. The angled rows of cars lining both sides of every canal, as tight as books on a shelf, made it easy to understand why such signs were needed.

Mark left the others in the car while he went to number 8 to collect the keys. These were handed over without undue ceremony. Mark was expected, and therefore trusted; English, and therefore who he said he was. He opened the narrow door of number 6 to reveal the steepest staircase he had ever seen. The others were wrestling their bags from the car onto the pavement. He stood aside to let them drag them up the steps and to the top of the staircase, while he opened up the garage from inside and pulled the car into it. It was a cavernous space. The owners' obsession – a beautifully preserved Triumph TR3 in pillar-box red – was parked at the back of the garage, but there was still room for another car in front.

They had been on the road for almost fourteen hours, nine of them in motion and five taken up with stops: several on the French motorways; a longer visit to Antwerp; fuel and coffee once in Holland. They'd shared the driving, working in two-hour shifts. They had talked a little and slept a lot. Mark had been back in Portivy for less than twenty-four hours before leaving again, and was struggling to shake off his jet lag. He did his best to make his back seat position comfortable with the aid of two pillows brought from Miriam's house. He had contacted friends Jos and Mica while he was still in Canada, as soon as the decision to go to Amsterdam was made; had discovered that they were in Malaysia, but had as usual left a key with their neighbours. They were happy for the house to be used, and glad to welcome Mark to Amsterdam, even in their absence. They had been urging him to visit again since he had been a guest at their wedding three years earlier.

For the second time in a matter of weeks, Fiona had explained to Colom that they were moving on, chasing their adventure to another country altogether.

"Does the name mean anything to you?" she had asked him, once they had decided that Amy was the girl they would go searching for.

"I don't think so," he said. She could see that he was trying hard, and there was something in his eyes. It was a question, not an answer, but it caught her attention.

"We don't have to go," she had assured him. "We won't, if you don't want to."

He was fighting tears. How could she expect him to make such a decision, to know what was right in such a circumstance? He was the victim here. He hadn't chosen any of this. He needed help, not pressure.

"I want to," he said at last. His voice was pinched, as if he only had breath for a few words and had to make the most of them. It was enough. He spoke little on their journey, but she took it as a silence of agreement, not of defiance or anger.

She had been grateful for the relative silence of the journey. Watching kilometre after kilometre of France flash by in a blur of unchanging autoroute, she reflected on the decision she had come to, and how she had explained it to Thierry. He had not been surprised; had sensed all along where her heart was taking her. They had walked again; a late evening on the beach-front, the sea unusually calm; a muffled stillness settling over them. It wasn't a decision to try again with David, not yet at least. But it was a decision against deciding not to. It was her duty; she owed it to their history. It was also, in the end, what she wanted. She had known it as soon as she had decided to seek out Amy. She was not a quitter. She couldn't jump ship. Not yet. They parted company as good friends. Friends, she hoped, who would see each other again. She had left him a gift, propped it against his front door just before they pulled away to leave the harbour a shrinking symbol in the rear-view mirror. A pastel of the beach at day's end; the tide low; a hint of evening colouring the sky; the edge of the fort's silhouette just visible. She had spotted it among others on Colom's bedroom floor; had asked if she could pass it on to Thierry as a thank you from them both. She had taken it to Quiberon to find a suitable frame. Had written on the back of the frame – her thanks; her appreciation of a friendship that had helped her – had helped them both – at a time of great need. Oddly, it wasn't the last words she had heard from Thierry that she would remember him by – it was the first, more or less. *Je suis enfin chez moi.* A confession. A statement of faith. For Fiona, a new ambition.

Mark pulled the sliding door closed and made his way upstairs. The first floor was taken up by a single, front-to-back room that served as living room, dining room and, through a small alcove in its back wall, kitchen. Sturdy wooden beams, in various thicknesses, crossed the ceiling from left to right. Layers of paint had softened their contours over the years, but could not disguise their strength. This was a house built to stand. Where the beams met they were joined with heavy bolts, as if from a giant Meccano set. Exploration revealed two even steeper staircases leading to a maze of small bedrooms, more heavy beams in evidence throughout. At the very top and back of the house a final ladder gave access to a tiny roof garden.

They briefly discussed room allocation. Colom got one of the captain's bunks; Miriam and Fiona the two other single rooms. Mark, as the friend of the owners and therefore surrogate host, was treated to the master bedroom, a vast, low-ceilinged room at the front of the house with windows overlooking the street. Miriam's hunch that the back rooms would be quieter made the distribution a little more even-handed. It was well past midnight by the time they had manhandled bags to the appropriate rooms. Those who'd driven were tired; those who hadn't were more than happy to sleep anyway.

Mark drifted off to the sound of three drunks, a poorly maintained scooter engine and a very drawn-out domestic confrontation, all of which sounded close enough to be on the pillow beside him. He was faintly aware, in the night, of movement inside the house. Someone on the stairs. Had someone cried out? But he had forced himself by then to screen out incoming noise, and didn't fully wake.

Fiona's journey into sleep was more protracted still. She had missed a call on her mobile while travelling, the number withheld. It was only as she prepared for bed that she saw she had a voicemail message. Tempted to leave it until morning, she was too curious not to check it. Which was how she found herself lying, sleep-deprived and anxious, wondering what it was that Sergeant White needed to speak to her about.

The street noises of early morning were more cheerful, but sounded just as close. They woke Mark early, and he slipped out for provisions. Miriam and Fiona were both up when he got back. Both looked tired, Fiona more so. No sign of Colom just yet.

Mark had sourced coffee, wholemeal rolls, Gouda cheese and thinly sliced bacon: a breakfast menu based on recollections of his last visit. As they ate they planned their day. Mark would occupy Colom with sightseeing while Fiona and Miriam shopped for more substantial provisions and contacted Amy's parents to see if they would be open to a visit. They had emailed from France, and had let David know of the connection with James O'Brien, but had not yet heard from either quarter. They wanted to test out the lie of the land, even make a preliminary visit today if such was offered. At the very least they would find out where the house was and establish that the family did indeed exist; that there was an Amy to be visited. They had no clue as to what might come of a visit. They knew only that it had to be done; that for Colom, it was the only way forward.

Leaving Colom to his day with his uncle, Miriam and Fiona spent the morning getting lost; getting stuck in traffic; struggling to locate a supermarket and, having found one, to park close by. Half the day was gone by the time they'd stashed a few meals' worth of food in the back of the car. Knowing that Mark and Colom would be gone for the day, and that the temperature of an early spring in Amsterdam would be no threat to the freshness of their food, they left the car where it was and set off on foot to find lunch. In this, at last, the city was more friendly to them. Their frustrations evaporated over a good quality café latte and filled rolls made with a bread dark enough to satisfy the most demanding palate. Fiona took advantage of the less stressful setting to make the call she had been dreading.

Sergeant White picked up immediately. No need of a switchboard for today's modern detective. "Thanks for calling back," she said once Fiona had introduced herself. "I have some news about the Daniel Tripp investigation. We've made an arrest."

"You have? Who?"

"You won't know the name. An older man Daniel met through a Youth Service project. They had been talking for some time by email – but he's the one who introduced Daniel to the suicide site. He did more besides, and we have a full record of it from his hard drive. We won't struggle to get a conviction."

"Well, that's good news. Thank you for letting me know."

There was a pause. Something else to be said. Fiona sensed that they were moving off the record.

"Only I thought you ought to know," the sergeant said. Another pause. "It wasn't Colom. It wasn't your son who told Daniel about the site. I thought you ought to know that."

"Thank you," said Fiona, relief working its way through her body like a massage. It had taken her a moment to realize the significance of the arrest, the reason for the call. Now it flooded into her. It was like sunshine after endless days of rain; like arriving home after a long and arduous journey. Good news at last. The smell of coffee; the view of the canal through the café window; the buzz of conversation: these small signs of life were all at once benevolent. The world was not, after all, against her. Her son was not a monster.

It was a brief respite. The afternoon brought no more progress than the morning as they set off to find the address they had been given for the Porters, Amy's adoptive family. The trip involved more traffic; more experiences of being lost in an alphabet soup of street names. At last they found themselves inching along the narrow strip of tarmac that marked the contours of the Amsteldijk. On their left, the long and lazy river filled their field of vision. Further into the city, the Amstel was crowded with barges and houseboats, some moored three deep. Out here the occasional pleasure boat tied to a jetty and the rowing crews pitting muscle power against the current didn't come close to filling the wide expanse of water. The resultant vista was spacious, peaceful; the far bank a green and unspoilt pasture – a view no doubt adding to the price paid for the detached villas that lined the right-hand side of the road. In a city of cupboard-sized apartments the ample proportions of these homes and their gardens marked them out as millionaire mansions, even if the Dutch disdain for ostentatious wealth kept their appearance as humble as comfort and security would allow.

Fiona drove, while Miriam strained to discern the numbers of the houses. They were in the low hundreds, and looking for 130. She called stop as they crawled past 129, and they found themselves alongside a high brick wall and blue-painted metal gate. The brickwork looked new; expensive even in this row of high-end homes. A sophisticated video entry system at the gate told them that the residents of 130 had possessions worth protecting.

The house appeared deserted. The shutters on the upstairs windows were down; the gates closed; an unbroken stillness resting over the property. Taking her courage in both hands, Fiona tried the bell at the gate. Both video and audio were captured by the entry system, but no response came. She tried again.

They retired to a nearby café to regroup. Fiona once more called the mobile number Mark had found, wondering if it was even the right number. She had left an initial message from Portivy; another first thing this morning. Had tried again twice since without adding further messages for fear of spooking her quarry. There had been no response, just as her emails, last time she'd checked them, went unanswered. Her second had been long and detailed, telling as much of Colom's story as she could bring herself to tell. The number went to voicemail again – the generic voice of a female Dutch computer telling her which number she had reached, but not whose it was. She hung up, despondent.

They finished their coffee in silence. What was there to say?

"OK," Miriam said, trying hard to inject some energy into their task. "Let's try once more at the house. Then once more by phone, while we're here. Then we'll head back across town – there's little point in staying here if they're not in. We can try the phone again from home this evening – maybe email again?"

They drove back past the house. Stopped at the gate. Tried the bell again; three times now, the last a long and lingering press. Still nothing. Fiona got back into the car; tried the number again; waited; heard once again the voice of Beatrix – a computer she now knew well enough to christen. Rang off before her virtual friend had finished speaking her way through the number.

CHAPTER THIRTY-NINE

*I always like walking in the rain, so no one can see
me crying.*

Charles Chaplin

Colom sat on a white concrete block under a bank of flat-screen TVs advertising upcoming events. The underside of the stairs seemed to float above him: huge slabs of concrete with no visible means of support. Glass-walled balconies rising up into the high roof space: clean lines; light-filled spaces; blocks of strong, bold colours in the posters and pictures on the walls.

A Japanese tour group came in, shuffling and chattering; pulling off and shaking out their matching see-through rain capes. One girl broke away from the cluster. Giggling, she turned to take a picture of her friends. She was short; a round face framed by jet-black hair; her eyes and teeth bright in her deep-tan skin. Laughter poured from her as she clicked. She smiled. He stared.

Mark broke the line of sight of his young charge, holding out a ticket for him.

"Let's go," he said. "We have a lot to see."

Colom got up to follow.

"The main rooms are upstairs," his uncle said, "but before we see them, there's something I'd like to show you first."

Turning aside from what appeared to be the obvious route, he led the way along a narrow walkway that took them downstairs to a lower gallery. Pushing through the double doors, they entered a white-walled room: spotlights hanging from the ceiling; the clean lines of a bare wooden floor. Around the walls, pools of light fell on glass-fronted frames that held the yellowing paper of letters and notebook pages. Beside these, larger framed sketches and, in some cases, paintings. Looking more closely, Colom saw that the paintings were of the subjects roughly mapped out on the notebook pages. In the letters, tight lines of handwritten script were interrupted by more sketches.

They began their slow journey around the room's circumference, stopping briefly before each frame, the drawings in ink or heavy charcoal: some small, a single subject or object, others larger and more complex, testing out the potential of a fuller painting. Many involved human faces or figures – working people in traditional dress, the drawings capturing a sense of respect, of reverence. Several were self-portraits: the face of a man disturbed by his own mirror image. And there were the landscapes: sweeping compositions that even without colour were vibrant and alive, the charcoal applied sharply; deep lines following the contours of the land and sky.

Colom knew at once why his uncle had brought him here. The style was not his, but there were similarities enough for the point to be made. Here was an artist, perhaps the greatest ever, who had worked with lead and charcoal to capture the form of the world he saw. Who even in letters found life easier to draw than to describe.

"Do you like them?" Mark asked.

"They're amazing," Colom said, unashamed of his enthusiasm. He was enthralled. There were passages where the artist had drawn lines that nature didn't carry, and yet they played their part: the swirling of the wind around the trees; the patterns of fields or of water. This was not the work of a draughtsman but of a storyteller: each picture a folktale of his own design. He had seen prints before of some of the paintings. He knew about the wild colours; the harsh brush-strokes. But he had never seen the drawings, and they told him that this man could also tell his stories without colour.

"He never knew, you know," his uncle said.

"Never knew what?"

"How good he was. He never knew. He was tortured by his own sense of failure. He sold no more than two paintings in his entire lifetime – and these to his brother. He knew that he was mad, but he never knew that he was great. People will pay millions now for just one of his canvases – but in his own lifetime he was unheard of."

Colom laughed, remembering, "They showed him once," he said, "in an episode of *Doctor Who*. They brought him forward in time so he could see how famous he had become after his death."

"A nice thought. But it never happened. I wish it had, really. I've always been very moved by his story."

"Do you think that's why he killed himself?"

"Because he didn't think he was any good? No, not really. It seems likely that he had a depressive personality, was perhaps mentally ill. I sometimes wonder what would have happened if he'd been alive today. Probably he would have been diagnosed as bipolar and prescribed drugs to level off his moods. Perhaps he would never have taken his own life, and we'd have had a lifetime's worth of art to look at, instead of these few short years…"

"Maybe not."

Mark's look of puzzlement dissolved as understanding came. "You mean the paintings?"

Colom shrugged. "Something drove him to suicide. Maybe that same something was what inspired him to paint. Maybe without the depression he wouldn't have taken up painting in the first place."

It was a remarkable observation for a fourteen-year-old boy seeing these works for the first time.

"You could well be right. He wanted to be a missionary, you know. He was for a while, in London. But it didn't work out. It's a good theory though: a life that is balanced but unproductive versus one that is unstable but inspired. I know a few scholars who would go for that – though I know others who would deny it flat-out. Some won't even accept that he was depressed in the first place."

"Well, he looks it to me." He was standing completely still, his gaze locked onto a canvas from which dark eyes stared back across a gap of 120 years, beneath the curving brim of a felt hat.

"Do you enjoy it? Drawing?"

"Yes."

"It shows. You're very good, you know."

He shuffled slightly, embarrassed, incredulous. "Not like this I'm not."

"No, I don't mean that. Maybe one day, who knows? But I mean now, for your age. You're good. You have something."

"Thanks."

"I just wanted you to know. I didn't want you to grow up without knowing. I didn't want you to give up, or think that it's not worth trying."

"I enjoy it. I want to carry on – maybe study it later."

"Good. You should. I just wanted you to know."

"Thanks, Unc, and thanks for bringing me. This is good."

They moved on through the gallery, taking in the rest of the letters and sketches before heading upstairs to the paintings. These were set out in blocks, named for the artist's location at that time: Paris; St Rémy; Arles. They talked about colour and line; about which paintings most struck them. For Colom it was the self-portraits, always with the deep, troubled eyes. He wondered how an artist could even know himself, let alone paint himself, so well.

Mark had never quite understood what the duties of an uncle were. At first he had assumed it was mostly about fun: doing the things parents didn't want to; buying sometimes inappropriate gifts. He never knew if he had done enough. He had no children of his own and was rarely in the company of the under-eighteens. He felt as awkward around them as he assumed they did around him. But he loved his nephew and the boy was clearly in trouble. Someone needed to throw him a lifeline. It didn't need to involve any kind of lie, not even an exaggeration, because Colom's drawings really were good, perhaps exceptional for a child of his age.

They talked again on the walk back to the tram stop. A light rain was falling from clouds that hung low over the afternoon, threatening to bring dusk even earlier than expected. Wet leaves bounced and danced along the pavements; cyclists pushing hard against the wind. The streets were not crowded, offering the opportunity for the kind of private conversation only open spaces provide. They reached a point where three canals met; an M. C. Escher sketch of intersecting footpaths and bridges; each brick perfectly and precisely placed. One of the bridges was movable, with a complex system of pulleys and chains, the metalwork recently painted; black gloss standing out against the dark red brick. A glass-topped canal boat, two-thirds empty but persevering nonetheless with its part-load of early tourists, entered the intersection by one canal and executed an impossibly tight turn before exiting by another. Colom watched its long, flat shape gliding through the water, the pilot's perfect guidance honed in the rhythm of a dozen daily trips. He saw the speckled pattern of rain on the curved roof windows; the empty seats within.

"There was something I wanted to ask you," Mark said.

"What's that?"

"I wanted to say that if you ever feel tempted to give up on art – if you think you're not good enough, or feel drawn to other things – would you ask someone before you do? I mean, find someone who really knows art – or ask me and let me find them – and ask them what they see in your work?"

Colom hunched inside his coat, the wind playing with his dark curls. "You think I'm that good?" he asked.

Mark stopped; turned. "I think you can be. There are people who know far better than me how to tell. Will you ask them – or let me ask them? I mean before you think of throwing in the towel to become an accountant or something?"

"OK." They started moving again. Row after row of uniform, tall houses, some of them hotels. Then a break; a view to other canals and their bridges beyond.

Later, back at the house, Colom took himself off to his room while his uncle went online to catch up on work emails. Mark suspected, quite rightly, that his nephew would be sketching; pouring onto paper the inspiration he had found in the richly talented, suicidal Van Gogh.

Mark broke away from his work at the sound of the doorbell, buzzing Fiona and Miriam in and watching as they climbed their weary way up the Everest ascent. Colom had obviously heard it too because he came down just as they arrived. Unusually, he said he was hungry and showed every intention of joining them for dinner. Once the shopping was unloaded and the dinner quickly assembled, he showed an unexpected willingness to engage in conversation. Fiona couldn't quite believe it, but didn't dare say so. They talked their way through the meal. As if it was their normal habit. As if they sat to eat together every evening.

"So what did you two get up to?" Fiona asked. Nervously. Anxious not to scare away her rabbit-in-the-headlights son.

"We went to the Van Gogh Museum," Mark volunteered. "Spent most of the afternoon there."

"How was it?" she asked, leaving the door open for either to respond. Everybody knowing it was Colom she really wanted to hear from.

"It was good," her son said. An encyclopaedic answer by his standards. A million pages in three small words. But there was more. "Really good," he affirmed, a faint smile gracing his lips.

Fiona wanted to reach over and kiss him. Hug him. Slap him on the back. None of which she would dare do, of course. It was like the first day of spring; the moment she remembered from her days in Canada – usually a day in early April – when she would first notice little rivulets of water on the road because the thaw had begun in earnest.

She went upstairs later to see him; to say goodnight; eager to communicate, somehow, her pride in him. He was in bed, still drawing, completed sketches scattered on the table, some on the floor. She leafed through them, as she often did. Colom hated attention being drawn to his work, didn't enjoy talking about it, but he had never minded his mother subtly taking a look. It wasn't that he didn't want her to see them, he just wanted to pretend that he didn't know she'd seen them.

They were good, these new drawings, the lines stronger than she had seen before. She had long since stopped saying that she was amazed at his capacity to capture life in a few lines. His talent had been clear to her from a very early age. But she was moved to see something new here. Confidence? Eloquence? These were poems: readable, crafted, rich with finely coded imagery.

"Take one," Colom said shyly.

"I'd love to," Fiona said sincerely. "You're sure you don't mind?"

He shrugged rather than spoke. An affirming shrug. She caught herself realizing there had been less shrugging these past few days.

The girl looked Japanese or Chinese. She was wearing a rain cape. Colom had set her at a canal side; behind her, the outline of tall buildings, soldier-like, side by side. In the water a tourist boat, glass topped, turning in the narrow channel. In the air, on the water's surface, signs of rain. Ripples; dashes; a thin mist clearing only around the face of the girl. At the bottom corner above his name, a title: "Rain, Amsterdam". It was cartoon-like in technique, hinting at, rather than detailing, the setting and surroundings. But there was subtlety, too. It was recognizably Amsterdam, and recognizably raining.

"Thank you, Colom," she said. "These are really good. Can I show the others?"

Even as she said it, she saw a shadow come across his face. A flash of confusion in his eyes. He said nothing.

"That's fine," she said. "Just me, then."

She wished him goodnight. Leaned in to kiss him. Felt the usual, momentary resistance; delivered the most minimal of kisses and stepped away again quickly, as always. She accommodating his ambivalence. He accepting – enduring? – the kiss goodnight.

"Try to sleep now," she said. "You know where I am if you need me. I'll leave a light on on the stairs." She smiled her reassuring smile and closed his door.

There was now, at least, a glimmer of hope. Doug Porter had phoned at last, late in the evening. Had explained that they had not been available all day; that they had indeed received the emails, and the calls and messages, on his wife's phone, not his own. That they had talked about it and agreed to meet. Would coffee tomorrow morning be appropriate? Did they know how to find the house? And it was done. A long hard day that had, at the eleventh hour, proved fruitful.

"I'm afraid Amy won't be there, though," he'd said, his words suddenly muted, hesitant, as if a great distance had just opened up between his voice and the phone. "She's sleeping over at a friend's house, through to Friday morning."

He paused; the sense that something more needed to be said. "Let's leave it at that for now," he said at last, quietly. "Perhaps I can explain tomorrow?"

"Of course. We'll see you then. Thank you."

And he was gone, leaving Fiona to wonder what crisis they had blundered into. One thing she knew for sure. As a mother whose own son's grief had pierced her heart twice over – whose instinct for the ache of parenting had sharpened exponentially these past months – she knew she had just been speaking to a man in pain.

CHAPTER FORTY

Raindrops do not fall in a tear drop shape, they
originally fall in the shape of a flat oval.
"Rain", Wikipedia

Finding the Amsteldijk again the following day was easier, though it still entailed a stressful battle with the traffic. The house looked no more occupied than on their first visit. Miriam got out to ring the bell and Fiona saw, rather than heard, that she spoke into the entry phone. The deep-blue gates swung silently open.

They drove onto a block-paved driveway, lines of black bricks adding a diamond pattern to the beige. The house was a new-build, a three-storey villa forming an L-shape with the blue-doored double garage. A new black Mini Cooper was the only car on the drive, others perhaps too precious to live anywhere but indoors.

The big front door was already open. Standing in it was a surprisingly small man, probably in his late forties, his hair thinning to baldness, his beard perfectly trimmed. His shirt and jeans were casual but laundered. He wore soft leather moccasin slippers and put Miriam in mind of a New York rabbi. Liberal; intelligent; aesthetic; perhaps kind in the way that only rich people can truly afford to be. When he spoke in a soft British accent that was more Greenwich than Greenwich Village, she smiled at how wrong she could be.

"Mrs Dryden," he said, extending his hand, knowing somehow who was who, "Doug Porter. Good to meet you – please do come in. Miss Casselles, pleased to meet you."

He stood aside as Miriam followed Fiona into a spacious lobby. Beige-painted and lit by soft uplighters, its ceiling height covering two storeys, it opened through arches to a kitchen in one direction and in two others to a huge L-shaped living and dining area. Perfectly furnished, staged as for a photo shoot, original oil paintings on every wall. Doug Porter showed them through to a seating area that was clearly neither the formal sitting room nor the family den. A morning-coffee area. A space for visitors you don't yet know as friends but don't want to treat as strangers. A tray of coffee was already laid out waiting.

"It's very good of you to see us, Mr Porter. Thank you," Miriam said, keeping a formality to her voice as she tried to gauge her host.

"Doug, please," he said. "May I call you Miriam?"

"Of course. We really are grateful."

There was an awkward pause, which he filled by asking them how they drank their coffee, and duly pouring it.

"My wife sends her apologies," he said as he poured. "She had hoped to see you, but she really isn't well enough today. The past few months have been a terrible strain on us both – more on Genevieve than on me, I think."

He spoke her name with genuine affection; lifted his eyes very slightly as he did so to indicate, perhaps involuntarily, that she was in the house. The Victorian phrase "she has taken to her bed" popped into Fiona's mind: the generations for whom sickness had been the only possible retreat from overwhelming circumstance. Had we really changed so little?

"You've had quite a drive," Doug said, extending the small talk just a little further.

"Fourteen hours, all told," Miriam volunteered. "We stopped a few times on the way; took in a brief visit to Antwerp."

"A beautiful city," he said. "Deeply Catholic, if I recall. Statues of Mary on every street corner."

"There were some, yes. None of them less than eighty years

old, though. I'm not sure Mary gets that much attention these days."

"In Belgium? I think perhaps she does. Certainly more so than in Amsterdam. Here in Holland even the Catholics are Calvinists, it seems."

"And you, Doug – which are you?"

Fiona blushed at Miriam's intrusive question. Doug Porter didn't seem in the least bit fazed.

"Neither, I'm afraid. Agnostic born and bred. Now Genevieve, she's a different story. Had thoughts of a convent life herself, once upon a time."

It was Miriam's turn to be taken aback.

"How ever did you know?"

"The wonders of Google. You've made quite a name for yourself in certain circles, Miriam. It wasn't hard to research your background. Less on you, I'm afraid, Fiona, though your husband I know already, of course."

Fiona realized in an instant why the visit had been allowed; why Doug's apparent disdain for Catholicism had not led to him refusing Miriam entry; why he had changed his mind after initially ignoring every call. What he had been doing in the meantime.

"David called you." It was a statement, not a question.

"Emailed. It was my late uncle that knew him really, but we did meet. I did an internship at Memorial back in the nineties – it was where I met Genevieve. My memories of David are faint, at best, but it appears my uncle thought highly of him, and since I thought highly of my uncle…"

"I thought they had fallen out, just before we left Canada? Would have been around 2002?"

"I do remember something. 'Stubborn mule' was the phrase I heard used. But it was said with great affection. I don't think my uncle's respect for your husband was ever seriously threatened."

"Your wife is Canadian?" Miriam interrupted.

"Born and raised. And not just Canadian – a genuine

Newfoundlander. Her maternal grandmother was from a First Nations background – the Mi'kmaq tribe, reputed to be one of the oldest of the North American tribes."

"Which is how you came to adopt Amy in Canada." Miriam had decided to take charge, to move the conversation to where they needed it to be.

"We were married there. Had intended to stay. Soon after we had Amy, though, we began to dream of a European education for her. I was itching to come back, and Genevieve wanted to see the world. I got offered a European posting six years ago – first in Brussels then here in Amsterdam – so we made the move. Seemed like the right thing to do."

"Because of the circumstances of Amy's adoption." Miriam again, blunt as a log.

Doug paused. Looked at them both. A minuscule flick of his eyes upwards again, to the bedroom.

"Look, I'll be honest with you," he said. Nothing about Miriam's bluntness had deterred him. He was a man used to negotiating. "I agreed to see you because of David's connection with my uncle, but I didn't want to. I didn't want you to even waste your time driving here. And I didn't – I don't – want Genevieve to be burdened any more than she already is. Our daughter is sick, and we are trying our best to help her deal with it."

He saw on their faces what he had guessed on the phone – that they didn't know of Amy's troubles. Deeply wearied by the recitation, he offered them his most basic summary.

"Amy has been in treatment for the past three years for anorexia," he continued. "There have been some associated behavioural issues, as I'm sure you can imagine, but the eating problems were at the core of her condition. She and Genevieve have… struggled to see eye to eye on her situation. It's been hard on all of us. Then twelve months ago we found out that Amy is also a Type 1 diabetic. We had no warning, of course, because we don't know the medical history of either of her birth parents.

The combination of the two issues has been very difficult for her. She has found it hard to come to terms with the diabetes, and it makes her relationship with food even more complex."

"She skips on insulin to keep her weight down?" Miriam asked.

"Yes. Is that common?"

"Common enough, sadly. Diabetes is a tough diagnosis when you're already struggling with eating. She has a lot to deal with."

"She does," he replied bluntly. There was an edge of sympathy in his voice for his daughter, but there was also frustration; exasperation. "Amy is... troubled. It's been a traumatic year for all of us. My wife is exhausted with it. We just don't know what the future holds for our daughter. For all her difficulties, she is still a teenager."

They acknowledged this new information in silence. Tried very hard not to show that they were not surprised by it. Fiona felt the tingle of familiarity; of confirmation. This made sense.

"I'm so sorry," she said.

Doug acknowledged her empathy with a nod.

Miriam sensed the words behind his words.

"You didn't want her to go?" she asked, leaning forward. "To the sleepover?"

"No, I didn't. We wanted her here, where we could keep an eye on her. But she's a strong-willed girl, for all her troubles. She and Genevieve fought about it. In the end it was me who gave in to her. She's sixteen. She's young for her age, and her conditions require a lot of care – but all the same, we can't keep her here forever..."

She felt she could hear the echo of the argument Doug and Genevieve had almost certainly had after their daughter had gone out. Accusations. Recriminations. The tensions in Amy's life bursting their banks; splashing wildly in her parents' raised voices. Fears played across Doug's face like searchlights. The terrifying chasm of incompetence. The nightmare of not knowing.

All at once he found his resolve; rallied behind a form of words he had evidently used often; turned to perhaps daily these past weeks.

"... but she is receiving the best medical support that money can buy," he said, looking up, "and we are doing everything we can to help her. Like I said, I didn't want you to waste your journey, but I'm afraid you have – there really is nothing we can do to help each other."

Fiona was shocked by this reversal. The refusal he had been working his way towards all the time. "But Doug," she said falteringly, "if Colom could just meet Amy, just see her once..." Where Miriam's voice had been confident, hers was tinged with desperation.

He hesitated, but only for a second. "I'm sorry – it's just not possible," he said, a little more firmly than he had intended. "I know you came here hoping for something else, but I just can't allow it. I'm sorry. As I said, Amy is being professionally cared for. She's in good hands. We trust her doctors – and in my wife's case, your God – to bring her through."

He looked in turn at Miriam and then Fiona, making sure that he had made eye contact with both; that there could be no misunderstanding. This was a man used to making unpopular decisions. Delivering them. Ensuring their implementation. Mother bears were known the world over for their fierce protective instincts, but father bears, and husband bears, could also do their share of growling.

Knowing that the conversation had run the course of its usefulness, Miriam sent up a silent prayer. She hoped it would do more than bounce off the high ceiling or rattle the modernist chandelier. When she looked at Fiona, she saw that her eyes were fixed not on Doug, but on the room behind him. Miriam wondered for a moment if the mysterious Genevieve had crept downstairs to join them. But there was no one. Just an empty room and, on its wall, lit by a spotlight angled for the purpose, a framed drawing: a portrait she assumed was of a First Nations woman. She was unsmiling but was looking directly at the artist. There was an endearing awkwardness to her pose; bright eyes framed in a bob of jet-black hair.

"Your mother-in-law?" Fiona asked.

Doug turned in his seat to follow her gaze.

"My wife's maternal grandmother," he said. "The sketch dates from the 1950s. It was posed, to be quite honest. Even then, things had moved beyond fur hoods and trapping. But it was her culture, her roots. We don't know who the artist was, but the picture has stayed in the family."

"She's beautiful," Fiona said, getting up to leave. "Thank you for seeing us, Doug," she said softly. "It was kind of you. We won't trouble you any further."

Both Miriam and Doug were, in their way, surprised. Was that it, the end of the interview? Averting the confrontation he had dreaded; the conversation she had hoped for?

Fiona stopped as Doug rose from his seat to see them out. She took something from her handbag, a piece of white paper, folded. A note? When had she had time to write a note? Had she anticipated his rejection; prepared for the worst? If so, Miriam was impressed – the thought hadn't occurred to her.

"Could I ask just one favour of you, Doug?" Fiona was saying. Her voice was soft, but strong now, the desperation gone.

He looked at her, puzzled.

"Would you give this to your wife for me? To Genevieve?" She spoke her name as if it were that of a friend. "Could you say it is simply a gift, from one mother to another."

Doug took the note. Went to open its folds. "May I?" he said.

"Of course," Fiona said quickly.

He unfolded it. Saw that it was harmless. Miriam couldn't see what was written. The paper was thick, no letters showing through. Doug Porter, armed with the instinct of a father, decided he would trust the instinct of a mother.

"I will," he said kindly. "I'll give it to her." He had no idea what it might mean. What it was for.

"Thank you," Fiona said. "We wish you all the very best. Do we have your permission to pray for Amy? I don't mean here, now. I mean when we are praying, over these coming days."

He looked momentarily vulnerable. Alone with the burden of a daughter who was sick and seemingly couldn't be cured and a wife whose spirit had been crushed by cruel circumstance.

"I'd appreciate it," he said sincerely. "Please do."

He stood in the open doorway as they got into the car and pulled out of the driveway. Just before the blue gates swung closed, he turned to go inside. Miriam was sure that he was talking to someone in the hall as he did so.

She wanted so much to ask Fiona what she had given him for Genevieve, and why, but something told her not to. It was a private moment between one distressed mother and, via an intermediary, another. If she wanted to explain she would.

But she said nothing.

CHAPTER FORTY-ONE

Raindrops can fall at speeds of about 35 km an hour.
"Rain", Wikipedia

They drove in silence for several minutes, each caught in the swirling dance of her own thoughts. Fiona was at the wheel, the river to her right as they headed towards the city. They passed a windmill, next to it a statue of Rembrandt, and they were away from the Amstel, heading into the lunch hour traffic and towards the centre.

"So what's next?" Miriam said at last, unable to sustain the silence any longer. "What do we do now?"

Fiona sighed deeply. "I don't know," she said, wondering if she was sounding just a little like her son. "Do we try again?"

"I'm not sure it will help. His mind seemed made up, I would say. I can't blame him – they've got a lot to deal with right now, without adding the interfering oddness of two strangers."

"Do you think he thought we were a little crazy?"

"I don't know what he thought. We never really got the chance to find out. He just hasn't got the capacity to pursue some whole new avenue with his daughter – introducing strangers to her; asking her to talk to them; explaining to her what it is that they're doing there. We could have been Mother Teresa and he'd still have said no. He was just doing his job: protecting his family."

"You think he feels guilty?"

"Wouldn't any of us in his situation? Did I do enough? Did I say enough? Was I away from home too much? Should I ever

301

have taken her away from her roots in Canada? I suspect poor Doug Porter has felt little but guilt these past few months."

They were caught in heavy traffic now, heading towards a junction where the road into town cut across the inner ring road: a bottleneck of delivery vans, bicycles, and cars; a few tourists trying to get their bearings in a metropolis planned by a puzzle-maker. Fiona abruptly switched lanes and turned left, finding a gap in the oncoming traffic to cut across and down a side road. She pulled into a bus stop lay-by; engaged the handbrake; killed the engine.

"Sorry," she said meekly. "I just needed to stop for a moment."

"Do you want me to drive?"

"It's not that. It's… Miriam, what are we doing here?"

"In Amsterdam?"

"In all of it. What are we doing? She's not our daughter. We know almost nothing about her. Do we really have the right to come blundering in, breaking into someone else's tragedy? We've driven a thousand kilometres and I don't know why. What were we even expecting?"

"I know, Fiona," Miriam said. "It seems strange. But it's… a shred. When you're in the dark, even the smallest light is better than nothing. I do think that coming here was the right thing to do. It's a slender hope, but it's the only hope we've got."

"Had."

"I'm sorry?"

"It's the only hope we had. You said it's the only hope we've got, but it isn't. As of about twenty minutes ago it's a hope we thought we had. Now we have… nothing. I'm sorry, Miriam. I'm grateful for your help, I really am. But I think I've had it. I don't think I can do this any more."

Miriam said nothing; had nothing to say. Fiona was right and at the same time wrong. They sat in silence, the noise of the traffic like the breaking of distant waves. And then another noise: closer; muffled but insistent.

"Is that your phone?" asked Miriam.

Fiona snapped out of her reverie, grabbed for her handbag where she'd left her phone on silent while they'd been speaking with Doug Porter. It was vibrating as she took it from the bag, but stopped the instant she had it in her hand. She looked to see who it was but saw only a number she didn't recognize: a +31 dialling code.

"I don't know who this is," she said, frustration bubbling up in her. She handed the phone to Miriam.

Miriam read the number slowly.

"I do," she said.

* * *

When they reached 130 Amsteldijk again, coming this time from the direction of the city, the high blue gates were open for them. Once again Doug was at the door by the time they got out of the car, but not, this time, alone. Beside him was a tall, finely featured woman whose jet black hair fell like a curtain to her waist. She towered above him, confounding again Miriam's habitual pre-judgement. She had expected a mouse, a diminutive "little lady" hiding in the shadow of her husband. Genevieve Porter had been crying, that much was obvious. But that took nothing away from her stature. This was not a trembling servant girl. This was a princess of the Amazon. No question now how the heart of a young English intern had been so comprehensively conquered.

Doug, a little paler than when they had last seen him, took care of the introductions.

"Thank you for coming back," he said, when they had arranged themselves around the chairs they had not long vacated. No coffee was offered this time around: both hosts were too preoccupied to even think of it. On the table where the tray had been, there was now a piece of paper, the folds of which identified it as the note Fiona had left for Genevieve. But it wasn't a note. It was a drawing. Miriam saw a girl; a boat; buildings that looked to be Amsterdam canal houses.

"I apologize for not having met with you before," Genevieve said, the strain of recent tears still tugging at her voice. "I'm afraid I just didn't feel that I could face it. The past few weeks have been too much for me. I've felt so exhausted. The thought of new people coming; of talking about Amy all over again with them; going over all that has happened. I couldn't face it. I am truly sorry."

"There's really no need to apologize," Miriam replied. "You've been through – you're going through – something that would strain the health of any parent. Believe me, we do understand…"

I'm not sure I do, Fiona thought. *And I'm certainly not sure why we're back now.*

"Your husband said you wanted to talk to us after all?" she said. "To ask us some questions?"

"About the picture," Genevieve said, as if that made sense of everything.

"Maybe you could explain," her husband interjected, "why it struck you so."

"Yes, of course," she said, collecting herself. She coughed, clearing her throat. "Fiona, did your son draw this?" She flattened out the picture on the table so they could all see it: the girl; the signature; the title.

"Yes. Yesterday afternoon. He went to the Van Gogh Museum and was really struck by the charcoal sketches. He spent three hours or so at home afterwards just drawing. He loves to draw."

"Do you know who the girl is?"

"I have no idea. He didn't say. Somebody he saw in the museum maybe. I'm never sure where Colom's ideas for subjects come from."

"You said before, in your email to us, that your son dreams of a girl – that he feels he needs to rescue her."

Fiona nodded assent, not sure if she was supposed to explain more.

"Do you think this is a picture of the girl he dreams of?" Genevieve asked hesitantly. Because she didn't want to hear the answer? Or because she did?

"Are you saying... that this girl looks like your daughter?" Fiona ventured in disbelief. "Is this a picture of Amy?"

"No, no, I'm not saying that at all. Sorry, I'm not explaining myself very well. The girl in this picture clearly isn't Amy. Amy is much taller, her face not so round. No, that's not it at all."

They waited for more.

Doug took the hint, aware that his wife was struggling to make herself understood. The look of utter shock that he had seen on her face when she had first unfolded the picture was still with him. A combination of disbelief and terror, but then the emergence, under both, of something else. Hope? He had not understood, had not at first looked closely enough at the sketch to see what she had seen. But when she pointed it out he too had paled with shock. Could he really believe? That the boy knew? That it wasn't some bizarre coincidence, or worse still, a set-up? In the end it didn't matter whether he believed it, because he saw that she did. She was up and out of the bed in an instant. "Call them," she had said, unflinching. "Get them back. I need to speak with them."

"Perhaps I can explain," he said. His voice soft now. Every effort made to distance himself from his earlier, more abrupt responses.

"I told you earlier of Genevieve's roots in the Mi'kmaq tribe," he began. "What I didn't tell you was that Amy, too, has native ancestry. Stronger even than my wife's, we think. We know that her birth mother was of Mi'kmaq descent, and we suspect her father was too. It was one of the reasons we decided so quickly to adopt her. We already knew that we could not naturally have children. We'd told the adoption people that we would gladly give a home to a child of native descent. Amy's case was special. We weren't told much, but we did know that her need of a new home was considered urgent – she was a priority case, and we were thought to be her best hope. Once we saw her, it took us less than a second to say yes. She was beautiful. I knew when my wife was halfway through the doorway that she had fallen in love. Amy's hair has changed somewhat over the years: she loves to try different styles, and has worked hard at curling it. When she first came to us she did have the most perfect jet-black bob. She beamed out from it with the brightest eyes I had ever seen in a child."

Genevieve was staring at the picture again.

"The thing is," Doug continued, "Amy was the name she was given in the foster home but it wasn't her birth name. We were told by the adoption people that it would be best to keep it, since it was the name she had grown used to. We had actually always wanted an Amelia – it was one of the first decisions we ever made together – so we were more than happy, and Amy she became, and still is."

"But it wasn't her birth name?" Fiona said, sensing a tingle of where this might be going. A hint of something. A train, still in the distance, but on its way.

"Her mother was part of a whole hippy subculture. Her childhood dream, so we were told, had been to reclaim her native heritage. When her daughter was born she felt a moment of hope, and named her baby in honour of her dream."

Fiona looked first to Doug and then to his wife. Alert. Expectant.

"She called her Rain," Genevieve said, her eyes fixed on Colom's drawing.

Fiona's hand went to her mouth. Miriam's eyebrows arched. No one spoke. They all knew what they were all thinking, but they were all afraid to say it. They had crossed now into new, unknown territory. Where they went from here was far from certain. But it would not be where they would have thought, ten minutes ago, they were each going.

"Tell me about your son," Genevieve said. Unmoving. Her eyes still on the drawing.

It took Fiona fifteen minutes to recap the basic facts of Colom's life so far, including what they'd learned of McAllister and his conviction. Once or twice she stopped and looked to Miriam to confirm the story, or fill in gaps. In the end she felt that Genevieve and Doug could build the most accurate picture possible, in the circumstances, of her adopted son.

"And you think these dreams are… real?" Genevieve asked. "That there really is a girl and that Amy might be her?"

Fiona took from her bag the photograph of Amy that Mark had found. She passed it across.

"This is a picture of your daughter, we believe," she said. Genevieve nodded, tears pricking her eyes.

"The soft toy beside her – we call him Oscar – has been Colom's companion for as long as I've known him," Fiona said.

"We think that Colom and Amy were together in the McAllisters' home," Miriam said. "And we think this means that they did develop a particular bond. Is it impossible to believe that he would dream of her as his missing sister?"

"No, it's not impossible," Doug said, "but it is unusual."

"It was an unusual home," Fiona said, "and not in a good way."

Genevieve spoke again. "And you think that seeing Amy might help your son in some way?"

"We think it might help both of them," Miriam suggested.

"But why?" asked Genevieve. It was a genuine question. She wasn't trying to be obstructive, but she was trying to understand, and nothing in her experience to date was helping.

"The truth is," Fiona interjected, a little more loudly than she had intended, "we don't know. We don't know if the dreams are real; if Colom somehow remembers Amy without knowing that he does. And we don't know if them seeing each other will help in any way at all. But it's all we've got. And it feels like the right thing to do."

"Fourteen hours," Genevieve was smiling. "You drove for fourteen hours straight to come and do this?"

"We did," Miriam and Fiona replied in unpractised unison.

"I don't see what harm it can do. One visit. On Saturday morning, if she is well enough. Doug?"

"I'm willing to give it a try," Doug said. "God knows we've run out of other ideas."

"Genevieve's parents fly in tomorrow," he continued. "It's her mum's birthday next week. But Amy will be at home all Saturday morning, and I think that could work. If you come for around 10:30, that should be all right. I'll call you if there's any need to change the time."

"Thank you," Fiona was saying, already getting up to leave; already inhabiting a new and different future, casting off her old, despondent self like an unwanted coat. "Thank you so very much."

CHAPTER FORTY-TWO

In heavily populated areas that are near the coast… there is a 22% higher chance of rain on Saturdays than on Mondays.

R. S. Cerveny and R. C. Balling, "Weekly cycles of air pollutants, precipitation and tropical cyclones in the coastal NW Atlantic region", *Nature* 394 (6693), 6 August 1998

They filled their Friday as any tourist family in Amsterdam might, a tingle of anticipation bubbling under their canal walks and pancake lunch. They visited the home of Anne Frank; the newly refurbished Rijksmuseum, brick-red and palatial under a steep grey roof, the permanent collection a history of Dutch art through the ages. Fiona had expected it to be a positive day; had been so encouraged by the progress Mark had made with Colom. So lifted by Doug and Genevieve's agreement.

But she saw, all day, that Colom was on edge. He seemed strained; tired. He barely spoke, returning to the shrugs of old. Where Van Gogh had triggered something in him, Rembrandt didn't even register. She was reminded sharply that however far they'd come, their journey wasn't over.

Even more so that night. She was woken by a shout more shrill, more urgent than any she had heard from him. She clambered up the steep stairs to him; found him sitting up in bed, his knees pulled to his chest, rocking; crying; whimpering. She tried to soothe him; waited for him to find sleep again. But he didn't. She talked to him but got nothing in return. She watched as pain and confusion played across his face. His breathing was fitful, as if he was flinching from the pain of third-degree burns. She asked him what was wrong but knew, as soon as asking, that he didn't know. Just the same mumbled words, "I couldn't save her." She sat with him for almost an hour, until he seemed to be asleep, albeit fitfully. She crept out, only to be back within the hour as he again woke, screaming.

This time, exhausted, he let her hold him. She rocked with him, stroking his back. All the time muttering, "It's going to be all right," but all the time battling the overwhelming feeling that it wasn't. In time he found sleep again. But in time, again, the terrors of the night found him, and she was back at his side. The last time she left him, when he at last had fallen back asleep, she saw at the window the pale pink glow of dawn's first light.

She had no choice but to wake him on Saturday, determined not to miss the meeting they had at last been offered. Her own sleep so badly broken, she felt as haggard and unrested as he looked. They breakfasted quickly and, leaving Mark to himself, set off as a threesome to the Amsteldijk house.

It was 10:35 by the time Fiona tried the bell for the third time, leaning on it for longer than was polite. They had said they would be there, grandparents in tow; that Amy would be back; that she and Colom could meet. Surely they would not have cancelled without saying something? It was a big house – maybe there were parts where the bell could not be heard? She thought she had spotted a pool house – was that where they were?

She tried again. Nothing. No noise or movement; the door resolutely locked. But the gates were open – that was the thing that seemed odd.

Then a voice – not from the house but from the pavement; beyond the open gates.

"They're not in." The accent North American. Canadian? A West Coast nasal twang.

They turned to see a small woman, almost hidden by the volume of her sheepskin coat, coming onto the driveway. Long rust-red hair, thick and flecked with grey. She was holding a thin green leather leash, on the end of which was a pocket-sized dog; pinch-faced; rat-like. The leash went not to a collar but to a body harness – the neck too weak to take the strain. The animal was gleefully sniffing every inch of the block-paved driveway, thrilled to be admitted to a new world of unknown smells.

The woman looked at the small gathering on the doorstep, sizing them up. They were too colourful to be Mormons; too numerous to be Jehovah's Witnesses; too smart to be beggars or burglars.

Miriam saw her hesitation.

"We were looking for Doug and Genevieve – Mr and Mrs Porter," she said quickly. "We had an appointment to see them, and to meet Amy."

Knowing the family by first names seemed to do the trick.

"She's not well," the woman said, pulling the leash to bring her own tiny terror into order. "She was taken sick on Thursday night – at a party." She paused at this moment, enjoying the salacious nature of this information; the fact that she was the only one who had it; that these people had turned up just at the right moment for her to share it – no one else was even on the street so far this morning.

"Mr Porter was here briefly, earlier this morning," she continued, "but he went straight back to the AMC."

They looked confused.

"The Academic Medical Centre, in the Bijlmer. She's been treated there before, but this was an emergency admission."

She emphasized the word "emergency" as if it was an exotic flavour of chocolate. Perhaps her favourite. She looked at them expectantly. Would they ask her more questions? Could she share all she knew of the poor girl's story?

"Well, thank you," Miriam said firmly. "We didn't know."

No one moved. No one spoke.

"Well. Good day to you, then," the woman said finally, entirely failing to disguise her disappointment. She pulled her paperweight dog away from the flower bed he had become interested in.

They watched her go.

"What do we do?" Fiona said, exasperated. "Should we call Doug?"

"I think we should," Miriam said, "but not from here. Do you have any idea where the Bijlmer is?"

* * *

The Academisch Medisch Centrum proved to be a concrete spaceport of a hospital a ten-minute drive from the house. Four main blocks were connected by air ducts and walkways and a host of mysterious hoses, with two multi-storey car parks at their heart. The whole complex ready to receive incoming interstellar liners or perhaps, itself, take off and fly.

The impression of a starship was reinforced inside the main lobby. White-uniformed personnel from a kaleidoscope of nations moved purposefully across and around the central welcome area – a concrete well at least four storeys deep. High on balconies above, the offices of different consultants advertised their positive approach to sickness with brightly coloured curtains.

Fiona, Miriam and Colom had all the appearance of a grieving family as they made their way to a coffee area and took a table. Miriam phoned Doug's mobile number to say that they were there and ask if they could see Amy. He replied that he would meet them in the lobby, and quickly hung up. They waited in silence, and in little more than three minutes, Doug appeared. He shook each of their hands, but instead of leading them away, pulled up a chair to join them. He looked pale; sleep-deprived.

"There have been some developments," he said, anxiety playing at the corners of his eyes. No one else spoke. Six eyes looked directly at him.

"Amy was brought in late on Thursday evening. She had collapsed at the party and slipped into a coma. We think that she had probably missed an insulin injection earlier in the day, perhaps two, and we know that there was a lot of alcohol circulating at the party. It pushed her system into collapse. They think they have stabilized her, she's on an insulin infusion, but she hasn't yet regained consciousness, and they don't know when she will."

He was passing on blunt facts now, as if by their very solidity they could wake him from this nightmare.

"It seems likely that she was unconscious for quite some time before the ambulance was called," he went on, his eyes closed. "Her friends know she is Type 1, but they weren't exactly sober themselves. It took a while for anyone to notice. Genevieve is with her now and the doctor is there."

Miriam's hand went immediately to Doug's arm. "I'm so sorry," she said. "This must be a terrible shock for you."

He looked at her. Directly. Fear and pain in his look. A drowning man. "It is. More so for Genevieve." He spoke quietly, but there was a tremor in his voice. He didn't know how much more his wife could take – nor what he would do if she were to lose hope entirely. Then into the silence, his voice expressionless, his eyes to the floor, he said, "Her arms were cut. She'd bound them with tissue and tape, but there's no question she had been cutting herself."

He had said it. In the sharing of such horror, there was an intimation of trust; a bond among them.

"Have they told you what is likely to happen?" Fiona asked.

"It's too early to say. She could be fine in a few hours. She could wake up brain damaged. She could stay asleep forever…"

They said nothing. Held their thoughts in a solidarity of silence.

"I'm really sorry," he said distractedly. "I should have phoned you earlier, but it's been chaotic here and I completely forgot our arrangement. There's no point in seeing her now – she won't even know you're in the room."

Neither Fiona nor Miriam knew what to say. He was right, of course. There was no point introducing an unconscious girl to her long-lost cot buddy. And yet they'd come so far. Was there nothing they could do?

Colom's voice was so quiet that it was a moment before Fiona realized he was speaking. He directed his words at the floor; curls hanging down over his eyes.

"Please," he said.

Doug, too, was taken by surprise. Colom continued.

"I could just sit with her," he said. "I don't need to say anything, or do anything. I could just be there with her."

Doug looked at Fiona, who silently mouthed back to him the word "please". He paused for a moment. No one moved. No one spoke.

"Well, I guess it can't do any harm," he said at last. "Even if it does nothing for Amy, maybe it will help you."

Colom stood, ready for action. The others followed suit, and Doug led them back the way he'd come and to one of about a dozen possible lifts. There was something in his stride; an intimation of confidence. Did he believe, after all, that this might help?

They rode in silence to the fifth floor. Doors swung open before them as they followed signs to general medical and then to ward six. They couldn't see which room Amy was in, and Doug showed them to a *Familiekamer* – a room set aside for visitors and family members. The room was an Ikea merchandise display, comfortable but dull seating balanced out by floor cushions covered in fake cow skin. There was a TV; a computer; DVDs. Subdued lighting; a coffee machine; a miniature desk and chair set out for colouring and games. Pictures on the wall of oak trees and sunflowers.

"If you could wait here," Doug said diplomatically, "I'll go and see how things are and come and get Colom when there seems a good moment. Is that OK?" The implication, that neither Fiona nor Miriam would be admitted to the room, was accepted without question. This was hardly a time for re-negotiation. Having brought Colom this far, they would simply have to trust him with the final straight.

Doug was back within minutes. He looked directly at Colom.

"You sure you want to do this?" he asked.

Colom nodded, though he didn't look sure. He followed Doug out of the room and down the corridor.

314

CHAPTER FORTY-THREE

If people were rain I was a drizzle and she was a hurricane.
John Green, *Looking for Alaska*

She had a room of her own, forming a corner. Windows on two sides, a view to a railway line and a lake beyond. There were four people in the room, aside from Doug and Colom. A woman was standing near the bed, fussing with the flowers and clutter on the bedside cabinet. An older man and woman were sitting on matching chairs against the wall opposite the bed. They were both dark and wrinkled; both wearing glasses; both mumbling and crying. Colom thought they might be Chinese but then realized they must be the grandparents.

The fourth person was on the bed; asleep but propped up on several pillows; present in body but in every other sense absent. Frail. Thin. Dark hair curling on the pillow. She was dwarfed by the machines around her – monitors beeping; a pump rhythmically whirring; tubes connected to drips and drains. As if she were no longer human. Frankenstein's Monster, ready to rise. Her arms were bandaged. Did he know this paper-thin ghost of a girl? He wasn't sure. How could he even tell, in such circumstances?

The woman who had been re-arranging the flowers saw him come in, and stepped aside, moving to the window ledge, where there were curtains, instead of clutter, to be arranged. She had long, dark hair. She was wearing slippers. Doug also stood back, letting Colom take the chair beside the bed. He pulled it around so that he was looking straight at Amy, his knees pressed up against the hard metal frame of the bed.

She was breathing but unmoving. Her eyes were closed. As if she were asleep, but forever. As if sleeping was what she now did; was her new life. Colom knew how that felt; how often he had thought how great it would be to just fall asleep and stay that way. What was there to wake for, after all?

He leaned forward, and took her hand in his. It was warm, but limp. The fingers were thin. As light as matchsticks. Skin like the leaves of autumn. He knew there was life pulsing through it, but it didn't feel alive; like a house that no one lived in any more. He let it fall.

At the far end of the room the old man and his wife were rocking backwards and forwards, muttering and crying. A mournful, hungry sound. As if she was already gone. As if the time had come to mark her passing. Doug was standing beside them, watching Amy. Colom looked at him, at them, at him again. Pleading with his eyes.

"Maybe you guys should come and get a drink or something, Nanny?" Doug said at last. "Take a break for a while? Pops?"

The woman ignored him, lost to her tears, keening still. The man looked up; stopped muttering for a moment. He hadn't noticed Colom come into the room but he saw him now, bunched up close at the side of Amy's bed. He looked from Colom to Amy, from Amy to Doug, and all at once got to his feet. His wife sensed the movement, opened her eyes and looked around, confused.

"Come on, hun," he said. "Let's go get a drink. Leave the young guy to his visit, eh?"

She nodded mute assent. He placed his hand under her elbow to help her up; guided her towards the door. Tenderly. All the time looking to see that she was OK and could make it.

Silence filled the space they left behind. Amy's mother stood motionless by the window. Looking out. Listening in. Colom became aware of the bleeping and burbling of the machines. From somewhere, a trickling sound. There was the faint noise of traffic, but it was distant; muted. He could almost hear Amy's breathing now. He leaned in closer.

He took her hand in his again; turned it palm up. Laid the two fingers of his other hand across her palm. Squeezed tight to urge her to grip; his hand in hers, in his. When he let go, her grip loosened. It was his strength, not hers, doing the holding.

He part-leaned, part-fell towards the bed, his forehead falling onto the bedclothes beside her. His fingers still in her hand. The top of his head pressed, through the blankets, against her. He closed his eyes. Mouthed her name, "Amy."

And all at once he remembered.

Not everything. Not the details. But the feelings. He remembered the feelings, as you do when you wake from a dream. Like a colour you know but can't name. A swirling sense of fear. Pain. Abandonment. He remembered crying; wishing and longing for sleep. He remembered how his heart beat faster when he sensed the man near him; faster still if no one else was there.

And he remembered her. Amy. How she would come to him; take him in her arms; pull him close to her. Hold him as he cried. "Boy" she would call him. "It's all right, Boy." Rocking back and forth as she held him. "I'm here, Boy." And when she couldn't hold him for fear they would be stopped, when the man was watching them, how she would take his two fingers in her hand and grip them tight. Holding on. Sometimes he hardly noticed the movement, had not known she was near, but he would feel his hand taken in hers; two fingers squeezed in her palm – and the very pressure she applied would give him courage. How she tried to protect him. Hustled him from room to room when moving was a good idea. Stepped in between the man and him sometimes. Warned him when to be quiet; when to still his tears. "Be brave," she would whisper. "Be brave, Boy." And sometimes simpler words still: "I'm here." "I'm here, Boy."

He remembered how he had cried for someone to come who was never coming, and then she was there. Amy. Rain. The girl who had chosen to make him her friend. Barely two years older than him, but bigger than the sky in his eyes.

He remembered and he wept. He wept and he remembered,

his head burrowing into her bed; his tears absorbed by the covers.

He saw her now, in imagination; remembered from his dream but her face clearer now than ever he had dreamed it. Her smile. Her crystal eyes. The dark hair straight, not curled, framing her olive-toned face. Knowing now, in memory, who she was. Not his sister. Not his twin. Not a projection of himself. His protector. His guardian. His friend. His body registered again, in memory, how it had felt for her to hold him. The safety. The absolute trust. Her small hand holding his two fingers. Squeezing tight.

He stirred when a nurse came to check the machines and change a drip. Her soft shoes made no sound, but the clicking of the beads in her hair as she turned her head woke him from his reverie. He remembered where he was. He didn't know how long he'd been there. Minutes? Hours? He didn't know what time it was. He was surfacing from deep memories, sensations still lingering. The joy of her presence. The pressure of her hand, squeezing his.

She had squeezed his hand. Was that in his imagination, or in the room? Did his memory conjure it from nothing? He looked down at his hand, in hers. Willed her to tighten her grip.

There it was again. A tiny pressure, but a pressure all the same. He was fully awake now, alert. He looked at her, kept his hand where it was but leaned forward. Placed his face close to hers. Whispered.

"Wake up, Amy. Wake up."

She squeezed again. A little stronger this time. He stood; looked at her face. She seemed as still as before; as absent. Had anything changed? But then he saw something: a tiny twitch in the corner of her eye; then another. Enough to know that something was happening. He stood unmoving; his hand in hers; his eyes fixed on her; his breath held.

She opened her eyes.

She seemed confused, not knowing where she was. Keeping her head still, she scanned the room with her eyes; right to left; seemed to remember. Then looked at him. Considered. Found his eyes.

"Boy," she said.

EPILOGUE

He came to find me.

I couldn't believe it at first. I felt his hand in mine in my dream and didn't realize that I had woken up. Of course he's changed since we were kids; it's not as if I recognized him or anything. But I knew. He's still Boy. And he came to find me.

There was quite a lot of weirdness when I woke up from the coma. Mom said I'd been out for about thirty-six hours; something like that anyway. I could see when I woke up that she'd been crying, but then she started shouting and hollering. I think I even saw her jump up and down. Then she hugged Colom. I think maybe she scared him a little. Then his mom came in to see me, and a friend called Miriam. It was all a blur, but I've spoken to them all since, so I know who they are now. Colom has an uncle, too; Mark. He seems cool. Apparently he's something big in the art world – writing about it, that is. He took Colom to the Van Gogh Museum. I've been with school, so that was something we could talk about, once I started talking again.

I'm still in the hospital. They kept me on the drip for a few days, but I started to take some water, and then food. It's still only soup and tiny pieces of bread, and maybe one slice of fruit. But it's a start. Colom keeps "happening" to visit during mealtimes. He says it's by accident but I think he's checking on me. He doesn't need to. I've decided to eat again and that's that. The whole chewing marbles thing has just gone. Don't ask me how. I didn't know where it came from in the first place, so how am I supposed to know where it's gone? They think I'll be able to

319

go home in a few days. We're going to take a holiday – just the three of us. To Portugal. We've been before and it's great. I won't be able to do much, but I can rest and catch some sun. I am so pale. They brought me a mirror and I scared myself.

Miriam is also cool. She's old, but really good to talk to. She's been four times, and we've talked for maybe half an hour each time. I've told her all sorts of stuff and she's told me some stuff that's pretty icky, but OK to know now that I feel safe. I've known for a long time that I was adopted. My parents were way cool about telling me. But I didn't know about this freaky man and his house of horrors. I guess I'd pushed the memories away. Kids do that, Miriam says, when it's too hard to bear. Makes sense of a lot of things, now that I know. It's going to take me some time to get used to it all, but I think I'll make it.

One cool thing that happened was that Colom's dad came. Colom was scared about it, but in the end it was good, and they seemed cool together. I told Colom he should be grateful about having a dad who loved him. I'm pretty cool with mine, but it isn't like that for everyone. He has a picture now, too, of his mom. The real one. She was an addict, back in Canada. I wouldn't say she was pretty or anything – she was sick when the picture was taken – but she has nice eyes, and she looks a lot like Colom. I'm guessing he'll hang on to that picture for a long while. Fiona, his other mother, is cool with him having it. I told him the most I have from my real mom and dad is the name of some tribe that we were part of three generations back. Not a lot to go on. He should be glad for everything he's got.

I'm glad he's here. I like him. I think maybe we'll be friends forever.

I told him, just today, "It's going to be all right, Boy."